THE VILLAINS CLUB
A DELIGHTFULLY DEVIOUS ANTHOLOGY

EDITED BY

JANINA SCARLET

EDITED BY

E. M. NOLLER

CONTENTS

Text copyright © 2026 by Divine Feminine Publishing
Divine Feminine Publishing
www.divinefeminine-publishing.com
For information about special discounts for bulk purchases, please contact the publisher
using the contact form:
www.divinefeminine-publishing.com/contact

Cover illustration by: Sasha West and Paul Miehl

Acquisition editor: E. M. Noller

Copy editor: Paxton Alyssa

Sensitivity Reader: Dr. Harpreet Malla

ISBN: 979-8-9929404-4-2

Publisher: Divine Feminine Publishing

Copyright © Janina Scarlet, 2026

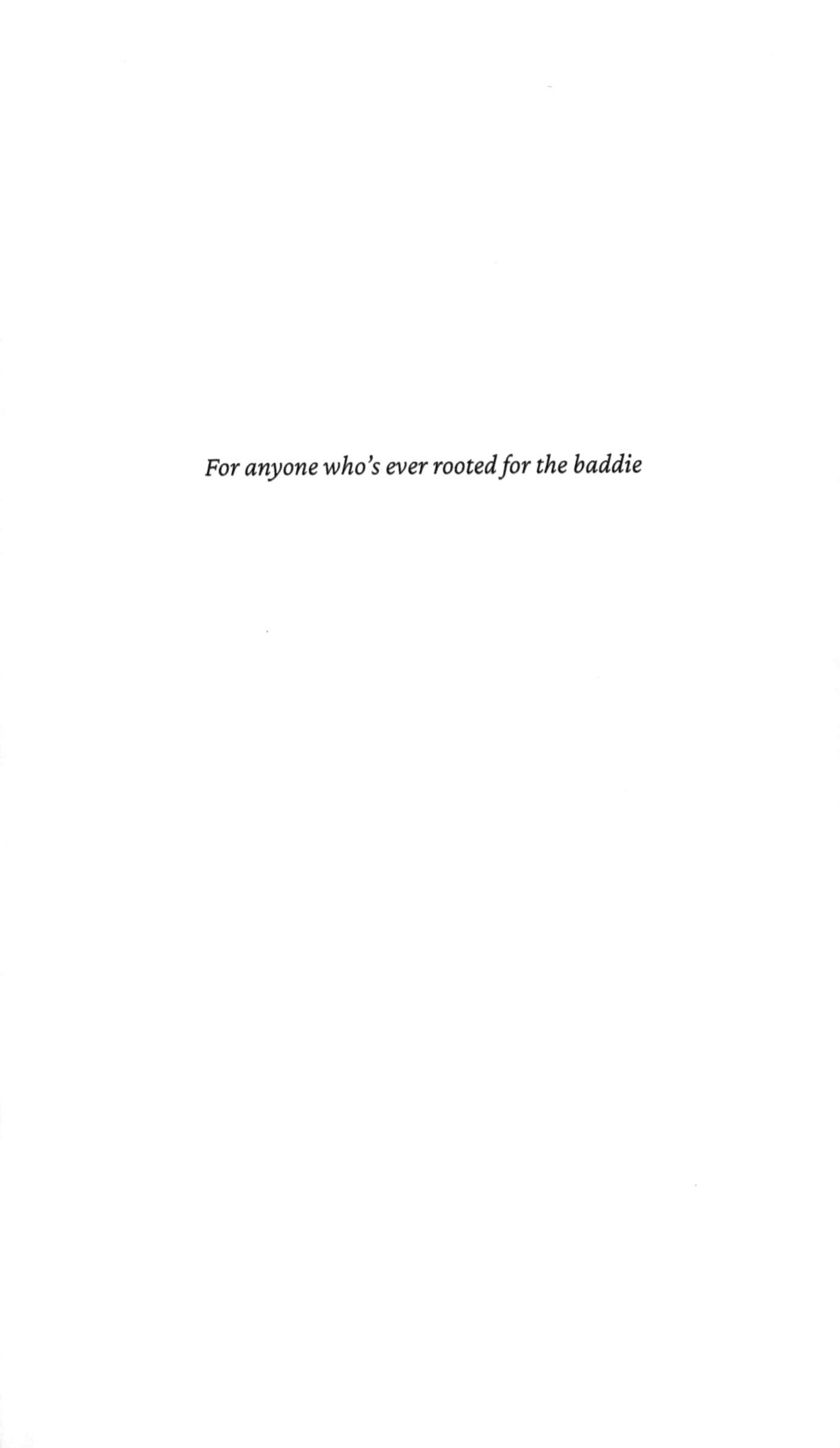

For anyone who's ever rooted for the baddie

LETTER FROM THE EDITORS

From Erin:

The beauty of a well-written villain, or of any unreliable narrator, is that they illuminate the gray areas of life. They confront us with uncomfortable questions, like, what makes a person bad instead of good? Was it their choices? Are there extenuating circumstances that led to these supposed bad choices? When faced with a lady-or-the-tiger style choice between a bad outcome and a worse, are bad choices excusable? What if a bad choice goes too far? Where is the line? When faced with a similar choice, what might I do?

What is the difference between a villain and a survivor?

Questions like these remind us that even when nothing feels simple, when figuring out how to do the "right" things feel overwhelming and impossible, we still have agency. We can listen to our intuition. We can listen to each other. We might make mistakes, but we can keep trying. We can laugh at a funeral, or cry at a wedding.

And if all else fails, we can plan a pudding heist and watch the sun set.

The villains in these pages are faced with all kinds of complicated, messy choices, and they respond in the messiest, most human ways. They are bitter, battered, and bruised. They wrestle with the complexity of their desires for love, connection, and the ways this desire conflicts with their equally powerful desire for greatness. In these pages you'll find haunting whimsy, caustic sarcasm, the perpetual ache of loneliness, and the psychological aftermath of betrayal. Some stories are cackle-out-loud funny, some tastefully macabre, and some rely on excessively satisfying gore to avenge their broken hearts.

Some of their stories are redemptive, many are not. Some villains learn how to love, some learn how to hate more efficiently, and some, regardless of the evidence before them, just double down on their inherently flawed worldview. Or is it flawed? Villainy is sometimes just code for not adhering to the status quo, for daring to challenge established norms and authority. Our interpretation of who is the "good guy" often depends on who is telling the story.

It was an honor to edit every single one of these stories, not least because the process made every member of The Villains Club quite real to me, and I sincerely hope the same will be true for you. I hope you leave this book with a brand new posse of sketchy, unpredictable friends squatting in your brain who remind you that context matters, that truth is slippery but not impossible to grasp, and that every voice—even the impolite, loud, wildly inappropriate, or a difficult one—still deserves a chance to share their tale with the world.

E. M. Noller

Co-Editor, *The Villains Club*

From Janina:

I've always been fascinated with villains. Not because they are devious, mischievous, and evil.

No.

Villains in most (well-written) stories are complicated. They are deeply flawed, yes. But they are also misunderstood, often longing for a specific goal only they can see. They are allowed to be messy, dramatic, and powerful, all at the same time. And most importantly, for many of us, they are relatable. Although we might not choose to emulate their devious actions, many of us can empathize with their intentions or their origin stories. Many villains are lonely, overlooked, dismissed, and made to feel "othered."

I wanted to put together a book in which villains take the front stage. Unapologetically, openly, and honestly. I wanted to invite villains to share their truth. But it was also very important to me that this anthology was fairly light, in terms of its emotional content. Due to heart-wrenching global tragedies taking place as of this writing, I wanted to put together a book which would offer a heartwarming smile, and even a laugh or two, during these trying times. Just villains doing everyday villain things that many of us can relate to, such as having a hard time stepping away from a job that's wreaking havoc on our mental health, needing braces, needing clothes that fit right, or just wanting to prove their worth.

And that's how *The Villains Club* was born.

This book is playful, yes. But it's also devious. It's sharp. And strange. And sometimes, it is laugh-out-loud funny. But beneath the humor, there is something deeply familiar: the ache of being unseen, unheard, or undervalued. The longing to belong *somewhere*.

Every contributor to this anthology brought their own flavor of villainy to the table, some tender, some chaotic, some whimsical, and some deeply moving. Together, these stories remind us that complexity is not a flaw, that humor and depth can coexist, and that sometimes the most honest stories come from the shadows.

If you are reading this during a time when the world feels overwhelming, I hope this book feels like a small refuge.

Welcome to *The Villains Club*.

We saved you a seat.

Dr. Janina Scarlet

Co-Editor, *The Villains Club*

SWEET TOOTH
BY HANNAH KATE KELLEY

Gryer was just about to rest her aching knees and prune her hirsute wings by the crackling hearth when she smelled it—a tart, syrupy whiff that sent a frisson through her. Somewhere out there, a child had just lost his tooth.

The young witch sighed before she splashed her ribtruffle tea onto the burgeoning fire, extinguishing it before it could grow to its full height. She'd been looking forward to that tea—a rare one she'd snatched from an unsuspecting vendor in the scrappy little town of Aveenly. It had taken not one, but two hours to brew to smoky, earthy perfection. But it was too hot to slurp down and she didn't want the crows—the damn rascals forever stationed outside her towering, teetering home— to break in and avail themselves of her effort. Better to waste the tea than share it.

Her exquisite evening must wait. There was a new prize to steal.

She shrugged on her cape and approached her parlor window. She had no need for doors. Gryer never accepted visitors, and her home was balanced on a stone trunk stories and stories above the ground.

"Caw," the fattest crow spat when she wrenched her latched windows open. Gryer shooed it away.

The sun was nearly set when she leapt into the icy, cloudless sky. Gryer reveled in the thrill of the flight, her massive oxblood wings stretching high, horned tips slicing through the oncoming fog. She knew better than to fly above the villages when night hadn't settled yet—but she couldn't let her sister beat her to this tooth. Havalla's nose was almost as good as Gryer's. In a few hours, she would know just as well as Gryer that the tooth's former owner was a boy, nearly ten, the tooth was a second molar, and it was worth nearly four hundred gold crowns from the elves, though her sister, the *saint* she was, would never charge even half that much.

The scent lured Gryer to a seaside village with frenetic, crashing waves and a long brick building housing a great number of young denizens. A boarding school, Gryer remembered. She'd visited just a fortnight before when a girl had lost her top right canine. Those fetched the highest price of all.

Gryer sold teeth to the elves because stealing from them was nearly impossible. Through their business arrangement, she'd already secured a brown cow that produced the purest, coldest sweet cream every new moon and a banned novel about a witch who conquered the world, which Gryer intended to use as a rubric.

Even now, deep in one of the many pockets of her cape, Gryer carried a wooden music box that would sing the first nursery rhyme the listener had ever heard, just once, then shudder and turn to dust. Gryer intended to use it later this very night.

Gryer never asked what the elves did with the teeth; it wasn't any of her business. She suspected, though, that human teeth, when crushed to a fine powder and sprinkled into their metalsmithing, fueled many of the elves' magical creations. Though she was a witch, Gryer's enchantments paled in comparison to the elves'. Their craftsmanship was unparalleled, and Gryer's collection of finery was her sole comfort.

Only when Gryer descended onto the boy's windowsill did she notice fluttering behind her. The crows had followed her, perhaps seeking entertainment from her escapades since she'd dashed her fire and tea. Again, she tried to slap the pesky, nosy birds away. But they were mocking and unmoving. She'd been too lenient the other night when she tossed them the crumbs from her grundleberry and caramelized orange rind cake. She would have to be more frightening. And infinitely more threatening.

A witch in her position couldn't afford to lose her edge.

Gryer folded in her wings like an accordion and slipped on her lace gloves, enchanted to render her as soundless as butterfly wings. She hopped into the dark room on padded feet, shut the window behind her to keep the crows out, and crept toward the closest four-poster bed, ignoring the five other snoozing boys down the row, since the tooth's scent still clung to the boy sleeping nearest to the window.

First, she checked if the boy was truly asleep. If he wasn't, he could alert the older humans that Gryer was here rather than her doting, sickeningly sweet sister Havalla, and then Gryer would have to escape before they trapped her and demanded remuneration for all the teeth she'd stolen throughout the years. Gryer had never been caught, but there'd been some sightings and close calls—enough that by now, everyone knew Gryer left fake silver coins that dissolved within days, while her sister paid the real deal. They wanted compensation for their tiniest bones, which Gryer hardly felt was fair. The loss of a tooth was a biological imperative that required no hard work on the human's part. Really, wasn't her role as a recycler enough?

Next, she checked under the pillow. But her loot wasn't there. She sniffed again. Something gleamed in the corner of the room beside the door. Gryer quietly scoffed.

The children were getting clever.

She strode silently to the corner where the second molar sat in its cozy, wooden trap. Not just any old mousetrap, but a deftly altered one that would smash the tooth to smithereens if she mishandled the box or failed to extract the molar in one fell swoop. The few cowering children who'd spotted Gryer throughout the years had clearly spread word. They learned that though Gryer had the longer, pointier nose, it was Havalla who had fingertips delicate enough to pluck the tooth free from the trap without harm. Gryer's clunky fingers were topped with thick black claws, and in spite of how clumsy they made her hands, she enjoyed the extravagance of her long talons too much to ever trim them to stubs.

But now she was at a loss. Gryer had squandered her precious tea, dampened her fire, and rushed here for *this*? Oh, how her sister would cackle when she arrived.

Gryer was getting desperate. She glanced back toward the window, where the crows were still perched on the outside sill, silently mocking her. Gryer crept back over to the window and opened it a hair.

"Come now," she whispered to the large crow amidst its murder on the sill. "That fine beak might as well be put to work."

The crow blinked its beady black eye at her through the glass, then threw its head back and squawked caustically.

Gryer growled, baring her needle-sharp teeth. The crow jumped back but did not acquiesce to help. In all of this, Gryer failed to notice the door creak open behind her.

"You're letting the draft in," a tiny voice said.

Gryer's attention whipped toward a girl, who couldn't be a day over six, standing in a weak stream of light from the hallway beyond. Her bare feet toed the twisting vines on the carpet beneath her as she held the door open with one pudgy hand and twisted her black locks in the other. With the light casting the girl's face in shadow, Gryer couldn't read her expression, but by her tone, she betrayed no fear. Not in the least. How could that be? Gryer's teeth were on full display. Were the girl's eyes still blurry with sleep? Though perhaps her lack of apprehension was best since Gryer couldn't have the girl screaming, not before she freed her prize. She decided to hide her fangs and squeeze her wings further back.

"I was just tucking him in," Gryer whispered. She shut the window. "He had a nightmare."

"Oh." The girl yawned, which further aggravated Gryer. Even with her teeth and wings hidden, Gryer should be terrifying—why was this girl so at ease? "Can you tuck me in next? The warden said she would, but I think she forgot, which happens sometimes. There are so many other children here."

Gryer blinked at the girl. Behind her, the crows tittered beyond the window.

Her, a bitter witch who was the stuff of nightmares, *tuck in* a human child?

"I'm already quite tired, but I can never fall asleep without being tucked in. Please."

Gryer sighed heavily. If she tucked the girl in without inciting any screams, she could sneak back to the boy's molar and try extracting it with her long claws or a nearby needle. But she'd have to be quick about it. The sugary scent had surely reached Havalla's tiny, pert nose by now. Gryer had perhaps an hour, maybe less.

"Fine," she grumbled. "Where is your room?"

The girl, unbothered by Gryer's long claws and hairy skin, took her hand and led her to a room down the hall. Gryer, however, disliked how clammy the girl's small hand was. The girl's room was posted at the far end of the school, and a finger's-width gap in her window was drawing in a frigid gale. It appeared to be broken in such a way that it couldn't close fully. There were only two other beds in the room besides the girl's, both empty. Most annoyingly, the crows had flown over to the girl's windowsill, now thoroughly amused even though they couldn't squeeze through the window's aperture. The girl climbed into her tall bed with effort and pulled her scratchy, pilled blanket to her chin. "Well?"

"Well, what?"

"You must tuck me in."

"I'm aware of our arrangement."

"You're just standing there. Have you never been tucked in before?"

Gryer had, actually. Since their parents were typically away on decadent travels, Havalla had always been the one to sweep Gryer into her bed. Even though Gryer was always bigger, Havalla was older, so Havalla carried her younger sister to Gryer's bed. Funnily enough, Gryer had been thinking about their childhood nighttime routine just before she'd settled into her chair earlier that evening. She remembered the music box nestled in her cloak pocket, just waiting to be savored later on that evening.

"I know who you are, you know," the girl said.

Ah, so the girl was not oblivious. Just unfazed.

"And you're not afraid of me?"

The girl shrugged. *Shrugged.* Gryer could hardly believe it. Again, Gryer was disconcerted that she failed to terrify the girl. For just one selfish moment, her desire for the tooth subsided, and all she wanted was to prove herself. She extended her wings to their full, imposing length and bared her teeth. She had to elicit a scream; the tooth be damned.

"Your teeth are creepy. But I know what it's like to be odd-looking." The girl lifted her hair to reveal two tiny ears. Gryer searched for horns or scales or even a second head hidden behind the little leaves of olive flesh—finding nothing but two completely human ears. "They stick out like an elephant's. Johnny Briggs told me so."

"I ..." Gryer felt deflated. "Well, if you know who I am, you know that I won't be able to tuck you in. You've got the wrong sister."

"If you tuck me in, I'll get the tooth for you tomorrow. Just put the trap under my bed."

Gryer's protest was on her tongue, but she reconsidered. If the girl could transport the trap without triggering the release, and find something to mask the scent from her sister, well then ... But was the tooth worth dealing with this perplexing girl a second longer?

The crows had somehow needled their way into the girl's room to huddle on a nearby bed, the bastards. How they managed to do that, Gryer might never know. The girl didn't seem disturbed by them either.

"Deal?"

"Fine," Gryer agreed. She folded her wings in once more and perched on the girl's bedside, squishing the mattress down with her heavy frame. "What do your parents do to help you fall asleep?"

"I can hardly remember."

"Surely, it hasn't been that long since you've seen them."

"They died a few years ago."

"But I thought ..." Then Gryer realized this was not a boarding school at all, but an orphanage. That explained why the children were always here, never away on summer holiday. And why the girl sounded far more mature than six. Something tugged inside Gryer's belly. A nasty, raw pull that nearly made her clutch the folds of her soft stomach. It was a long-dormant feeling she despised and usually dismissed as hunger pangs. "Oh."

"Will you sing to me?"

Gryer scoffed, composing herself. "The crows can attest to my voice. It's hardly sleep-inducing."

"A story should do, then."

"Does it have to be true?"

"No."

But Gryer told a true one, anyway. She wasn't particularly inventive on the spot. She told the girl about a young witch and her sister who grew up in a vast cave and spent hours contriving games to chase their boredom away, and how they discovered which trinkets they could sell to the elves for the highest profit. They made an excellent team, if only for a while. She blinked at the wide-eyed child. "Shouldn't you be asleep by now?"

"I was expecting a duller story. This one is quite thrilling."

"Well, I can tell another—"

"What happens next?" The girl's brown eyes widened.

Gryer told the ending as she knew it. Havalla tried to convince her to file their horns to nubs and bleach the skin of their wings into a light, candy pink. It was less scary, she'd claimed. That, and Havalla wanted to reward the children for their fallen teeth. She called her plan a "business" but called Gryer's own plan a "scheme", even though they were both bargaining with elves. *You have no heart*, she'd told Gryer the last night they'd spoken, some years ago.

"Why do you steal so much and don't give anything back?" the girl asked Gryer.

"The story wasn't about me."

The girl crossed her soft arms. "I told you, I'm not stupid."

Gryer drummed her claws on the bed frame. "My comforts demand a high price."

"But are they worth it if you've no one to share them with?"

Gryer laughed. "That is the *only* way they are worth it. No one else to hog."

The girl's gaze settled on one of the empty beds in her room. "That hardly seems a way to live." Then she just laid there, unconvinced, and not nearly as somnolent as she should be. "Perhaps you should try singing now."

The large crow hopped onto the girl's bed and, for a moment, Gryer was afraid that the bird was going to pluck the girl's eye out. But the thing nestled against the child's neck and she grinned, petting the crow's inky feathered head with one tiny finger. The bird shut its eyes slowly, relishing her touch even though it would reek of human oils for days after. Gryer didn't know what mortified her more: how the girl was cozying up to the vile nuisance that was the bane of Gryer's existence these days, or that Gryer had felt fear *on the girl's behalf.*

"No singing." Gryer was running out of time before Havalla arrived. And that was the only reason she was desperate enough to pull the wooden box from her cape pocket. It was pure luck that she hadn't unpacked it before leaving to retrieve the boy's tooth. Perhaps with the molar, Gryer would be able to start saving up to buy another box. But deep down she knew this was impossible. The elves were masters of craft, not industrial manufacturers. They would never create another. "This box holds one song. However, I can't open it, or it will reveal a comforting song for me, not you. You must open it."

"How do I know it's not a trap?"

"Because I very, very much want you to fall asleep. We have a deal, remember?"

The girl yawned—a good sign—and nodded. She slipped the twine off the box and freed the lid. The slow song was a duet sung by a man and a woman in a language Gryer didn't recognize. Though Gryer couldn't comprehend a word, the girl could. She hummed along, fighting a creeping smile. Within a few verses, the girl was fast asleep. Gryer didn't even need to snap her fingers to check. When the song ended, the box sighed and collapsed into wooden powder. The next gust of wind scattered it all away.

The crow gently weaseled out of the girl's embrace and eyed the witch. Perhaps it meant to mock her for wasting her prized purchase on this little girl. Gryer didn't stay to decipher its glare. She stole away to carefully retrieve the boy's trap. After she stowed it beneath the sleeping girl's bed, she covered the thing with a bowl and three pungent socks from the boys' room to disguise the scent, wrenched open the window, and flew out.

Her wings beat quickly, but not quite fast enough to out-fly the creeping feeling that had started when the girl's eyes fluttered closed. The girl had wrenched up an unwanted heaviness that Gryer had, so far, managed to keep buried for all these years. She could hardly bear the weight of it. She felt sorrow for the girl, but something else far more dangerous. Warmth.

Gryer did not return to the orphanage the next night. Or the next. For a long month, she kept to herself. Gryer convinced herself the girl had forgotten their deal or pawned the tooth off to Havalla, instead. The molar's scent had diminished, as all teeth do after a while. Gryer spent her days reinforcing the inside of her tower walls with wooden boards, hellbent on locking the nasty crows out once and for all.

When she was finally done, Gryer collapsed onto her chair in front of a blazing fire to warm her swollen feet and the tip of her long nose. At last, she had peace and quiet, and the chance to indulge in the expensive chocolates the elves claimed tasted exactly like the twelve seas —fish, kelp, foam and all.

"Caw."

Startled, Gryer whipped her head up, accidentally dropping the chocolates before she could even lift one to her maw. They landed in a series of discordant thuds, scattering across the carpeted floor. On the mantle in front of her perched the large crow. Before Gryer even had a chance to react, much less unleash her talons on the intruder, it dove for her chocolates and snatched the one with white swirls.

"Not the Azkaiin Sea," Gryer hissed. It was the one she was *most* looking forward to.

The crow lifted its head all the way back and the chocolate swam down its throat. Then the thing coughed and spat it back out.

"And now you've wasted it!"

Gryer chased the bird around her home until her hair was frazzled and she'd thrown so many vases and chairs at him that she nearly undid all her hard work reinforcing the tower's walls. She stopped, panting. And without another word, she abandoned her blazing fire and took to the dark skies, not even bothering to close the window behind her. Let the crows sate themselves on her chocolates, warm themselves in front of her fire, relax in her big, comfortable chair. They would leave soon enough, anyway. Everyone always did.

The girl was in her bed, awake, as she'd been the first night they'd met. "Took you long enough," was all she said when Gryer strode in through the creaky window.

"I was busy."

The girl extended a small hand toward her tiny desk. "It's over there."

Gryer snatched up the second molar, grinning with the heft. It would fetch a fine price, indeed. Beneath it, she was surprised to find several sketches. The girl had tried to sign the drawings with the name *Ammi* but the A wasn't right yet—it looked like a punctured O. Most sketches were of Gryer. Some were of her sister, or at least, the version of Havalla that Gryer had described to the girl. Snakes spun out of her sister's hair and ears. Havalla would be peeved by the inaccuracies and anything that made her look unpalatable. Gryer nearly chortled.

"The lullaby worked," Ammi said. "I had forgotten some of the words and now I will never forget again. Thank you."

Gryer could hardly choke it out: "You're welcome."

"Will you sing it to me? Your voice can't be *that* bad."

"I have to go home."

"Oh, alright."

But Gryer hesitated. The warden had forgotten to tuck the orphan in again, it seemed. And it was too late now. Ammi would be up all night. And for once, Gryer was not eager to fly home to her fire and her solace and her tea.

Though it hurt her to admit it, Gryer understood what it was like to feel alone at night with no one to tuck you in anymore. Despite how aggravating Havalla had become, Gryer still missed her sister dearly. Plus, Gryer was finding she didn't mind as much that the human girl wasn't disturbed by Gryer's appearance. Maybe Gryer was becoming less scary. Maybe that wasn't such a bad thing, not if it meant she could have some company who didn't annoy her beyond compare.

"Perhaps I remember a little of the song."

The girl smiled and settled in. "It doesn't have to be perfect."

"Good, because it won't be. And don't complain that I sound like a toad or a screeching cat," Gryer said, and sang what she remembered.

When the large crow and two others snuck their way into the girl's room again, Gryer nearly shooed them away. But they knew the song better than she did, for they whistled jarringly with their razor-sharp beaks so Gryer could continue beyond the first verse. She added her own lyrics when Ammi's eyes started to close, a small smile fading from her mouth as she drifted off to sleep. Gryer sang of a witch who invited her sister to tea.

When Gryer flew home with the tooth in hand, her cape weighed far less. She'd given the girl twenty silvers for the tooth, the going rate of Havalla these days. Ammi could share the money with the boy or keep it for herself.

Gryer also left a bundle of spare charcoal. The next time Gryer visited, she expected the girl to have new drawings for her to admire. Maybe she'd even gift Gryer one to hang on her walls.

When she got home, Gryer fastened her window and nailed the fallen boards back into place. But even as she settled into her chair with a piping cup of spiced tea, stoked the fire to crackling perfection, and picked up one of her favorite tomes, she felt for the first time in a long while that everything was too quiet. She should be comfortable. And she mostly was; her day's work was done and she was surrounded by every little luxury money could afford. So, what was the matter?

That's when she realized the crows hadn't broken in again, as they should have managed by now. The irksome birds weren't tapping the panes incessantly either. Her heart dropped when Gryer saw the perch outside her window was as vacant as the chair beside her. She tried to ignore the silence as she fetched a slice of rum cake, but all she could wonder was where the crows had gone and if they'd found a new home with Ammi, or even a stranger who was less abrasive and sour than Gryer. She shouldn't care, of course. And she didn't. But she still left a small sliver of cake on the sill before clamping the window shut again.

Only when one crow, then two, then the whole lot, flew back to snatch up the cake did she relax back into her seat. When they began tapping the glass for more, she chided, "Oh, enough. What spoiled things you are."

Then she smiled, slid her book back into her lap, and resumed her reading.

The End

Hannah Kate Kelley is a writer and developmental editor living in Brooklyn.

FARADAY'S CAGE
BY CHANCE KISTLER

Faith Faraday sat alone in the den of her primary lair, musing. She wasn't sure what was wrong. It had started ... a week ago? Yes. Just after her last battle with the solar-powered champion, Pulsar.

Last Sunday, Faraday had unleashed her army of super-powered ultra-cats, only for them to be de-powered and rounded up. In retrospect, the plan had been rushed and ill-considered. Even with their intelligence increased, it was impossible to tell cats to do anything. More annoyingly, Pulsar had somehow made friends with them.

Before the hero could apprehend her, Faraday threw a gravity grenade into the air, temporarily trapping Pulsar in place. As the hero struggled against gravity similar to the planet Jupiter, Faraday donned super-speed boots made from stolen hypergel, a near-frictionless metamaterial that would quickly evaporate.

Pulsar called after her, "This is going nowhere, Faraday! Why can't we try something different? You could do so much more!"

Faraday launched into a sprint, covering a mile a moment later. Another two steps and she was on the highway, weaving through traffic. Two steps later, she skidded to a halt on the side of a mountain, the hypergel dispersing into silver ashes.

Why can't we try something different?

Ridiculous question. A manipulation tactic, of course, not a genuine call for a truce. Pulsar hated her, naturally. They were enemies.

Faraday then returned to her primary lair, just as she had done after many other battles against authorities and superheroes, most commonly the costumed champion, Pulsar. Faraday was tired from the battle, but she'd pushed the exhaustion aside. There wasn't time to waste. She had to find the key factors quickly so she could make true progress toward her end goals: world domination, recognition as Earth's greatest mind, and the defeat of Pulsar (not necessarily in that order). But now, seven days later, it was Sunday again and she'd yet to come up with anything.

As she mused, Robot Assistant Number 8 walked in and handed Faraday a hot cup of tea. Faraday breathed in the scent, sipped, and considered her options.

"Cats are too chaotic," she muttered. "Maybe ultra-dogs. Or penguins. With rockets. No one would be prepared for flying penguins. Maybe not."

Why can't we try something different?

She shoved aside the echoing question, the voice fading into a soft static hiss in the back of her mind. But she had to admit, maybe it had a shard of wisdom.

Long ago, during a strange adventure involving several self-proclaimed heroes and villains, Faraday had seen evidence of parallel universes, other versions of

Earth existing in different harmonic frequencies, each with their own histories. On some, she knew there were alternate incarnations of herself. There had to be Faradays who had won in the end.

After further work and with some stolen materials, Faraday activated a new machine that could tune into video and audio transmissions from parallel worlds: the World Window. It wasn't the same as visiting, but she could still learn something vital from these alterniverses and "what if?" realities.

As the days rolled on, looking through the Window did not bring the results she'd hoped for. Some Faradays gave themselves super-powers rivaling Pulsar's. They failed. Some created imperfect clones of Pulsar to defeat her. They failed. One Faraday created a "quantum golem" that drew power from the hero's fear. Pulsar offered the beast understanding and acceptance, ending the fight and gaining a comrade.

Annoyed that she had spent too much time distracted by hypothetical realities, Faraday shut off the Window.

The next day, Faith Faraday walked into a hidden meeting hub for villains who had agreed to occasionally convene. She hadn't let anyone know she was coming to this latest gathering, of course. A true villain never gives an RSVP.

Yet to her surprise, the mystical renegade Madame Arcane stood in the doorway, smiling as she gazed into Faraday with deep, amber eyes. "Security detected your approach," she said in her European accent (maybe Ukrainian, Faraday couldn't remember). "And I sense something of your reasons for visiting. Follow me. Maybe you'll find answers."

In the primary assembly chamber, the Steam Queen

saluted Faraday as she entered, raising one of her gauntlets to tip her stovetop hat. She looked ridiculous in her steam-powered battle armor, but Faith found her oddly charming.

Madame Arcane spoke to the group. "Many of you know Dr. Faraday, former military scientist, and arch-enemy to Pulsar. She joins us in the hopes of finding inspiration."

"Weak," remarked the cyborg Technolo-Jock. His robot arms were folded across a T-shirt that said *NO WEAK WARRIORS*. "A real villain doesn't need help. Life's a jungle, you learn to survive on your own. Maximum power, no apologies."

"Relax, Jock," sneered Zero-Chill, an ice-powered mercenary. "The whole point of us meeting is to trade ideas and resources in exchange for favors. Why else are you here?"

"Free snacks," the cyborg answered. "You want a plan? Stop arming animals with tech. Just do bigger tech. Flying tanks. Make yourself part robot with bigger arms. Arms with missile launchers. Bigger weapons always win."

"How has that strategy worked out for you?" Steam Queen asked. "Didn't that teenage elemental girl defeat you again?"

The cyborg left the table to do push-ups in the corner.

The evil app FaustWare™ manifested on Faraday's smartphone and spoke. "Greetings, user! I'm Faust-Ware™, your premium partner in morally flexible success! With my resources and strategies, you can synergize your sinister influence, enhance your engagement, and mute your rivals. Metrics don't lie! I'll help you in exchange for: *terms to be explained later.*"

Faraday swiped the app away.

One by one, the other villains each suggested a dynamic plan. Faith Faraday listened. And listened. Finally, she asked, "But none of this has worked, right? The plans. The inventions. The magic spells and weaponized thought-forms and alien technology and engineered monsters. None of us really win, not for long at least. We come back and repeat and reboot the same ideas. Are any of us making any real progress?"

"She's getting emotional," Technolo-Jock said as he failed to achieve a handstand.

"Any goal reached provides new challenges," Madame Arcane said with a shrug. "Reward is never as good as pursuit and competition, so the chase itself must be the reward. Don't you see?"

Faraday left the room.

Two weeks later, Faraday retreated to her lair after another loss. What did her next plan need? Where could she find the key to victory?

The static rose in the back of her mind.

You could do so much more!

Robot Assistant Number 8 asked her what it could do for her. And Faraday recalled Technolo-Jock's suggestion.

A month later, Faraday attacked Pulsar in Central Park, aided by her upgraded robot assistant. The robot was taller now with a reinforced body, standard circuitry replaced with data-encoded DNA-cells. She'd been given a personality, greater intelligence, and better yet: ambition. She was a living syntelligent machine. No longer simply "Number 8", the automaton had a new name worthy of her upgraded power: Mechani-Kill!

During the battle, Faraday observed the inner workings of Mechani-Kill's decision-making process on a hand-held monitor linked to the robot's neural network. The precaution seemed unnecessary as the battle ensued. Faraday felt pride watching Mechani-Kill fight Pulsar with admirable skill.

Despite Pulsar's efforts to avoid endangering others, the fight carried through Central Park and the combatants found themselves crashing into the middle of a live performance of *Twelfth Night*.

Confused by the sight of people in costumes, Mechani-Kill paused her attack, her synthetic brain rapidly searching the internet for an explanation of "Shakespeare in the Park", followed by a search for *Twelfth Night* and why it would draw an audience. The answers rapidly displayed on Faraday's hand-held monitor in 0.82 of a second. But rather than resume the fight, Mechani-Kill felt the electro-chemical spark of curiosity. She took another 2.034 seconds to do a deeper search regarding Shakespeare and interpretations of the bard. This led her to essays on ancient oral traditions, an article about the psychological impact of art, works by James Baldwin and Virginia Woolf, and a podcast about why some narratives seem timeless.

Faraday saw these discoveries fly across the monitor but couldn't stop or filter them in time. No more than 4 seconds after pausing the battle, Mechani-Kill was a changed automaton. She apologized to Pulsar for the fighting; she had been young and foolish and hadn't questioned her upbringing. She wanted to find deeper meaning and connect with others more positively and felt that art and theatre would help her do both. She was no longer Mechani-Kill. Her new name would be: Mech-Beth!

Since no one had been seriously hurt and Mech-Beth promised to help with repairs, Pulsar accepted the apology and shook the robot's hand. The audience cheered.

"I offer you conquest and glory and you want to make art and play pretend?" Faraday demanded with bewildered rage. "What do you know about examining life? You have nothing to be existential about! You know exactly where you came from and why you're here!"

"Oh, this is so like you, Mom!" Mech-Beth shouted. "You're emotionally stunted!"

Faraday then ended the argument the same way she had ended many others: smoke bombs and the use of an anti-gravity belt to make a quick getaway. Overall, the audience thought it was a great show, if a bit on the nose.

Days later, Faraday sat in her chair. How had her robot gone wrong? Too much free will in the bio-positronic matrix? Too much imagination? Maybe they should have talked more.

Her eyes drifted to a map on the north wall of her den. She'd made it fifteen years ago, a blueprint for her plans of conquest. Now, with none of those goals achieved, it seemed more like a crayon drawing made by a child who dreamed of being an astronaut or pirate. Well intentioned, but meaningless.

Faraday sipped at tea that didn't taste right and turned away from the not-map.

$\sim$

Days later, Faraday returned to her lair after another defeat. Flying penguins armed with laser guns were not the answer after all. She was too tired to bother trying to destroy her lab in anger, so she took a shower instead. Afterward, she stared at a reflection in the mirror that took time to come into focus. She looked at the newest lines around her eyes and the scattered gray hairs that didn't have the decency or ambition to grow together into a dramatic streak. She winced at the area above her left hip that now often felt tight after battle. Then she returned to her den, drank tea that didn't taste right, and stared at the map that wasn't a map.

Maybe the problem had been herself. Her heart hadn't been in these fights for ... well, for some time now. Why?

Over the next two weeks, she ran a series of tests on herself. No viruses. No tumors. Cholesterol, good. Heart rate, villainously steady. She was athletic for her age. No poisons in her system, no nanobots sent by an enemy to sabotage her mind, no gas leaks in the lair. No physical factors seemed responsible for her mood. That left possibilities such as villain's block or annoying feelings.

Nonsense. She was Faith Faraday. A genius in engineering, chemistry, and physics. She just needed to work harder. She could do more. She'd traveled to other planets and back. She'd outsmarted magical sprites from other dimensions. She'd created a true living robot who could dream its own dreams.

Had she wanted to be an astronaut as a child? There must have been a time before her true goals had formed in her mind. She could ask her mother. No, that wouldn't be worth it. She needed to focus on the future. One day, the map could become real.

A week later, Faraday was still mulling things over. No plan felt right. She returned to the World Window. To her delight, she tuned into an alternate universe with a Faraday who had used trickery to kill her world's version of Pulsar. But then this version was almost immediately captured by other heroes and imprisoned. During the trial, this Faraday didn't seem to hear the charges brought against her or her sentence. She didn't boast about her victory over Pulsar. She just looked tired.

Faith Faraday was shaken at first, then dismissed this world. There was nothing to learn.

In another sideways reality, a version of herself became President of the United States. This President Faraday turned public opinion against Pulsar and succeeded in legally imprisoning her. It was incredible to see!

But the President Faraday of this Earth did not trust her own victory. She became paranoid, shouting about new conspiracies, flying into public rages when she felt people were not loyal enough. Her allies wondered if she needed to be removed.

Faith Faraday's confusion boiled into anger. Why was this other incarnation sabotaging herself when a true path to total victory was within reach?

Faith searched further. At last, she found another Earth where an alternate Faraday seemed to have achieved some form of victory and satisfaction. But this version had abandoned her goals for domination and her conflict with Pulsar. Instead, this Other Faraday now created technology to address social ills that couldn't be punched into submission or solved with super-powers.

It was appalling. To disregard all her plans, effort, and brilliance? To decide suddenly that years of trial and error had all been the wasted efforts of a fool? To settle for a life of … of community service? Cowardice. Insanity.

How was it she still hadn't found any Faraday who had really succeeded? Was there no other outcome for her than just different flavors of defeat?

She sat and considered this for several nights, her mind shifting through reactions and moods faster than the World Window had shifted through dimensions. Finally, she started to calm. These other Faradays, these doppelgängers and equivalent twins and hypothetical people … none of them represented her fate. They were warnings against weakness. They hadn't had the will needed for victory or understood true endurance.

But she could be the exception across realities. She could still figure out how.

Victor Faraday didn't look up when his daughter entered his office. Faith wasn't surprised. He had always claimed his attention was a currency more valuable than time itself. She took a seat, quietly judged the office rug, and explained recent events.

"Honestly, Faith," he said as he scrolled through his black tablet, "why waste any time consulting with theme villains and pop art criminals when your own father has been running hostile takeovers and criminal operations for years? You could still join one of my operations."

"All you do is play the same game all politicians and robber barons have done since they decided money works best when it's hoarded," Faith remarked. "All your work and you still never have enough money or influence. I am trying to do something worthy. Something creative that changes the world in ways only I—"

"Do you want me to say I'm impressed, Faith? That I admire your determination to repeatedly take the harder road just to prove a point? That I respect your determination to stand against your enemies in direct confrontation instead of learning where they live and killing them in their sleep? You could have been a political player by now if you accepted that cheating is a good strategy. We could have made something together."

Faith shook her head. "There's no end goal with corporate conquests. You think stability is weak and accumulation is victory. You're caught in a loop and turn your back on the horizon. I have a vision."

"Your vision has changed more than once already. Consider your life, Faith. You were a teenage genius with fantastic inventions. You got government funding and a path to fame, even political leadership. But Pulsar publicly debuted as a superhero, and you resented her spotlight. She sought friendship, the naïve idealist. You responded by challenging her again and again until your rushed, ill-considered inventions endangered people that *she* then had to save. You could have recovered with some PR, some right-worded apology. You could have played the redemption arc card, gathering influence. But you had no patience or self-awareness. You blamed others for the dangers you caused and doubled down. More inventions. More fights with Pulsar. The government removed your funding, so you attacked them next. The teenage genius you used to be ... would she agree with your dreams now?"

Through gritted teeth, Faith answered. "That's ... a

simplistic and inaccurate summary. I've done incredible things, even in defeat."

"Like making a window that says your failures are a multiversal constant? Or a robot who wants to be an actor and writer? Imagine. You build an heir, teach it to think, then watch in dread when it dreams of a life contrary to your plans. Typical child. You have my sympathies."

"The fact that she developed personal ambition is a breakthrough in syntelligence," Faraday snapped. "Her existence will prove—"

"And there it is again. You want to prove yourself publicly when you don't need to. Just tell people you're the hero. Tell them you already won. Shout at a few crowds. Do podcasts and interviews. Bribe the right supporters. Tell people Pulsar's the problem, that her presence holds them back. Sell yourself as the solution and tell them it was their idea to think of you that way."

"More corporate advertising that won't work long term," Faraday said. "You fall or someone knocks you down with a better story. You can't stand firm on lies if you have nothing real beneath you."

"You can with mass marketing," her father chuckled. "You don't need real victory. Just good branding."

Faith stared at her father. Victor Faraday shrugged, saying, "You don't see it. You have your mother's romantic heart. Will you see her while you're in town?"

"You know I won't."

Victor nodded and returned to the reports on his tablet. A receptionist came in and showed Faith out.

~

In her lair, Faraday examined the World Window again. It was probably pointless. But she needed distraction. The static was back in her mind.

Why can't we try something different?

After days of further searching through multiversal frequencies, she was surprised to find an Earth where she and her solar-powered rival were fictional characters in a TV program. She dug deeper and found a podcast interview with an actor named Clarissa Collyer who played this world's fictional version of Pulsar.

"Do you think there's hope for her?" the podcast host asked. "They were friends first, before Pulsar started getting attention as a superhero. If Faraday got past her envy and her insecurities and the rest, could they be friends again in the future of the show?"

"I don't know," the actor Collyer admitted. "That question is part of what fans love about Faraday's character. Some of them cheer for her to double down on being a villain, even though defeats keep piling up and she keeps ignoring lessons she could learn. Some fans keep hoping that one day she'll realize she can do something else, anything else. But I don't know if she'll accept that. If you define yourself by a limited view of what it means to be accomplished, it can be difficult to challenge that idea and ask yourself whether you've been wasting your time. I don't know if Faraday has the will to face that possibility."

Faith Faraday shut off the World Window. Clarissa Collyer vanished from sight.

"That sounded insightful," a synthesized voice said.

Faith Faraday jumped and turned to see Mechani-... Mech-Beth standing at the entrance to the room. A red leather jacket adorned her metal frame and a blue scarf hung loosely around her neck.

"Hello, Mom," Mech-Beth greeted.

Faraday tensed, still not used to being called such a nickname.

"Beth," Faraday greeted flatly. "Are you here to lead the police and Pulsar to me?"

"I have no interest in your conflict," Beth responded. "Violence isn't my path."

"Of course," Faraday sighed, rolling her eyes. "You're an artist. Well, at least people seem to like your work."

"This is for you." Beth produced a small envelope from her pocket and handed it over. "Tickets. It would be nice if you could see one of my shows."

Faraday held the envelope and considered several responses. Then, she put it on the table and said, "I'm often busy."

"When was the last time you did something outside of work? When was the last time you rested your brain from your big goals and did something for its own sake?"

"You're young," Faraday sighed. "You don't under-stand endurance."

"I understand that changing your mind's program-ming starts with pausing long enough to think and then trying a new choice."

Faraday was silent. Beth turned to leave. "There's a seat reserved for you. There will be one at my next show, too. I hope you'll come."

"You could've helped me build a better future," Faith called after her.

"I still might," Beth said without turning back. "If you really consider the possibilities."

Faith Faraday sat looking at the map that was not yet a map. Artists. Actors. They had dreams but no insight, not really. Changing her "mind's programming." Starting a new path from scratch. Romantic ideas to justify giving up. She wasn't that weak. She was close to victory, she could feel it. She only needed to try harder, think smarter. Just for a little longer.

But there was still static in the distance. Whispered questions.

She sipped tea she didn't acknowledge was cold.

She never should have looked through the Window.

The End

"Chance" Alan Pablo Kistler (he/him) is a writer, director, storytelling consultant, and former bartender. He has worked in film and live theatre in New York City, video game marketing in Los Angeles, and contributed to the direction and production of video trailers for titles including Star Wars: Jedi Survivor and LEGO Batman: Legacy of the Dark Knight. He is neurodivergent, half-Peruvian, all nerd, and fueled by a blend of coffee, tea, and benevolent lunacy.

MONSTER SMUT IS RUINING MY LIFE
BY MEGHAN SPELBRINK

Krampus <krampus@almythos.org> Dec 6. 2024, 5:42AM
>To: IR Holiday Division
>Subject: Hell Hath No Power Against a Horny Human

To Whom It May Concern:

I don't even know who my department rep is. I've never had to contact you before. But I can't keep working under these conditions! Last night was Krampusnacht, my night to shine, the night of terror and punishment that keeps me fed for the rest of the year. But instead of screaming and gnashing of teeth, what did I find? Lust. Wet, sticky, sordid lust. No remorse, no bargaining for forgiveness or more time. Just "Spank me, Daddy. I've been a very naughty girl," and "Finally! I've been waiting all night, my dark lord," and "You want me to beg? I can beg, big guy." What has gotten into women these days? No fear whatsoever! They're confronted with a strange, horned, half-goat demon in their bedrooms and are turned on? I even tried taking them up on their offers in an effort to scare them with how far a being like me would push them. I don't think I even came close to their limits. Not one safe word was uttered. Not one ounce of delicious fear dripped from their souls. It was all excitement and libido. They wanted me to keep going all night with the filthiest filth you can possibly imagine (and yes, that's saying something for a Knight of Hell). I'm not an incubus. I'm not built for these unrealistic expectations! I'm drained almost completely of magic due to the expenditure and the lack of fear to feast on. I'm about ready to throw in the towel and transfer to an in-Hell torture chamber. Sure, it's more hours, but at least I'll get to eat! Tell Management to fill the Krampusnacht position with an incubus or succubus if she can't make a change because I can't do this for another year.

Insincerely,

Krampus, Terror of Winter Nights (or, at least, I used to be)

Mari Lwyd sat back from her desk after reading the email a second time, and ran a soothing hand down her long, bony muzzle. *Another one.* This was the third such complaint in as many months. Just to her inbox. She wasn't even the only Inhuman Resources Assistant that dealt with the Holiday Division.

"Hey, horse face." Belsnickel's voice dripped honey, despite its usual grit. He poked his grizzled, antler-crowned head around the cubical wall separating them and winked. His choice of words might be considered an insult to humans, but here in the Under Realm it was pure flattery. And accurate. She was a therianthropic horse demon after all. "You wanna grab a cup of decaf after work today?"

Third day this week. He is persistent. She tried not to preen. The busy season was upon them, she was prepping for her own trip Above in a few weeks, and she had an IR mystery to get to the bottom of. She didn't have time for canoodling with a coworker, however persuasive, persistent, or pretty he might be.

Mari tossed her mane and played coy. "Not really my drink of choice."

"More of a blood of the martyrs kind of gal?"

"Nope."

"Milk stolen from the hands of babes?"

She chuckled, which came out as more of a whinny. *Flirt.* "Not even close. And I doubt I'll have time. I just received an email that might require some field investigation."

He glanced at the subject line on her screen. "Is it the demon kink thing?"

"I think so?" She sat back in her chair and swiveled to face him. "Unfed fear-based demons. You too?"

"Mmhmm. I got at least two this week. Wild, huh? Something's definitely going on Above. Sex Division's been recruiting a lot. Weird stuff too." He rolled his chair closer. The scent of pine needles and woodsmoke tickled Mari's sensitive nose. It wasn't unpleasant.

Maybe it's not just the Human Realm being affected. Could it be a contagious pheromone issue?

Belsnickel leaned in and lowered his gravelly voice. "A

buddy of mine down in SD Acquisitions just told me he onboarded a fork after Thanksgiving."

She reared back. "Like ... the inanimate object?"

"Not so inanimate from what I hear, but yeah."

Mari whiffled air through her lips. "Humans are so weird." She rolled back to her desk and added a meeting to the team calendar for next week to discuss the matter further. Whatever this was, they couldn't dump it all on Sex Division, and she needed to know how widespread the problem was before initiating a field investigation.

Something big was shifting in the Human Realm, and if they didn't catch up, it could spell disaster. Hungry, unsatisfied demons could break free of their bonds and easily ravage humankind. They might cull more of the food supply than they should, or wipe out entire belief systems, effectively killing magic for connected supernatural beings, rendering them mortal. It wouldn't be the first time. It's why A.L. Mythos existed as a company.

Belsnickel stroked his chest-length beard and moved back to his cubicle. "Want me to help? I'm headed topside next week. I could scope out the issue."

"That'd be great actually." The more data they could gather, the better handle they'd have on the situation. "I'm not slated until after Christmas."

"Maybe we could grab that drink when I get back? You know, to go over my notes."

"I'd love to." She smiled at him and popped a sugar cube into her mouth from the tin on her desk. "If you can manage to guess my order."

Mari Lwyd <mari@almythos.org> Dec. 12, 2024, 4:23PM

To: Krampus, IR Sex Division
RE: Hell Hath No Power Against a Horny Human

Dear Krampus,

I wish I could say this was the only instance of humans losing their fear of demons, but it seems to be a common complaint in our inboxes recently. I'm copying Sex Division on this email, but they've been extremely overworked and understaffed taking on so many referrals from other departments. I also wish I could say it was only the female human population affected. It's not. We had a department meeting to discuss the matter this morning, and based on preliminary data, it seems all genders are represented (though the female demographic is the largest). Rest assured your complaint has been filed and will be investigated and addressed before the next Krampusnacht. I hear there's a support group forming for the affected demons. Contact the organizer here if you're interested. You may use this link to follow the status of your complaint in the employee portal.

Worst Regards,

Mari Lwyd, The Grey Death

A.L. Mythos, Holiday Division, Inhuman Resources Assistant

~

Krampus <krampus@almythos.org> Dec. 22, 2024, 11:59AM

To: IR Holiday Division, IR Sex Division

Subject: Krampusnacht

Dear Mari Lwyd,

Have there been any developments on my previous complaint? The link you sent seems to be broken. At least, it takes forever to load, and the progress bar hasn't moved at all. Which makes it a fantastically evil software, but it's hard to appreciate Glitch Division's genius with my current level of anxiety and malnutrition. It's been almost two weeks in the Human Realm with no word. I've had to pilfer fear from a war zone to keep from burning out of magic, and I joined that support group to try and make it through New Year's without hyperventilating in a dark corner or destroying a small village in the middle of nowhere without authorization. Tell me there's new information.

Insincerely,

Krampus, Terror of the Night (hopefully again soon)

"Diet Dr. Pepper."

Mari turned at Belsnickel's voice and let her gaze travel up his impressively tall form as he strode toward her desk. He was windblown and ruddy-cheeked with a fresh dusting of snow clinging to his beard and fur-trimmed coat.

He's back. The office had been quiet for the last week while he was Above. Too quiet.

"Nope."

"Plain-ass water."

She smiled and shook her head. She'd missed this, missed him.

"Oh, Hell. It's eggnog, isn't it?"

She rolled her eyes. "No one in their right mind likes eggnog. Weren't you on the Torturous Traditions Development Team for that?"

"Its inventor, actually." Belsnickel's beard twitched with a smile. "You been reading my resume?"

Her heart stampeded in her chest. *Woah*, she scolded it, worried it might run away and leap the distance between them. *Steady, girl.*

"More like paying attention. Unlike you, Flirty McLumberjack. You're welcome to keep guessing beverages, but I don't have high hopes based on your choices after a week of contemplation."

He stilled, towering above her seated form. No, drooping above her seated form, leaning on the back of her chair. Exhausted, haggard, drained.

She sobered. "It happened to you too."

He nodded, and snow drifted down from his antlers to sprinkle on Mari's nose. She licked it off out of instinct.

Belsnickel tracked the movement then shook his head and groaned. "None of that today, Mari." He slumped into his own desk chair. "I can't handle anything remotely sexual right now. Those *humans*. Gods above and below!"

She wasn't jealous, it clearly hadn't been a positive experience for him, but she was concerned. They needed to get to the bottom of this mess, preferably before she went Above herself in a few days. "Tell me."

"You're never going to believe this."

She waited, silent.

"It's books."

"Books?"

"Books."

"I guess that's not completely outlandish," she replied. *Though we usually have a little more notice when a new faith crops up or a religious sect shifts texts.* "Holy books from a variety of faiths have neutralized demons in the past. Along with sigils, spells, amulets, totems—"

"No. No, no, no." He waved his glove-clad hands as if warding off the idea. "These aren't holy books. If anything, they are the exact opposite. They're romance novels."

Mari opened her mouth, but nothing came out. *Romance novels?*

Belsnickel lost it. He doubled over and cackled, drawing the attention of the few beings still in the office at Yule. "Your face!"

"I—There must be a mistake."

He continued to laugh.

Mari whiffled, annoyed. "Erotic literature is older than the Bible."

"Erotic literature is *in* the Bible. That's not the point." Belsnickel wiped a tear from the corner of his eye, humor still shading his words. "Monster Smut is a new subgenre blowing up the online charts, social media, and fan fiction forums everywhere. It's the source of our issue."

Her mind went blank. The words he was saying made no sense together. *He must have gotten something wrong, misinterpreted, lost his mind with hunger.* "Monster Smut is an oxymoron. Smut is based on happiness and indulgence, a joyous, sensual fantasy. Monsters are reserved for horror, science fiction, terror legends, nightmares—"

"Preaching to the choir, horse face." Belsnickel's laugh lines crinkled, and he held her gaze as he used the endearment, but it wasn't sexual this time. There was no heat. His eyes were the crisp cold of a perfect winter morning dawning on an untouched blanket of snow. Comforting. Deep. Patient. Clear.

He's lucid. He didn't get it wrong. She looked away, shaking her mane. "Monster Smut?"

"I know. But it's true. Seems that led to Demon Erotica with holiday spinoffs, and here we are. Readers are practically inviting us in, as long as we're there to fulfill their darkest fantasies. No fear. No terror. Just desire."

"Wow." She brushed her hand down her muzzle. "Santa's got a brand-new bag."

"Pretty sure that's a title, actually."

"If it's not, it should be." Mari flashed him a smile then smoothed her skirt. "You think even someone like me—"

"Definitely. You've always been beautiful by demon standards, but humans are finally catching on to the finer things in life." He said it so casually, like it was pure fact instead of flattery.

A bashful nicker escaped her lips before she could contain it.

"There are entire book universes dedicated to shifters, but even standard half-humans like minotaurs or yourself, and nonhumans like aliens or dinosaurs get play. I finally asked one of the humans about the specifics and got *way* more information than I was looking for." Belsnickel bent over his knees and shoved his fingers through his hair. "We are so screwed."

"Pun intended."

He half-groaned, half-chuckled. "Too soon."

"This is bigger than us," Mari said. "We need to get Management involved."

Belsnickel nodded, his antlers grazing the edge of her skirt. "Sooner rather than later."

Mari swiveled toward her desk to send the email, but not before brushing a comforting hand on his back and whispering, "Wassail is my drink of choice."

~

Mari Lwyd <mari@almythos.org> Jan. 6, 2025, 2:36PM
    To: Krampus, IR Sex Division
    RE: Krampusnacht Update

Dear Krampus,

Yes, there is new information regarding your experience. After a data gathering mission by an undercover operative and an exhaustive internal inquiry, we have linked the issue to a PR initiative put in motion a decade ago by the Mythological Monster Division in an effort to garner some respect in the age of "pics or it didn't happen." People just weren't believing in monsters like they used to, and the whole department was in danger of being let go. Management approved the initiative then quickly forgot about it when her focus shifted to the Political Discontent Division, the World Conflict Division, the Plague Division—you get the idea. But the PR stunt worked, for MMD at least. It seems Monster Romance (aka Monster Smut) has seen a huge boom on the eReader market. Humans of all genders are begging for the stuff. But writing about sexy monsters naturally led to authors writing erotica featuring other traditionally scary creatures, including demons. And there's a lot of it. (Some of it is quite good actually. Here's a <u>link</u>.) But it's turned many previously terrifying beings into objects of intense and often kinky sexual desire, which is creating a division of labor issue for the company. We are currently in meetings with Management about next steps. I'll keep you posted.

Worst Regards,

Mari Lwyd, The Grey Death

A.L. Mythos, Holiday Division, Inhuman Resources Assistant

Steam curled upward into the crisp winter night from the mug of wassail clutched between Mari's fingers as she and Belsnickel cuddled on an outdoor couch, stargazing. It was the most relaxing date she'd ever been on, which was exactly what they both needed after such an insanely busy month at work.

"Will you take the deal?" Mari asked him softly. It had been a wonderful evening, and she hated to spoil it with reality, but she needed to know. It had been a very long time since she'd gone out with anyone, and she liked Belsnickel. But with all the shifts the company was making, they might not have more than tonight.

He sighed, his warm breath blowing a cloud into the air. "I might not have a choice. I'm a demon of justice, not torture. If the company's program can help me channel that into a job at Sex Division ..."

"It's better than mortality." She nuzzled into his chest. He smelled of pine and snow-dampened wool.

"Yeah."

Silence stretched between them, heavy with the weight of change. Belsnickel stroked a glove-clad hand down her neck, soothing and repetitive. Mari closed her eyes and enjoyed it. She loved being touched this way.

He finally whispered into her mane, "What about you?"

"I've already accepted a new position." A promotion, a big one. But he'd find out soon enough. She wanted to keep their easy repartee tonight while they were still on equal footing. "My job should shift smoothly. I've never been a fear demon. I was born of joy, singing, and wassail." She lifted her head and smiled at him. "These books are bringing happiness. It's got a slightly different flavor than I'm used to, but it'll sustain me. I'll see you in Sex Division once you graduate. I'm sure the inventor of something as heinous as eggnog has a few more ideas up his sleeve."

Belsnickel's laugh lines deepened with his smile. "Save me a seat, horse face. I won't be long."

She lifted her mug in salute and clinked it against his. "First day's round is on me."

~

Krampus <krampus@almythos.org> Feb. 15, 2025, 3:56AM

To: IR Holiday Division, IR Sex Division
Subject: Monster Smut is Ruining My Life

Dear Mari Lwyd,

I can't do this anymore. I got propositioned. Me. Summoned. On Valentine's Day. I AM OFF THE CLOCK PEOPLE! Please consider this my two weeks' notice. I plan to retire to a remote island that has no internet connectivity to start over. I know it's a step down in my career, but at this point, it's worth it. A small food source is better than no food source. I'll send a forwarding address for my final check once I'm settled.

Insincerely,

Krampus, Terror of the Night (once more ... fingers crossed!)

∼

Mari Lwyd <mari@almythos.org> Feb. 18, 2025, 9:12AM
    To: Krampus
    RE: Monster Smut is Ruining My Life

Dear Krampus,

Before you go, would you consider rebranding instead? The company is offering paid courses in the Sexual Arts and a higher position in Sex Division upon completion (pun intended). Management wants to capitalize on our viral popularity in this area and is willing to greatly increase your salary, as well as offer a food stipend in Hell's Torture Kitchen for all your fear consumption needs during the transition. If you're interested, you can apply internally at this link. If not, let me know, and I'll initiate your offboarding paperwork.

Many Sexy Returns,

Mari Lwyd, The Grey Death

A.L. Mythos, Sex Division, Holiday Smut Director

P.S. Just a little career advice from one demon to another: it's only a matter of time before the missionaries bring the Good Word and the internet to those islands (which will lead to books about much more than the missionary position, if you know what I mean). No pressure, but it might be better to bite the bullet and make the shift now. Either way, I wish you luck and terror.

The End

Meghan Spelbrink was raised in Missouri on a steady diet of fairytales, mythology, old school Star Wars novels, and making up stories for her brother's Lego battles. She now lives in California, is a stay-at-home mom to a feisty four-year-old, wife to a wonderfully nerdy virologist, and a dog-mom to an ornery rescue. She is an award-winning writer (The Emily Contest 2024), President of the Bay Area Romance Writers, and holds BAs in English Literature and Secondary Education from William Jewell College and an MFA in Writing Popular Fiction from Seton Hill University.

THE ZEPHYR

BY DENNIS K. CROSBY

"**H**ere you go."

Jenisys Jones took the cup. It was as nondescript as the room she was in. Both were plain white. No style, but still warm in a lazy way. Like they were working hard to appear pleasant and comfortable but didn't really care if they achieved the look or not. It didn't impact her mood, though, because today was an important day. She'd planned this for a long time. She'd been patient—more so than she'd ever been in her life.

It was time.

"Oh, wow!" Jenisys exclaimed. "Thank you. You folks *actually* have soy milk in this place?"

"No. What we *do* have is a fancy schmancy gourmet coffee shop about a block away."

"And you sent someone? Just for me? Oh my god, thank you!"

Jenisys removed the lid from the cup and inhaled the sweet aroma. It cleared her head. Centered her. Made it possible for her to do the things she needed to do. What she needed to do now was get through this interview with Detective Omar.

She took a sip.

She closed her eyes.

And she smiled.

"Oh yeah, that's doin' things for me," she said.

Despite the display of generosity with the special coffee, there was a slight look of annoyance on Detective Omar's face. It didn't slow Jenisys one bit. In fact, it only added to her delight. She enjoyed dysfunction. She reveled in it. Took pleasure in being its agent. Jenisys was a loyal employee of chaos.

And today was Employee Appreciation Day.

"Okay, Miss Jones—"

"Oh, you can call me J.J. All my friends do. Well, some of my friends do."

The detective's arched eyebrow told her that she'd be addressed as "Miss Jones" throughout the interview.

"I'm just saying," began Jenisys, "this doesn't have to be all weird. It's ... a conversation between two professional women, right? I mean, you have questions. I have answers. But I also have questions. Maybe you can help me. I can help you. We can help each other. Wouldn't that be amazing if we just helped each other? Let's show the world how it's done."

Jenisys held out her fist. After a few seconds, she smiled, nodded, put her hand down, and drank more coffee.

"Miss Jones," the detective began again, "can you confirm for me that your name is, in fact, Jenisys Alia Jones?"

"I can."

"And that you are currently thirty-eight years old, residing at 515 Garfield Street, in Oak Park, Illinois."

"I mean, you didn't have to call out my age or anything like that, but yes, that's all true," Jenisys said with a smile.

"Is it?" asked the detective, knowingly. "Because … that's a park. Would you have us believe you're homeless and living in a park?"

Jenisys giggled, shrugged her shoulders, and drank more coffee.

"Tell you what, we can move on from that. We'll get you fingerprinted and see what that yields," said the detective. "Moving on to the good stuff. Can you account for your whereabouts on the night of Friday, June 11th?"

"Are you talking the whole night?" asked Jenisys, sitting up straight, eyes focused on the officer. "Because some things are private, detective."

She held out her fist once again and, just as before, received no reciprocity. It wasn't an arched eyebrow this time, but an eyeroll that let Jenisys know how the detective was feeling. Butterflies were fluttering about in her tummy, and Jenisys couldn't help but giggle.

This is going to be fun.

"Listen, Miss—Jenisys," said the detective, softening her tone.

"Ohhhh, we're using first names now. Nice! What's yours?" she asked hurriedly.

Several beats of silence passed, and eventually, though with some visible discomfort, the detective spoke.

"Rania."

"Rania," repeated Jenisys. "Detective Rania Omar. That's pretty rad. I dig it. I know a Rania. Haven't seen her in a long time, though. Maybe after I get out of here, I'll pay her a visit. What's a thirteen-hour flight to Jordan between friends, am I right?"

Jenisys sipped more coffee.

"You know, I've read a lot about you," the detective replied. "I know you like to catch people off guard with this kind of flighty, flirty, nonsensical behavior."

"You think I'm flirting with you, Rania?" asked Jenisys, biting her lower lip.

She meant to disrupt and disturb, and, as usual, she succeeded in both. The detective's flushed cheeks spoke volumes. Jenisys had no sexual interest in Rania Omar. None of what she was doing now was rooted in sexual attraction, though the detective was a beautiful woman. Her olive skin, hazel eyes, and brown curly locks were, in every sense of the word, attractive. Actually, they were much more than that. But the detective's degree of desirability was not the focus of the day.

Disruption was.

"Okay, just so we're clear," began Rania, "I have had women and men in that chair—"

"This chair?"

"That chair," confirmed the detective, clearly annoyed. "And they've all done their best to get under my skin, or in my pants. I have all the patience in the world, but at some point, even *that* cup gets empty, you know?"

"Preachin' to the choir, sister."

"So, before we get there, how about you answer my questions. I'll be more than happy to answer yours. And then we can move on to next steps. Whaddaya say?"

Jenisys took another drink of her coffee. The butterflies continued their gentle assault in her tummy. Things were progressing nicely.

"I'm sorry. I promise, I'm much better after coffee," said Jenisys. "Thank you, again, for getting this."

"You're welcome," said Rania.

"Okay, so … you asked where I was Friday night. Let me think. I went to get my hair cut at ten that morning. I decided to try something new. I remember seeing Halle Berry in *Boomerang* and I absolutely loved that look. And since I already kinda look like her, I decided to give it a shot."

"Looks great," said Rania.

"Thank you," said Jenisys with a grin and an eyelash flutter. "Okay, so after that, I went home and packed a bag for some late-night shenanigans. Then grabbed dinner with a friend to kill some time after the Field Museum closed. And then … around eleven that night, give or take a few minutes, I robbed it."

A beat passed.

"You robbed it?" asked Rania.

"Yes, ma'am."

"To be clear, you're not talking about the restaurant you had dinner in?"

"No, ma'am," said Jenisys.

"You're confessing to robbing the Field Museum on the night of Friday, June 11th of this year?"

"I am, indeed. Yes," said Jenisys.

There was no eye roll or arched eyebrow this time. Just the look of utter disbelief on the face of Detective Omar. For Jenisys, though, the butterflies were in a frenzy —causing a grin so wide that her cheeks hurt.

It took a few moments for her to collect herself, and when she did, she sat back, crossed one leg over the other, and said, "Can I get another cup of coffee?"

It had been over an hour since her very casual confession, which included providing the location of the stolen artifact. Jenisys assumed they were taking the time to verify that information and collect the item. There were some questions about how to proceed, because according to the confession, the item never left the museum. She had had trouble actually getting it out of the building. So, was it even theft? Maybe it was just mischief. Jenisys was fine with either.

She was spinning around in her chair to kill time when the door to the interview room finally opened. Detective Omar stepped in. She had a rather pensive look on her face. A man walked in just behind her. He was tall and lean. Fairly fit. His face was pockmarked beneath a struggling five o'clock shadow. If not for the badge, he could easily be mistaken for a criminal.

"Miss Jones?" he said.

"Yes?"

"You're not going to ask him to call you J.J.?" asked Rania.

Jenisys giggled. "Him? Nah. I told you, only my friends can do that," she said with a flirty wink.

"My name is Lieutenant Hoffman," said the man, cutting in. "I'm just stopping in to verify your confession."

"Verify?" asked Jenisys.

"Yes. You know, to make sure that it wasn't made under duress, or with the promise of anything?"

"Wait a minute," began Jenisys, turning her gaze to Rania. "Is he trying to say there's no way you coulda got a confession outta me? Isn't he supposed to be ... like ...

happy?" Jenisys shifted her attention to the lieutenant. "Also, how can you not be supporting one of your detectives for a job well done? What the hell is that about? Sexist much?"

Jenisys watched the good detective stifle a laugh. The lieutenant on the other hand …

"It's nothing like that. I'm here to make sure that you did, in fact, willingly write and sign this confession. Because in my experience, with something like this, no one just says, 'Hey, I did it'."

"Well, that's because you mess around with bush league crooks, Lieutenant. Respectfully."

"Bush league?" asked Rania.

"Oh yeah. Punks and braggarts. That's all you really get in here. You've never had a … well … me … come in here. I'm a whole different breed."

"Of criminal?" asked the lieutenant.

"I prefer to think of myself as a global liberator of illicit goods," said Jenisys.

"A liberator?" asked Rania.

Jenisys nodded.

"You stole the Scarab of Osiris. One of the oldest and most famous artifacts in existence," said Rania.

"Yeah, but I wasn't the first, was I?" asked Jenisys.

The officers shared a look before turning their attention back to Jenisys.

"The religion of the ancient Egyptians goes back thousands of years. It predates Christianity. Worshippers of Osiris created the scarab. True believers. It was created to honor their god and show their fealty. Then it was lost for ages. When it was found, instead of being returned to Egypt, it was put in a museum *not* in Egypt. So, yeah. Stolen."

"Please don't sit there and tell me you stole it with the intention of returning it to the Egyptian people. Tell me this isn't some political stunt," said Hoffman.

Jenisys wasn't political. In her business it paid to have as few affiliations to anything as possible. She'd passed on beautiful condos because she wouldn't join the HOAs. She cared about politics only when they infringed on her rights. At her core, she had empathy for others, so she would act on their behalf in certain circumstances. Particularly when the action also benefited her or caused discord within the system.

"I don't get into politics," said Jenisys. "I just try to be the best that I can be. Growth, in any industry, is important. Wouldn't you both agree? I mean, it's not like the two of you just walked into your respective roles, right? You had to learn. Evolve. Adapt. Think about where you started, and where you are now. It's been a long road, right?"

Her question was answered with blank stares.

That suited her fine.

"Do you remember your first big one, Detective? Nothing like it, is there?" asked Jenisys.

"Excuse me?"

"Your first. You know? Your first big arrest."

As the lieutenant snickered and returned to his normal look of annoyance, Rania answered the question on the table.

"Yeah, I remember. It was this wannabe jewel thief. Valerie Meeks. Called herself Valley Girl. I still don't know why. She was from the suburbs."

"What stuck out about that case?" asked Jenisys.

"I don't know. The name? I wasn't even a detective then. I was plain clothes, just helping out. But I broke it.

I broke her," said Rania. "We argued because I could tell she was smart. Couldn't figure out why she was wasting her life. That got her going. She said I got lucky catching her because she was the best. We went back and forth a bit before she declared she'd be escaping from custody. I told her if she ever got away from me, I'd give her my badge. She flipped me off and said she'd take it from me one day. There was a look in her eyes when she said it, though. A look of hunger. Maybe that's what stood out."

"Sounds like my kinda girl. What happened to her?"

"Did time. Got out. Haven't seen her since. She was my first bust, but it was *not* hers. She was a hot mess, too. Ratty brown hair. Split ends. Make-up caked on. Definitely *not* your kind of girl. Nothing like you, Jenisys."

"Aww. You flirtin' with me, Rania?"

"Don't start that nonsense, Jones," Rania scoffed. "I just mean, she wasn't as ... upscale as you, shall we say. Could have been, though. Hell, could have been anything but what she was."

"Sounds like you hope she made it," said Jenisys.

"I hope everyone makes it," said Rania. "I'm not heartless. I even hope *you* make it. Your sheet has you down for two arrests, though you're suspected of a string of robberies around the world. If it's true, your scores have been huge. Yet you've been quiet the last few years. Why the change?"

"Maybe there's been no change, Detective," said Jenisys. "Maybe I'm just. That. Good."

The silence that filled the room was electric. While the lieutenant stood there, his stare a volley between the two women, Jenisys captured Rania's gaze. Wheels were clearly turning, and it brought her immense joy.

"Detective Omar," began the lieutenant, "get this woman processed and find her some lodgings till—"

"Wait," said Rania. "Sir, if I may."

The detective gestured for him to join her outside. After sighing deeply, the lieutenant acquiesced to her request. Jenisys stood after they left. She stretched, ran in place, then dropped down and did twenty quick pushups, followed by twenty jumping jacks. Feeling a little more energy, she sat. Again. In the dull, non-descript room with sweaty white concrete walls.

When Detective Omar returned, she did so alone. She carried a file filled with paper. It didn't look official, though. It was more scrap-bookish.

"Where's your boss?"

"I gave him something else to consider. In return, he gave me a little more time."

"Time for what?" asked Jenisys.

"To talk," said Rania, leaning back against the door, hugging the file.

Is this the moment?

"About?"

"About a story floating around out there," said Rania. "Rumors of a thief so prolific that he's stolen an artifact in every major city on Earth without leaving so much as a fingerprint."

"Impressive," said Jenisys.

"Right?" said Rania. "And here's the thing. They say he's got something of a Robin Hood complex. A thief for a cause. The crook with a heart of gold."

"Ugh! How boring," said Jenisys.

"Well, it is a tired trope," agreed Rania. "Between movies and TV shows, the gentleman thief bit is a bit played out."

"Tell me about it," said Jenisys. "Except for the French guy on Netflix. I like him. He's so … tall. Yeah … I like him a lot." Jenisys drifted away for a moment. Some of it was genuine. She did fancy the man, after all. "Anyway, what's your point?"

"Well," began Rania, "it's weird. There's been this international manhunt for the guy. No stone unturned types of investigations … and nothing. No prints. No hair. No DNA. Not so much as a grainy photo."

"Guess he's that good," said Jenisys.

"Yeah," began Rania, smiling, "and … maybe … he's not a *he*."

Jenisys was giddy. The butterflies felt like the Blue Angels turning barrel rolls in her belly.

"You're not suggesting *I'm* this thief?"

The detective moved slowly, purposefully, toward the chair opposite Jenisys, and sat. She placed the folder on the table and opened it. Inside there were various newspaper clippings and sheets of paper with scribbles. Jenisys accepted the unspoken invitation to go through it and read some of the headlines. They were from all over the globe.

All stories about the Zephyr.

"I'm saying … something," said Rania, and flung her arms up, grinning from ear to ear. She sat back in her chair, never losing eye contact. "Come on, Jenisys. Are you going to tell me that you don't know about the Zephyr? You seem savvy. You have the aloof thing down pat, but deep down I know you're brilliant. I can see it."

"You're too kind," said Jenisys.

Several moments of silence lay between the two. Jenisys finally closed the folder, pushed it toward Rania, and sat back in her chair.

"Yeah … I've heard of the Zephyr. Everyone out there has. But it's just an urban legend. It was a rumor started by someone to get reduced time."

"Say more," said Rania.

"Look, the story goes that some guy, years ago, got caught after a big heist, and let me tell you, he was not equipped to do hard time," said Jenisys, tapping the side of her head. "So, to try and get out of a potentially hellish future, he said he'd give up the mastermind behind all the major heists. Well … up to that point, at least. Anyway, he made up this elaborate character called the Zephyr, an alleged criminal genius. He robs, steals, grifts, all to teach the privileged a lesson, or, in some cases, to right the wrongs inflicted on certain nations or cultures. But it was a ruse. A smokescreen. Something completely made up so this guy could get off light and confuse the hell out of law enforcement for years to come."

"That's a pretty elaborate lie," said Rania.

"Yeah … well … desperate times and all. You know?"

"Hmm … desperate indeed," said Rania. "Okay, let's say it is all fake. How do you explain the alleged sightings across the globe?"

"I mean … the lie just grew legs and took off running. I don't know."

"You don't know?"

"Not a single clue," insisted Jenisys. "I can tell you this, though. That guy, the one that was caught… he got his deal. He did light time, I'm talking *light*. He was supposed to stay on as an informant to help them catch the Zephyr, but instead he just … vanished."

"Vanished?"

"Vanished."

"And the rumblings about the Zephyr continued?" asked Rania.

"Well, yeah. Before you knew it, the legend grew too big. Everything was getting blamed on the guy. It was the perfect patsy. A masterclass in misdirection," said Jenisys.

"So, you don't think the Zephyr is real?"

"Think about it. One person? Doing all those jobs across the globe and never getting caught? It's simply hard to fathom. Besides, the mark of a true, bona fide international criminal is to have a nemesis. One cop who makes it their life's work to capture you. The Zephyr had legs, but no nemesis. There wasn't enough evidence out there to convince the world that he was anything more than an urban legend," said Jenisys.

Once again, the silence settled in. It was awkward. Uncomfortable even. For most. It was a tool used by many professionals to get people to talk. PIs, HR Managers, law enforcement, and countless others used silence regularly because people, in general, always felt the need to fill it. They talked more. Sometimes too much. Jenisys knew this trick well. She'd used it on many a mark in her career. She knew how to manipulate it.

I've got you, Detective.

"I mean ... if he were real—"

"Or she," countered Rania.

"Sure. Or she," agreed Jenisys. "If this Zephyr was real, I'm not your girl."

"Not good enough?"

"Oh ... see ... now you're trying to bait me. I see you, Detective. Trying to bruise my ego," said Jenisys, pointing a finger playfully at Rania. "Whether I'm 'good enough' or not isn't my point."

"Then what is?"

"If I were this guy—"

"Or gal."

"Whatever," said Jenisys, feigning annoyance. "If I *were* the Zephyr, why the hell would I allow myself to get caught here? If I'm international, I want one of the big dogs to catch me. It would help with my clout. Gettin' caught here is like a serial killer gettin' caught because of a busted taillight in Coal City. Nothing against Coal City, but sheesh! C'mon."

The comment got a slight chuckle from Rania.

"I got nothin' for you on the Zephyr other than it's a ruse."

"Hmm," said Rania.

"All I know is, I robbed the museum, and I'm ready to do my time. Did you find the scarab?"

"We did. They brought it in a while ago," said Rania. "It was right where you said it would be."

"Well, there you go."

Jenisys held out her arms, preparing for handcuffs.

"Just like that?" asked Rania.

"Honestly, Detective, I'm crashing from the sugar in that coffee, and I'd love to just get through this so I can lie down. Even if it's in a cell."

Rania sat there for a while, as if contemplating more. Jenisys watched the wheels turn. She thought they were moving as fast as the butterflies in her tummy.

"Tell you what," began Rania. "We'll get you processed and taken to a cell. It'll be a while before we get you over to County. In the meantime, you think on some things, and if you decide you want to say more about the Zephyr, you have someone come and get me. Deal?"

"Why do you care about the Zephyr so much?" asked Jenisys, pretending to be exasperated.

"Because if I'm right, and you're her ... well, this ain't Coal City. And if it's a nemesis you're looking for, who's better than a detective with the Chicago Police Department?"

Got you!

"Sure, sis. I get it. Big score and all for you. But I'm not the Zephyr. When you check my prints, you'll see. I'm just a regular, but brilliant, international thief," said Jenisys.

Rania went to the door and called in a uniformed officer who escorted Jenisys through processing. They took photos, fingerprints—all the things. The officer walked her past the evidence room, the door wide open. She caught sight of the scarab on a desk next to an officer typing away—likely logging the artifact into the system.

Jenisys was led through some heavy metal doors to the holding cells.

When the doors closed behind them, the lights went out in the precinct, and all hell broke loose.

Jenisys giggled.

Rania Omar sat on a bench near the evidence room and stared at an envelope left in the spot where the scarab had been. It was plain white, completely non-descript, but there was something peculiar written on it.

To Officer, Now Detective, Rania Omar.

After everything had gone dark, there were twenty or so minutes of pandemonium before lights in the precinct returned. The uniformed officer who'd escorted Jenisys Jones was found on the ground, unconscious. Handcuffed. Jenisys herself was missing.

So, too, was the Scarab of Osiris.

"Detective?" said a voice.

Rania looked up from the envelope to see a uniformed officer standing in front of her. She hadn't even heard the woman walk up.

"Hey, Char. What is it?"

"Got the results on those Jones prints."

The officer handed Rania a folder. As the officer stepped back, Rania put the envelope on the bench and opened the file. She gripped it tightly when she read the information. Especially the name.

"No. Way," she said aloud. "This is bona fide?"

"I ... guess," said the officer, confused.

Rania dropped the file on the bench and grabbed the envelope. She ripped it open and pulled out a single note card. She read it, then quickly stood up and put her hand on her waist.

Her badge was gone.

Rania smiled. Wide. The smile turned to laughter. Then she looked at the uniformed officer and said, "Buckle up, Char. It's about to get fun in here."

Rania turned and walked away, leaving the file and the note on the bench.

The uniformed officer picked up the note and read it.

"Dear Rania, we all evolve into something else. Come and get your badge. See ya 'round. Sincerely, Zephyr aka Val the Valley Girl"

The End

Dennis K. Crosby is an author, editor, speaker, and workshop leader with an MFA in Creative Writing. Since 2020 he has published three urban fantasy novels in his award-winning Kassidy Simmons series, and seventeen short stories found in multiple anthologies. He is the co-editor of Dread Coast: SoCal Horror Tales and has been a panelist and moderator at multiple conventions including, WonderCon, Comic-Con International, Nebula, Bouchercon, and StokerCon 2024 where he also served as Co-Chair. In March 2025 he was awarded the Jonathan Maberry Inspiring Teens Award from the Creative Writing Club at Canyon Crest Academy. Dennis lives in San Diego, CA. where he is secretary of the local chapter of the Horror Writers Association, a member of Crime Writers of Color, and board member of Partners in Crime, the local chapter of Sisters in Crime. For more information on his work go to https://denniskcrosby.com.

FORGIVENESS
BY MORAG WEHRLE

The old woman hobbles onto the bog without hesitation, her feet finding the solid ground she needs without the help of her crooked walking stick. The day fades into flickering twilight. Darkness wraps around her as she moves forward into the creeping trees. The smell of peat, rich with rot, rises to greet her like a friend. She breathes deep. Her strides lengthen. She lets her shoulders drop.

She hums as she walks, and the bog opens up for her. She looks forward to the solitude of her little cottage, a fire and her chair and a glass of her own strong whisky. But for now, she hums a finding song, and her feet carry her in a different direction. The reed basket over her arm is not yet full.

In a dim clearing, at the base of a gnarled willow, she finds the inky-cap mushrooms growing in a thick cluster. The caps topping their pale stems are shaggy but have not yet begun to shade to black. She kneels, produces a sharp knife from the folds of her drab cloak, and harvests what she needs. Then she pricks her thumb with the tip of the blade and lets three drops of blood fall to the sodden earth. The bog rustles its thanks as she gets to her feet and wipes her hands against her knees.

Before she draws a cloth over the now-full basket, she can't resist popping one of the mushrooms into her mouth. She chews slowly as she takes a moment to lean against the tree. The mushroom's thick, pungent flavour makes her belly growl. She thinks of a thick stew, or perhaps a pan of butter and garlic, herbs from her garden. She lets her head rest against the tree's bark for just a moment. A deep weariness weighs down her bones. She allows herself a sigh.

As she rests, sucking the last filaments of mushroom from between her teeth, a pale light bobs toward her through the trees like a tiny moon. Misty, blue-white, it drifts closer, dims, nearly winks out, brightens again. It hesitates at the edge of the clearing, flickering like a candle. The light warms to a friendly, enticing silver. A whisper ghosts over her ears, a chiming bell-like voice. *This way, this way.*

The old woman straightens her back, narrows her eyes at the orb of light. "Foolish creature," she mutters. As the orb moves closer, she waves a hand as though swatting away a fly. With the other, she pushes back the hood of her cloak to reveal her long, tattered braid, bark-brown and threaded with silver. Her face, her hard profile, like a carving. "Don't you recognize me?"

The orb halts. In a blink, its light dims to nearly nothing. Then it swoops to the ground and hovers, quivering, near the old woman's feet.

"Don't *cower*," she says crossly, pulling her hood back into place. "I won't hurt you, you daft thing." The orb hesitates a moment, then drifts upward again until it's level with her waist. The woman sighs, turning toward home. "Don't you have mortals to be leading astray?"

Brightening, the orb bobs up to her eye level again. Keeping pace as she strides through the bog, it stutters back and forth, flies two loops around her head, and zips behind her, where it hovers like a dog following at her heels.

The old woman nearly misses a step, but she catches herself with a jab of her walking stick into a tuft of grass. "You saw *who?*"

The orb blinks on and off, a firefly.

The old woman mutters a curse and picks up her pace. The glowing orb zips along beside her, a faint buzz of excitement rising from its flickering light. She glares at it. "Get back to work," she hisses. Dimming with disappointment, it wisps away into the trees.

She stumps along, her feet finding the safe path through the treacherous bog. Beneath the soporific hum of insects and the distant, mournful hoot of an owl, she can sense it now: a heartbeat that doesn't belong here. The taste of mushroom rises at the back of her throat and she scowls, shifting the basket on her arm. So much for her dinner.

Out of the shadows of trees and vines, a humped shape gradually resolves from the dimness. Her cottage crouches at the edge of a small, open pool; the waters reflect silver and ebony with the wan moonlight streaming from above. A thin trickle of smoke rises from the chimney and twines with the mist that has begun to gather among the trees. The crooked cottage is near impossible to reach without a guide, near impossible to see in the twilight even from a few feet away.

And yet, a visitor.

As the old woman draws near, a smaller shadow detaches itself from the darkness of the cottage and moves forward with hesitant steps. Her face reflects the moonlight like a silver coin. Streaming tresses of pale hair lie against her long dark cloak. She is so young and lovely. They are always so young and lovely.

The visitor bobs a perfunctory curtsy, her wide eyes fixed on the old woman's. "Mistress, I've come to beg your help. I am Elia of—"

But the old woman is already shouldering past her, toward the door of the cottage. "No."

The eyes widen even further, blood drains from the pale cheek. "But I—"

She reaches the door, yanks it open, goes inside. "*No*," she says over her shoulder, and slams it shut.

The knocking starts almost immediately. The old woman moves to the banked fire, where she kneels to stir up the coals and lay some new wood. All the while, the knocking continues.

"Go away."

"Please." More knocking. They aren't usually this persistent. She hums a look-away song, but the girl has already seen her face and the knocking doesn't stop.

"Go away or I'll curse you."

"I'm already cursed." She hears the girl take a deep, shuddering breath. "Please, Bog Mother."

That gets her attention. No one has called her that in ... has it been decades now? In spite of herself, curiosity rises. She pushes herself back to her feet with a grunt and shuffles back to the door.

When she opens it, the moon seems to have drawn closer, as though she is curious too. The girl stands there, cloak pushed back from her shoulders. Her eyes are still wide, but perhaps less with terror than the old woman thought. Now that she looks closer, she sees determination. And a moment later, as her gaze slips down over the rest of the girl's body, she sees the curve of the belly under her dress, round as the moon hanging low in the sky.

The bog witch closes her eyes a moment. Her fingers curl into fists. Then, with a tight jerk of her head, she turns back into the cottage.

She goes straight to her tiny kitchen, where she plonks her reed basket onto the counter with more force than necessary. She picks up an ancient-looking glass bottle and eyes it for a moment, scowling. Then she shakes her head, pours a finger of dark gold liquid from the bottle into a clay cup, and tosses it straight back. Leans on the counter, letting it burn down her throat and chase away the taste of mushroom. Behind her, the faintest of footfalls and the rustle of fine cloth tell her the girl has followed her inside.

"You shouldn't be here," the witch says without turning around.

"I know." A chair creaks.

"I'm retired."

"So I heard."

She turns at that. Elia is perched on her chair—*her* chair!—her hands folded across the swell of her belly. She gazes up at the bog witch, who scowls back at her. "What's that supposed to mean?"

Elia flinches a little at that and drops her eyes. So, she does have some sense of self-preservation. But then she swallows and looks up again. "It means that I hope you'll help me anyway, Bog Mother."

The witch hisses between her teeth. She wonders

again how this child knows that name. "Then do you know what *retired* means? I don't do that work anymore."

The girl looks down at her belly, runs a hand slowly along its curve as she bites her lip. Her shoulders hitch, then quiver. The witch closes her eyes to stop herself from rolling them. She's seen all the moves and knows what's coming. Now the lass will start to sniffle—just enough to make her big doe eyes shine with tears, not enough to blotch her smooth complexion. Next, she'll wring her hands. Her chin will wobble. Then, finally, with a shaking voice, she'll lay out a tale of woe and heartbreak meant to tug at the witch's long-dormant heartstrings. And then the witch is supposed to laugh and say that she'll make the bargain, but the girl will regret it, and suddenly the whole thing just feels so exhausting that she sits down with a *whump* in the other chair and puts a hand over her face.

Elia clears her throat and begins in a whisper. "I have come to you at great peril, Bog Mother. I have—"

"Fine, *fine*," the witch says from behind her hand. "I'll help you if you'll stop calling me that." As Elia trails off, the witch drops her hand and points one long finger at the girl. "But I'm not interested in hearing your tale of sorrow. I carry many stories, but the ones full of tears and regret? I don't carry those anymore."

The girl opens and closes her mouth a few times. "Pah," the witch mutters, and heaves herself back to her feet. She stomps irritably back to the counter and twitches back the cloth that covers the reed basket. She wraps it around the bundle of mushrooms she gathered and ties the ends of the cloth in a neat hard knot. Returning to her chair, she thrusts the packet at Elia, who blinks at her like an owl.

"Mushrooms," the witch says, tossing the bundle onto the girl's lap when she doesn't move to take it. "Over-season them with salt to cause thirst. Have the strongest ale at hand to quench it for him. As for yourself, take only water or milk. And be sure that someone sees you eat of the same dish."

Elia looks down at the wrapped cloth in her lap and picks it up, turning it over in her hands. "Poison," she says slowly.

The witch shakes her head. "Only turning the body against itself. The mushrooms will stop his from breaking down the liquor." She shrugs, sitting back in her chair and popping one last shaggy-cap into her mouth.

Elia's eyes widen as the witch chews. "But I saw you drink something when we came into the cottage," she says, and points to the bottle on the counter. "Whisky, from the smell?"

The girl is observant. Annoyingly so. The witch feels, more than ever, the weary weight of time on her shoulders. "Nothing in this bog will harm me," she says. "Do you want the mushrooms or not?"

In answer, Elia tucks the cloth into a pocket of her cloak. They both sit silently for a while, gazing into the crackling fire. The whisky has settled into the witch's stomach with a pleasant warmth. She glances over at the girl again, at the smooth curve of her cheek, the fine cloth of her garments. She is as out of place in this bog as the witch would be in a royal ballroom. Still, the pampered thing found her way here. She is clever and resourceful. She and her babe will be fine.

Elia shifts in her chair to face the witch, graceful in spite of her swollen belly. She inclines her head. "I've brought payment for you, of course, Bog Mo — I mean, um ..." She falters, clearly unsure what form of address she should use instead.

The witch waves this uninteresting question away. "I have no interest in gold or jewels," she warns.

The girl shakes her head, reaching into another pocket of her cloak to withdraw a tiny bottle made of deep blue glass. A silver stopper hangs from the neck of the bottle by a fine chain. "I have brought neither. Instead, I offer you this: a memory."

The witch sits straight up in her chair.

Elia holds up the bottle, which winks indigo in the firelight. "Freely given, and yours to keep as long as it pleases you."

The bog witch thinks about protesting. A memory? Surely her help is worth more riches. But somehow, this girl came here, knowing her name, knowing what she collects, what she hungers for. So she does not bother with pretense. "Then give it to me."

The young woman nods. Without taking her eyes from the witch's, she lifts the tiny bottle to her lips. She speaks into it, her voice low but clear. "I give you my memory of coming to this place, of the tracks through the bog that led me here. Of asking for your aid and receiving it. Instead, I'll remember finding these mushrooms in the woods. Oversalting them will be a slip of the spoon, while the strong drink at hand—" Her lips quirk in a humorless smile. "This man can be counted on to provide that himself. I give you this memory of the kindness you have done for me."

It's hardly a kindness when it requires payment, the witch thinks.

The girl sits forward, her shining eyes fixed on the

witch's. "I do this in recognition of you helping me," she finishes, "when no one was there to help you."

It is the witch's turn to gape. Elia smiles, a smile so kind and compassionate it stops the witch's breath. With a delicate twist of her fingers, she screws the stopper into the neck of the bottle, now sparkling like the last rays of sunshine off a deep mountain lake. She holds it out to the witch, who watches her own hand rise to take it without any conscious thought. The bottle hums with warmth and comfort against her fingers, and she nearly clutches it to her chest. To cover her confusion, she *harrumphs* and gets up, hurrying to open the cottage door. Elia follows her without protest.

The girl steps outside, then turns back to face her. Before she can speak, the bog witch clicks her tongue. Within a heartbeat or two, a small blue-white orb bobs out of the misty shadows, flickering with interest.

"Take her back to the safest path," the witch says gruffly. The orb dims with alarm and she gives it a pointed glare. *Don't question me.* The orb pulses again; she softens. *Yes, it's fine. I'll be fine.* The little light warms to a friendlier glow.

The witch can see herself fading from the girl's expression as Elia turns away from the cottage. The rich darkness of the bog parts all around. The witch and her cottage draw back into the deeper shadows.

Elia finds herself moving forward, following a steady light through the treacherous ground with tonight's dinner tucked inside her cloak. How lucky to find such delicious mushrooms, she thinks, and she imagines a thick stew, or a pan with butter and garlic. She smiles.

As the girl and the orb vanish into the murmuring quiet of the bog, the witch looks down at the little bottle in her hand. The warmth of the memory inside pulses like a heartbeat against her fingers. She feels, again, the urge to cup the bottle against her chest, to see if that warmth can seep further: into her heart, her bones. Except this is not a memory, no matter what Elia said, no matter even what she may have intended. This warmth is meant to re-light a fire, but the witch does not want to burn.

Instead, she moves out of the doorway and toward the edge of the small pond. Starlight sparkles on its surface, cold and black and smooth. In its bottle, the girl's words sparkle too, serene and steady.

The witch lifts the bottle to her lips.

"I didn't ask for your forgiveness," she murmurs against the burning glass. And before she can stop herself, she hurls the bottle out into the middle of the lake. She doesn't wait to hear the splash before she hobbles back into her cottage, humming the look-away song. Next time, whoever comes looking won't find her.

The End

Morag Wehrle (she/her) is an author and educator who writes at the intersection of culture, health, and history. Her work spans fiction, non-fiction, and academia, and has been included in various anthologies and literary magazines. She holds a BA in Latin from the University of Victoria, an MA in archaeology from University College London, and an MFA in creative non-fiction from the University of King's College. Morag lives and writes on the traditional unceded territories of the WSANEC peoples on Vancouver Island.

THE INVITATION
BY R. V. THOMAS

You learn a lot of things in superhero school—first aid, crisis response, punching things real hard. But one of the final classes you take is Image Management 101. This is where you define your name, your brand, and yes, your costume. A good supersuit is not only functional, it's a calling card. It lets those you serve know who you are and what you stand for. A great one should send any two-bit criminal running.

You know what you learn in villain school? That supersuits are a *problem.*

I'm just kidding, there isn't a villain school.

But you know what there also isn't? A tailor.

The heroes figured this out a few years back. They started issuing licenses to the Utility Design students from the university. Wove trackers and dye packs into Kevlar and spandex. Any body armor and raw fiberglass coming into the city is under careful watch.

And I absolutely loathe that it's *working.* We look like crap. This is my last suit and it's falling apart. Every seam has been restitched twice, and I'm not much of a seamstress. The whole thing is one bad brawl away from disintegrating altogether.

Tonight, I've taken a fireball to the stomach. Don't worry, I'm fine. The mycelia in my skin have already stitched me back together. My suit wasn't so lucky. There's a gaping hole with melted edges that will take a lot more than a needle and thread to fix.

I climb into the alley, still clutching my gut and catching my breath as my insides put themselves back where they're supposed to be. There are a bunch of designers and fashion houses on this block. Sometimes you can get lucky with a scrap of material, though they're usually careful to burn anything robust enough to serve the purpose.

Don't get me wrong, I could grab leggings and a leather jacket anywhere in the city and call it a night. Hell, I'd be content to fight in sweatpants. But that's not exactly intimidating, is it? Polyester melts. Canvas has no give. My regenerative powers aren't invincible, and I feel every second of it. And a lot of us don't have that kind of power, or any powers at all. Body armor would be nice is all I'm saying. This suit used to have a plate of it down the torso. At some point it got too damaged, so I replaced it with leather. Then canvas. As of tonight, it's just a hole.

I clench my fist until enough phosphorescence builds up to create a faint light in my palm. It's barely enough to make out the difference between fabric and shadow and I can feel my pulse racing, struggling to sustain it.

Footsteps.

Down the street? Down the alley?

I don't have a lot of options, and even less energy. The light has left me trembling. I need to get out of here, but I don't think I'll make it to the sewer without being spotted, so I bury myself beneath the trash and wait.

We used to be better than this, the villains of this city.

I've never thought that name is fair, by the way. I prefer Adversary. There are the people in charge, the muscle that keeps them that way, and the people who oppose them with nothing left to lose. Most tend to call those last two *heroes* and *villains,* but I prefer Bootlickers and Adversaries. Status and Change.

What I'd really prefer at the moment is some goddamn fabric.

The footsteps recede, and I'm starting to pull myself up from the mess when something catches my attention, because it's shimmering, even in what little light filters through down here. A small swatch of something about the size of a business card. I go to pick it up, but I can't. My fingers fumble against the edges of the scrap, but it's stuck tight to the floor of the dumpster. I risk a little light in my palm again to get a better look.

It *is* a business card. Printed on a piece of dark Kevlar with some kind of shimmery ink are the words *Midnight Designs* and an address. That's it.

Huh.

I trace its outline with my finger. Try to peel it up but it's really cemented on there. This scrap is exactly what I need. Well, it and fifteen more just like it. Then again, is this a mistake, a piece of trash stuck to the bottom of a dumpster? Or is this an invitation?

No. What am I thinking? I can't show up to this address in my costume, even with the trench coat I threw over it. Doesn't matter where I got it; don't ask. I shouldn't even be here, honestly. I should be slinking back to my lair and doing what I can with a needle and thread.

But what are the odds of this swatch being here, face up, and perfectly centered? I know how to find out.

This is one of two dumpsters in the alley. I carefully drop onto the pavement and, regrettably, climb into the other. I thought I'd bottomed out on humiliation tonight, but now I need to know. I push aside bags of trash and scraps of flimsy fabric and slimy things I don't want to think about until I reach the bottom. There, again, is the same swatch.

A calling card.

I probably should not follow mysterious directions from the bottom of a dumpster. But why is this here, carefully adhered so it stays put when the trash is emptied, if not to signal someone who is doing exactly what I'm doing—scrounging for a very specific type of scrap?

I'm already beat up, covered in garbage, and wearing a melted suit. At this point, why the hell not?

I glance at the address again, shimmering like oil on pavement. *8 Weston St.* That's only a few blocks from here. I pull myself out of the dumpster and weave through the alleys until I'm close. No need to end up on camera.

It's an old brick apartment building, like every other structure in this part of town. I'm wondering how I'm supposed to know which apartment to target, so I climb the steps and look at the list of tenants. It's not like I'm expecting a neon sign, but a familiar name maybe? I don't have a better idea. I'm about to turn around when the names catch the moonlight. They're all scribbled on bits of paper and stuffed in the call box, but only one glimmers with that same oil-slick iridescence. *Chen. Apartment 12.*

I pass a fast-food delivery guy on my way down and circle around the building. Four floors. Any way you slice it, twelve will be on top.

The climb is worse than I thought it'd be. I carve a gripping texture into my palms but still almost fall from the fire escape when I first catch hold. I'm way too tired for this. I tell myself all I need is to get in, grab some fabric, and get out. I tell myself it will be easy. I almost collapse on the third floor. But no. I can't give The Infurnace the satisfaction. The next time I see him, I want him to wonder if he even managed to hit me in the first place. The next time I see him, he's crawling home with so much worse.

I haul myself onto the final landing and pray that this is the right apartment. I'm not holding myself together enough for a bluff, let alone a fight. My hands tremble as I feel around the window casing. I send tendrils of mycelia creeping under the frame, but after they push the lock aside, they won't settle all the way back into my skin. Through the window, I can see a worktable with bolts of fabric up along the wall, which is a good sign.

I slide the window open, trying not to let the old frame creak too much, and practically fall into the room. I have to get what I need and get the hell out of here.

Both hands are fraying now as I feel across the bolts of fabric, mostly the gaudy whites, blues, and golds of the Hero Alliance, with the occasional black and bruised purple at the bottom. They're labeled, but I don't really know what I'm looking for, only what it's supposed to feel like. Stretchy but durable. Like …

I pry a bolt of heavy black fabric from the bottom of

the pile. This will work. I have it shoved out onto the fire escape with one foot out the window to follow it when a voice behind me says, "I'll help you. If you want."

God, I really am slipping. I didn't even hear her come in. A skinny thing, still in school or just out of it. She's holding a bag of takeout, staring at me impassively.

"Or just take it. Up to you."

The girl dumps the takeout and her keys on the kitchen counter as if nothing's wrong. She's as far as she can get from me in the little apartment, but I track her every movement. When I stay frozen in the window, she throws up her hands and says, "Pretend I was never here." Then she unpacks a few containers, grabs a pair of chopsticks from a drawer, and sits at the tiny counter to eat. Her back is to me. I could flee. I could attack. She seems unconcerned.

This more than anything makes me hesitate. "Who are you?"

"You saw my business card, I take it," she says, still eating. "I thought that might work."

"Yeah, it's a great way to get your stuff stolen."

She shrugs. "Do you eat?" I raise my eyebrow and she goes on, "Some of them don't eat, I've heard. Or, I assume they consume something. Nutritional paste, sunlight, blood. I don't know."

"I don't eat blood."

"Do you eat five flavor soup?" She pushes a cardboard carton away from her, to the far end of the counter. "Only place in the city that makes it half as good as my gran did."

I do eat five flavor soup. At this point, I will eat anything.

So, the thing about mushrooms, is that they're very

good at decomposing matter. If I don't keep them fed, they'll start decomposing *me*. I can feel it beginning. It starts as an ache like you've just finished sprinting, that acidic tang in your mouth. Soon it'll begin to burn. I'll get confused. If I wait too long to give them a different form of energy, I'll go catatonic. Then I'll just be gone.

I let the window fall shut and take the soup. It's delicious. I would have loved to have met her gran.

We eat quietly. I stand near the worktable, ready to make an escape. At one point, she slides a pork bun on a napkin to the end of the counter. "You can have this if you don't drip on my fabric."

I stand a little farther away.

When she's finished, the girl cleans up as if there isn't a stranger in her apartment, then turns to face me. "So, what'll it be? You want fabric or help?"

I want help. Of course I want help. All anybody in the Villain's League wants is help with their goddamn costumes. But one dinner's not enough for me to trust this woman, although the threads on my hands have started folding back into my skin and the ache is easing up.

"That depends, are you a cop?"

"No."

"Then why are you doing this? You have to know the penalties for working with us."

I've been looking around the apartment for a while now, trying to get a sense of who I'm dealing with. In addition to the worktable with the bolts of fabric and a sewing machine, there's a dress form with half a costume pinned to it, sketches tacked up all over the walls, sketchbooks on the coffee table. No evening gowns or work wear for this woman. Every sketch is a hero costume. I recognize some as redesign concepts for a few of the powered clowns who work for the city. There is even a pretty good design for the jerk who tried to melt me, and I hope he never sees it because he doesn't deserve to look that good. She is, or was, a Utility Design student. She has to know what she's up against.

She shrugs. Not good enough.

"No, now. Why are you doing this, or the bolt and I ... bolt." Unfortunate turn of phrase I backed myself into, but I think I can make it down the fire escape now without melting through the grates, so that's something.

She sighs and strides over to a massive binder on the coffee table. It has to be three inches thick. "Have you seen this?" I haven't, but I recognize the seal of the Justice Enforcement Division on the cover. "The new brand guidelines for hero design. Each year they get stupider. I mean look at this." She flips open to a page for Captain Coruscant—Captain Croissant, we like to call him—and I have to laugh because it's so bland. Neat. Unified. But not threatening, or inspiring, or particularly ... anything. Then again, that pretty much describes Captain Croissant. "Do you remember what he used to look like? With the hat?"

"Pretty sure I punched that hat right off his head," I joke. Maybe that's revealing too much about myself, but honestly which of us hasn't?

I walk up to the wall where designs hang on a cork board. I point to the one for Invisibelle and try not to clench my jaw. "You're talented. You must be headed for a killer apprenticeship. Why would you risk that? If you're suspected of putting one stitch in my costume, you're done."

She huffs and glares at the board. "That design? This whole portfolio? I failed my senior thesis."

"What?" It's stunning work. I can't believe that.

The woman taps on the binder again. "Not compliant with the guidelines. You know what every collection that passed looked like? Exactly the same. Like they'd been spit out of a mix and match playdoh factory. I have three months to resubmit, but I've decided to take my skills elsewhere."

She picks up one of the sketchbooks and hands it to me. This isn't a hero outfit, it's for Walter, AKA Watt Savage. And it's good. Dark lines. Big shoulders. A nice homage to his electric power. I flip through a few pages, and I know instantly who each costume is meant for.

"There might even be one for you in there. Take a look."

At first, I think she's teasing me, because I've already passed two different redesigns of my costume, but as I watch her watching me, I start to suspect that she isn't. "You don't recognize me?"

Granted, I've taken off my faceplate and I look pretty stupid in this trench coat, but I thought I'd outed myself back at the pork buns.

"I've never been great with faces," she says.

I don't realize I'm going to do this until my hand is already on the tie, but I open the trench coat and let it fall off my shoulders. There's no mistaking me now.

My host, who's been doing a great job of being, or at least appearing, apathetic up to this point, snaps up from where she's leaning against one of the tables. Her eyes go wide. "Holy shit."

I admit, I'm something of a name. "Bet you didn't

think your little business card would work quite this well, huh?"

"Madam Mycelia, ma'am," she stammers. I enjoy the moment of panic.

"At this point, you might as well call me Cecily," I tell her. She already has more than enough to turn me in, though that would be the end of her side gig.

"Morgan," she manages. "Morgan Chen." She holds out her hand and I shake it.

"So, Morgan." With the coat open, the giant hole melted in the middle of my suit is plainly visible. "How serious are you about switching sides?"

In response, I'm given a pair of pajama pants and an old band t-shirt and directed to the bathroom.

Something happens when I'm free of the suit. It's not that I become a different person or no longer have to worry about my powers eating me alive. I'm still me. But I'm a different version of myself. I still haven't decided if I'm more at home with or without it. All I know is that in the suit, I would not be sitting on a college dropout's street corner couch drinking peppermint tea. Now, that is exactly what I'm doing while Morgan combs over the suit with a light and a magnifying glass.

"Yikes."

"I know."

"I don't just mean the blast damage."

"I know."

She looks back at me, as if a thought has just occurred to her. "Are you okay?"

"Hmm?"

She circles the damage with her finger. "Are you okay?"

"Physically yes, though my pride's in critical condition."

Morgan laughs. She draws something and scribbles some notes on a new page in her sketchbook, then shows it to me. "What I'd really like to do is a complete redesign. There's not much here worth salvaging."

"I'm aware."

"But that would take time and materials I don't have right now," she explains. I figured as much. My original suit took months to perfect. There were fittings and tryouts and a few warehouse raids for good measure. "For now, I can replace the torso. Unfortunately, the blast hit all three panels. If you can leave this for a few days—"

"Absolutely not." That's a great way to get her arrested and leave me without a suit. I'm back to considering that she might be a cop playing the long game.

"Then, get comfortable. Even a cheap job will take a few hours. Where is my ..." She starts looking through the bolts for something and when she doesn't find it, I open the window and retrieve the cloth I dropped on the fire escape. She runs it through her fingers and gives me a strange look. "You know what you like."

"In this business, you have to."

I watch as she takes my suit apart. Uses the panels to cut new pieces. Sews my identity back together. There's ribbing along the seams now, which wasn't necessary but adds a nice touch. She even added back the little collar that I sacrificed to a repair job months ago.

"Try it on."

In the tiny bathroom, I ditch the pajamas and slip into the suit, using my mycelia to pull up the zipper. I can feel the difference immediately. There isn't a giant hole, for starters, but it's more than that. The suit is snug, but not tight. The new panels move with me as I twist, testing their limits. I must be taking too long because Morgan knocks on the door and asks, "Everything alright?" with the restrained patience of someone whose work is up for review.

I try to keep my excitement down, but my mouth crooks into a hint of a smile. I haven't looked this good in years.

She wants to make a few adjustments but it's late now. I've been here far too long. "It's fine. Thank you."

I hold the coat over my arm and stand by the window. I'm safer in black now. Once I get to the tunnels I can ditch the trench coat entirely.

"What do I owe you for this?" I ask.

"Nothing. Call it a proof of concept." I don't believe her. I believe in debts. "Just send the next guy my way."

I'm opening the window when something occurs to me. "I can do you one better." I retrieve the notebook, the one with her villain work in it. I point to my suit and say, "When this gets noticed, expect to be raided by the Justice Enforcement Division. They'll cast a wide net. Destroy any evidence. Expect bugs. I'd keep working on that second take at your exams for all you're worth."

"So, I should give up my life of crime before I'm in too deep?"

"I didn't say that. I'll show this around. When things settle down, we'll contact you."

"Promise?"

"I'm a supervillain. I don't make promises."

I leave the way I came and disappear down the nearest maintenance tunnel. When I'm back to my lair, I admire the handiwork on my suit again before I take it off. This will definitely hold up for a little while. And after that, who knows. If Morgan hasn't been scared straight or arrested, well ... I open the sketchbook to her redesign of my costume. Not this patch job, the real one. It makes me feel invincible just looking at it. Beside it there are some scribbled materials and quantities, the things she'd need to make it, which will be a nightmare to get.

Then I see a note beneath it. *Whenever you're ready,* and a phone number. Then *(It's a burner).*

Hmm.

I just might.

The End

R. V. Thomas has an MFA in screenwriting from Boston University, which she occasionally uses to rewrite movies she didn't like. When she's not chipping away at novels, screenplays, and more, her hobbies include trying and failing to learn new languages, and amateur ceramics. The baristas at her local coffee shop are very patient about her endless parade of handmade mugs.

ROOMIES

BY M. B. BRUCE

The annoyingly cheerful Resident Services Aide, Brenda, held up two mini dessert cups. "Would you like sugar-free orange gelatin, Ms. G, or—" she squinted at the label "—lactose-free, no sugar-added butterscotch puddin'?"

I gave the perky brunette my coldest, dead-eye stare.

At eighteen grand a month for a shared room, you'd think this place would serve double-crème brûlée with fresh raspberries and a couple of those dark chocolate straws, artfully shoved into the baked custard—Sicilian stiletto-style.

"How about an Empress 1908 Indigo on the rocks with a twist," I said, offering my own version of a no-sugar-added smile. "Make that a double."

She laughed.

I didn't.

"You're so funny, Ms. G," she drawled, exposing her deep Southern roots.

Every day it was the same routine. I'd tell her what I

wanted. She'd think I was joking. And I'd resist the urge to shove a plastic spoon up her nasal cavity.

Well, perhaps *resist* wasn't entirely accurate. My commitment to do her bodily harm was perfectly intact. It was my ability—or should I say, limited mobility—that greatly reduced any chance of success.

I edged my wheelchair a quarter-turn to stare out the window. Spanish-moss-shrouded oaks stood at attention to either side of a gravel lane, terminating in a circular drive at the foot of this three-story, antebellum monstrosity. Once fallen on hard times, the old girl was now painted up, corseted, and rechristened Sunnybrook Retirement Home.

Sounds nice, huh? Evocative of peaceful afternoons swinging lazily on a whitewashed wrap-around porch, sipping mint julips.

Well, names—like most things in life—can be deceiving.

"I'll just leave them right here so you can take your pick." She set the dessert cups down on the tray table. "Have both, if you like. After all, it is your birthday."

Was it?

Hard to keep track when one day bled into the next. When my entire existence had become an endless loop of mediocre meals, sponge baths, and "occupational" therapy. When a life lived on my own terms—hard and fast, outside the boundaries of societal norms—had long since coagulated into a pool of lukewarm memories. Not so much haunting, as taunting me with all that I'd once been.

Times change, or so they say.

But really it's time that changes, slowing down in the day-to-day, and yet also savagely speeding up. Until one day, some obnoxiously sweet young thing, rocking a body like you used to have, reminds you that you're ninety years old.

How in the hell did that happen?

At the far end of that long gravel drive—my experienced eye pegging the distance at a little over 800 meters —a passenger van turned off the highway and headed our way. I lost sight of it as it rounded the parking circle, pulling up too close to the building to be visible at this angle. The crunching of gravel beneath tires ceased.

Brenda, with her two-legged height advantage, stepped closer and peered over the sill. "Looks like your new roomie just arrived."

"My new what?"

"Didn't anyone tell you?" She smiled at me in that big-brown-eyed innocent way that told me the staff had purposely withheld the information.

"Can't say they did."

"Well now, Sugar, you didn't expect to have this big ol' room all to yourself forever, did you?"

One could hope.

The truth was, I already knew they were gearing up to fill the vacancy. The other bed, stripped down to the mattress and disinfected after they hauled the last corpse out, had been freshly made this morning. With pillows fluffed and one corner of the thin blanket artfully turned down, it didn't take an intelligence analyst to figure it out.

Since becoming a resident of Sunnybrook, I'd had four roommates. The first, a wise old bird from New York City, had requested a transfer. The others had died—numbers two and three, of natural causes. But the last one, number four, a real talker, I ... helped along.

Nice side-benefit of hospice care. No autopsy.

"I'm sure you'll get on just fine together," Brenda prattled.

Oh, yes. One way, or the other.

She met my eyes and, seeing something in them—something dark and dangerous, no doubt—looked away.

"Well," she said in a breathy voice, that ever-present Southern charm faltering. "If you need anything, just ring."

She was out the door before I could say "boo."

It took nearly an hour before my solitude was disrupted by a light knock. Not one of request, but rather of warning, as the door opened.

"Hello, hello." The Director of Resident Services, a plain-faced woman with no fashion sense whatsoever, barged into the room like a drum major at the forefront of the parade of staffers ushering in the new arrival.

I only caught a glimpse before a nurse's aide pulled the privacy curtain. But that's all I needed. Out of deeply ingrained habit, I catalogued my observations: average height, medium build, dark brown hair gone mostly gray, and—

I knew that face.

For a long moment, I stared into space, riffling through imagery stored in eidetic detail. Though my broken and abused body had betrayed me, my mind hadn't. Arguably not as sharp as it once was, my memory—for the most part—remained intact. I never forgot a face.

Especially this one.

"There you go. All settled in," a female aide cooed in that singsong manner reserved for pets, children, and old people. "Welcome to Sunnybrook, Ms. Bishop."

Footsteps receded, the door closed, and the room went quiet.

Mary Anne Bishop.

What the hell was *she* doing here?

Silence dragged long seconds into a full minute. Then finally, from the other side of that curtain, "You still there, Giavanni?"

Where did she think I'd gone—out the third story window?

Tried that in Milan once.

Didn't work out too well.

"Isn't there a less obvious question you'd like to ask? One, perhaps, that you don't already know the answer to?"

Bed covers rustled and the mattress springs released with a faint squeak. A few moments later, Bishop tugged aside the privacy curtain. Her gaze, as frigid as a winter sky, took in my wheelchair-bound vulnerability and the battle-worn lines on my face, before finally meeting mine.

"You're right. That was a stupid question."

"Icebreakers often are."

We studied one another, assessing strengths and weaknesses with well-honed professionalism.

In nearly six decades of cat and mouse, it was the first opportunity either of us had ever had for a good look at the other. This close, anyway. That one time her face graced the crosshairs of my rifle scope notwithstanding, of course.

Oh, I'm sure there'd been obscure surveillance photos of me, poured over late into the night as she attempted to track my whereabouts, identify the next target, and stop me from fulfilling a contract; however, this was our first face-to-face.

"Aren't you curious how I found you?"

"Not particularly," I said—though I was. "The more compelling question is what took you so long."

Eyes narrowed, she pursed thin lips, her face scrunching into a crow's nest of wrinkles. "Everyone presumed you were dead. The agency stamped your file 'closed' after you went off that cliff in Gibraltar."

I sighed, remembering like it was yesterday. "How I loved that Jaguar."

"The car was recovered, but—"

"The body never was." I arched a condescending eyebrow. "Don't tell me you actually believed that I was—"

"Dead? No, I'm not that gullible. But I was surprised when you never resurfaced—pun intended."

That genuinely made me chuckle.

"So, why now? After all these years?" She cocked her head, as if her next thought had just occurred. "In Louisianna, of all places?"

I chose to answer the last question—the least relevant. "I like the weather."

"Most people don't."

"I'm not 'most people'."

I held her scrutinizing gaze long enough to make it perfectly clear I had no intention of saying more.

After a few moments, she shifted her stance—a visible indicator she was about to adjust her tack but not actually change direction. "You've always covered your tracks, Giavanni. Why not this time?"

Good question—one with an answer I preferred not to examine too closely.

Over the decades, I'd cultivated dozens of false identities, acquired millions in assets, and set up safe houses on every continent—save Antarctica, of course. Never was much for cold weather. But this time, for no reason I could identify, when I applied for lifetime residency at Sunnybrook, I used my real name.

"I have a better question, Agent Bishop—or rather a series of observations that leads to one. If the agency had concrete evidence on me and knew where I was, I'd already be in custody. I suppose you could be here in some volunteer capacity, playing the part of my arch-nemesis in the hopes of bating me into self-incrimination. But that, too—based on your sloppy approach—is also unlikely. In fact, I'd hazard a guess that no one at the agency even knows you've found me. So, unless I'm missing something—which, I highly doubt—the logical conclusion is that you are legitimately a new resident here."

I paused to give her a chance to comment. When she didn't, I pressed on, "Building upon that premise, even having waited well past standard retirement age to take your pension, you can't afford this place. Unless, of course, you were on the take—"

That elicited an indignant enough reaction to confirm that she wasn't.

"Which, apparently, you're not," I was quick to reassure. "So then, tell me. How and why are you here?"

Her gaze swept the room as if taking in the Southern opulence of intricately-carved, Rococo Rival inspired mahogany furniture, damask window treatments, and gilded—albeit, faux—accents for the first time. Dressed in frumpy, off-the-rack sweats and skid-resistant socks, she appeared markedly out of place.

"I devoted my life to protecting innocents, catching the worst of the worst, trying to make the world a better place. And I did a pretty good job of it. Then, one day, I realized no matter how good I was, no matter how many I put away or eliminated from the gene pool, I just couldn't get them all."

When she met my eyes this time, something in hers had changed. The coldness was gone, replaced with a subtle, but unmistakable, appreciation. Never what you might call beautiful, Bishop hadn't been unattractive, either. But now there was a gauntness to her features hinting at some chronic—perhaps even terminal—illness.

"And I'm the big one who got away."

She shifted position, her posture softening. Bodily fatigue, evident. "That's one way of putting it."

Without another word, she shuffled back around the edge of the privacy curtain to her side of the room and, based on the telltale squeak of mattress springs, got back into bed.

No, Agent Mary Anne Bishop didn't have sufficient financial resources to afford a place like Sunnybrook—at least, not long term—but perhaps, long enough.

Returning my attention to the beatific scene outside the window, I contemplated my sudden and thoroughly unexpected change in circumstances.

Leaving Sunnybrook was one option, I supposed.

That would be the prudent thing to do.

The truth was, I didn't want to.

Though disinclined to share with Bishop, or anyone else for that matter, my reasons for coming here—specifically Louisianna—I had them.

I'd chosen Sunnybrook, and this corner bedroom—

paying a premium, of course—not only because it afforded an unobstructed view of the mansion's driveway, but also because it overlooked a wooded area with a handful of private cabins tucked in between the trees. The fact that those woods provided the best covert approach to the building was an additional selling point, as was the visual I had on the parking lot, allowing me to monitor the comings and goings of visitors and employees alike.

Call it paranoia, but old habits were hard to break.

Outside the window, movement caught my eye.

Brunette curls bobbing, Brenda crossed the parking lot into the area designated for employees, heading toward her car—a restored, candy-apple-red Mustang convertible parked in the shade of a crepe myrtle in full bloom.

I glanced at the wall clock.

4:31 p.m. on the dot.

Brenda was nothing if not predictable.

From beyond the privacy curtain, Bishop groaned. Bedsheets rustled as she settled with a heavy sigh.

"You all right, Bishop?"

"Yeah." After a long moment, she said, "I almost forgot. Happy birthday, Estella."

After a few weeks, Bishop and I settled into a tentative relationship of tolerant, almost friendly, détente. As had become our afternoon habit, we retreated to a pleasantly shaded courtyard no one ever used. Me, to reminisce about my past exploits. Bishop, to fill in the blanks of over fifty years of shared history.

"What about that time in Helsinki?"

"Which one?"

"After Istanbul. Before Atlanta."

"Ah, yes. That *was* a close call." I sipped my sweet tea. "Blizzard grounded all flights, so I procured a dogsled team and—"

"Crossed the border into Estonia."

I raised an eyebrow. "Very good, Bishop."

"I knew it!" She rocked back in her patio chair. "I sent a team, but you still managed to slip through our net."

"That was the coldest eighty kilometers of my life."

We both laughed.

What I learned from our frank conversations was that Bishop had been one step behind me my entire, off-the-books career—but only just.

She was good.

I was better.

Even so, I found myself admiring her tenacity, the single-mindedness with which she had pursued me all those years.

"What about Cairo?" She didn't wait for an answer before pressing on, "My team was closing in, you had nowhere to go. Then, that damn sandstorm hit. When it cleared, you'd vanished."

I set my iced tea down on the shatter-resistant glass patio table between us and glanced at the sky. Though gray clouds threatened on the Eastern horizon, they were still a long way off.

Oh, what the hell.

"It was Bobby."

"Bobby?" She frowned, then those ice-blue eyes widened in realization. "Davenport?"

Watching her, knowing that my revelation risked

cracking the reality of everything she believed to be true about herself and those she trusted, I simply nodded.

"Robert Davenport? My—my team leader?"

Team leader. Trusted handler. Mentor. The works.

I'd done my research into the background of the woman who had made a career out of trying to catch me. Typical recruitment profile: Both parents tragically lost at a young age. No siblings. No relatives that gave a damn. Documented sociopathic tendencies that translated into a revolving door of foster homes.

It was only natural that Robert Davenport had become the father figure Bishop needed.

"After I ... satisfied the terms of my contract, Robert spotted me repelling off the building and gave chase. He managed to corner me in an alley, just as the storm hit. When it became apparent that neither of us were likely to survive without immediately seeking shelter, we put aside our differences and took refuge in the basement of a condemned apartment building. We were trapped there, together, for hours."

Thirty-seven to be exact, but who was counting.

"I remember that," Bishop whispered, more to herself than me. "That storm was so bad we lost all communications. We thought Robert was—that you had—"

"Killed him?" I smiled, remembering the two of us standing less than a meter apart, guns leveled. "I very nearly did."

"What stopped you?"

"Honestly, I can't recall," I lied, because the truth was, I'd never been able to find a satisfactory answer to that question. "What I can tell you is that our uneasy truce slowly gave way to a long, heartfelt conversation. And then, unexpectedly ... other things."

Mouth agape, she stared at me. Then, her initial shock simmered into a deep flush of anger, and she boiled over. "You seduced him!"

I should have expected that's the way Bishop would see it.

Always the villain.

Might as well lean into the role.

"Of course I did." I gave her a sly wink. "How else was I to persuade him to let me go?"

"You're despicable."

"Thank you."

She rolled her eyes.

"Once I overcame his initial resistance—and, I have to admit, Bobby was a hard one to corrupt, the honorable ones usually are—we discovered all sorts of pleasurable ways to occupy those idle hours."

"I've heard enough." Pushing out of the patio chair, she stormed off.

"Are you just going to leave me out here?" I called after her, laughing. "A helpless old woman in a wheelchair?"

She kept moving, didn't even look back, as my laughter faded into a lonely echo in the deserted courtyard.

～

"I think I figured it out," Bishop announced, out of the blue, one late night after we'd gone to bed.

She had hardly spoken to me in a week. Not since the courtyard incident. Couldn't blame her. I'd been particularly cruel that day. More like my old self. It felt good.

Though still awake, my mind had been drifting

toward sleep, so I was confused as to what, exactly, she was referring to. "Figured what out?"

"Why here." The creak of the mattress preceded her appearance at the edge of the privacy curtain. "Why Louisianna."

I pushed myself onto one elbow, peering at her through the safety-light-imbued dimness. "What are you talking about?"

"I can't even fathom how much money you have tucked away in Swiss bank accounts, offshore investments, real estate. You could have gone anyplace. Lived anywhere. But you chose here."

"I told you—I like the weather."

"Bullshit!" Bishop grimaced, her body nearly doubling over in pain caused, I assumed, by her sudden outburst. Her pale complexion went a shade paler, emphasizing the hollowness around deep-set eyes. She'd always been thin, but since her arrival, she'd become downright skeletal.

"Mary Anne. Please. Sit." I indicated the comfy recliner opposite my bed.

She didn't argue.

"I've never asked, but I think it's obvious that you're —"

"That I'm dying?" she said, in what I'd come to recognize as her sardonic voice. "Aren't we all?"

"You know what I mean." I waited, giving her the opportunity to say more. When she didn't, I decided to open the wound. "What type of cancer is it?"

This time, she didn't hesitate. "Pancreatic. Stage four."

As I processed the information, I nodded slowly, not

certain—nor even caring—if she could see me. "I hear it's painful."

"You have no idea."

"How long do you have?"

Apparently, that was a question she couldn't—or wouldn't—answer. Shifting in the chair with a barely audible groan, she asked instead, "Ever see the movie *Thelma and Louise*?"

I shook my head.

Frankly, I was never much of a movie-goer. Besides being a colossal waste of time, the idea of sitting in a dark theatre with my back to the doors, blinded by light-images flashing across the big screen, seemed at odds with my deeply-ingrained survival instinct.

I'd heard of the cult classic film, knew the basic plot-line and grand finale, but little else.

"What about it?" I asked in a deceptively neutral tone.

She must have sensed my utter stillness, the guarded-ness with which I awaited her answer, because she veered off.

"Nothing."

What remained unsaid hung in the air between us.

"As I was saying." She picked up the thread of our initial conversation. "I figured out why you chose Louisiana."

"Really—" I feigned disinterest "—and why is that?"

"Robert Davenport."

My heart—the actual organ, not the metaphorical one—fluttered in my chest.

"He was a Southern boy, born and raised. In fact, he grew up not far from here. His family had a weekend place—" she nodded toward the shuttered window "—in those very woods. Bet you might even be able to see it from here."

I was thankful the low light made it difficult for her to see my expression.

"Admit it. You loved him. And he must have felt the same about you. Otherwise, why take the risk?" She released a heavy sigh. "You think you know someone. Shit, Giavanni! The agency kept tabs on everything we did, everyone we ever met. Do you have any idea how dangerous that was? How the hell did the two of you pull it off—where, when?"

"Wherever we could. As often as we dared." I blinked away my goddammed tears before they could form. "The last time here, at his cabin in the woods."

"Shit," she said again, this time with less energy. Then, with obvious difficulty, she rose.

"Mary Anne," I whispered, fully aware of how emotionally vulnerable I was and, for the first time in my life, not caring that someone had seen so deeply inside of me. "He loved you like a daughter, you know."

She cocked her head in that way she had whenever something struck her as amusing. "Is that why, when you had me in your sights in Buenos Aires, you didn't take the shot?"

I shouldn't have been surprised, but I was. "How did you—"

"Sunlight reflected off the lens of your scope." Even in the dimness, I saw her smirk as she headed toward the privacy curtain. "Goodnight, Estella."

"Where are we going?" Bishop complained as she trudged along, pushing my wheelchair through the employee parking lot.

"Just keep moving. You'll see."

It was a gorgeous Southern morning, yet to be ruined by unbearable heat and stifling humidity. The nearby woods, a sun-dappled shimmer of greens and browns beneath a robin's-egg blue sky, beckoned. But that wasn't the direction we were going.

"There—" I pointed "—beneath that crepe myrtle."

She stopped pushing and the chair rolled to a halt a dozen strides short of my intended destination. "Giavanni, what have you cooked up in that insidious brain of yours?"

I produced the set of keys I'd lifted earlier that morning from Brenda's smock pocket, jingling them. "Road trip."

Behind me as she was, I couldn't see her face; however, I had no difficulty imagining her delightfully aghast expression.

"No," she said flatly, turning my chair around to head back toward the mansion. "We're not doing this."

"Oh, come on, Bishop, be reasonable."

"Stealing an employee's car isn't *reasonable*."

"Think of it more as borrowing."

"I'm taking you back."

I slammed on the hand brake. The thin wheels jittered, jerked to a stop, spun the chair enough so that I could see her. "Oh, for God's sake Bishop, you're running out of time. For once in your life, do something *bad*."

We glared at one another. Two fiercely opposing forces in a battle of wills that neither of us could win.

I was never quite certain which of us broke the stalemate first, but soon we were grinning at each other like idiots.

"Shit," she muttered as she turned the wheelchair around and headed toward that candy-apple-red symbol of daring and independence.

Once she helped settle me into the passenger seat with my belt secured—even when perpetrating grand theft, Bishop was a rules follower—I handed her the keys.

"I can't believe we're doing this."

"Feels wonderful, doesn't it?"

"We're bringing it back."

"Absolutely."

"I mean it, Estella."

"Of course."

Wincing, she eased herself behind the wheel and took a deep breath, mentally and physically beating back the pain.

"Do you want me to drive?" I teased.

"Very funny."

We sat there, engine running, staring off into the woods. Me, at one cabin, in particular. Barely visible amid the trees.

"Where to?" she asked, slipping it into reverse and backing out of the parking space.

I flipped down the visor, caught Brenda's gawdy, pink-framed, dime-store sunglasses as they dropped, and slid them onto my face. "I always did want to see the Grand Canyon."

Chuckling, she floored it.

Gravel spewed from beneath our tires as we sped between the neat rows of moss-draped oaks and out onto the highway.

The End

M. B. Bruce's love affair with speculative fiction began between the pages of a hand-me-down copy of Frank Herbert's Dune. She's authored short stories and scripted commercials, music videos, and short and feature films. A believer in supporting fellow writers, she facilitates critique groups, hosts retreats, and presents at writing conferences. An avid reader, roleplay enthusiast, and life-long skier, she resides in Southern California with her husband, children, nine chickens, four goats, three cats, and one very spoiled rescue dog. For what comes next, visit MBBruce.com.

A Necromancer's Reprieve

by Robin Talamas

Evandria sat on the manor balcony, drinking her tea. A zombie stood beside her.

"*Gruuuuuuh.*"

"What a mess this is, Louis," Evandria said, taking a sip from her cup. The recent insurgence had taken a heavy toll on the town. Buildings had been burned, lives had been lost, and her balcony was still stained black from the ash. It had been the second insurgence this year, and if Evandria wasn't careful, she could be looking at a third within a few months. "How soon can we get everything cleaned up?"

"*Gruuuuuuuh.*"

"Well, I suppose that's not too bad. We did lose half the northern quarter. Rebuilding that will certainly take a few weeks." Evandria refilled her cup. The teapot was antique ceramic, a porcelain white painted with delicate scenes of flowers and cherubs. It absolutely clashed with her midnight-black dress and matching silk gloves. But, spoils of war. She preferred to pour it herself, Louis's hands being unsteady.

She looked out over the town. From her balcony, Evandria had an unobstructed view, which was normally quite nice. It allowed her to see the developments to the town as they were made, and she was rather proud of the work she was doing. The previous government had done a horrible job maintaining the place: public sanitation and infrastructure were abysmal, to say the least, and don't even get her started on the roads. Now, though, the view was simply depressing, so much of her work having gone to waste because of a few discontents.

She wanted it rebuilt as quickly as possible.

Evandria took a sip of her tea. It was strong and tasted of the bright cherries she had grown in the garden below. They, at least, had remained untouched by the attack. "And what about the newest batch of undead? Any progress?"

"*Gruuuuuuh.*"

"Oh, you must be joking me." Evandria set her cup down. She couldn't believe this. "They're still hung up about that?"

"*Gruuuuuuh.*"

"Well, if they were going to complain about it, maybe they shouldn't have rebelled in the first place." Evandria massaged her brow. Naturally, when an insurrection broke out, it was the citizens who fought against her, but, when it came time to rebuild, Underworld forbid they do anything to help. That part always fell on her shoulders, and that required manpower. So what if she reanimated a few of the dead rebels? It was the least they could do to make up for the damage they caused. But *noooooo.* Always something about desecrating the dead, as if necromancy weren't a worthwhile profession. Sometimes, she thought they just hated her on principle.

"I don't suppose I can just kill off whoever's complaining and use them, can I?"

"*Gruh.*"

"No, I thought not." Louis was right: if she killed off everyone who complained, there'd be no one left alive in town, and, necromancer or not, that was no way for her to govern. "What do you suggest, then?"

"*Gruuuuuuh.*"

Evandria considered it. "It's not the worst idea, but walking about town in this state? The townspeople don't like me even on the best of days. Do you really think it will work?"

Louis paused before answering. Evandria admired her own work as she looked at him. He was smarter than most other zombies, a quality she had worked hard to preserve. Even in his desiccated state, he still managed to maintain the air of stately nobility he gave off while he was alive. It also certainly helped that she dressed him in a fine three-piece suit with a forest green waistcoat. That was just good fashion.

"*Gruuuuuuh,*" he finally responded.

Evandria let out a heavy sigh. "Well, in that case, I guess there's no point in avoiding it. Please arrange for a carriage, Louis, and check to see if Maria is available. The people seem more comfortable around her."

"*Gruuuuuuh.*"

That was true. Maria was a vampire, and even they needed to feed, albeit infrequently. "Then, I suppose we'll have to wait until after lunch."

⁓

Evandria sat in the carriage as she rode through the town's streets. The inside of it was comfortable, and the decor was much more to her taste than the rest of the manor. She sat on plush seats covered in a rich scarlet velvet, and the interior walls were a deep mahogany brown. She had even arranged for dark violet curtains to be draped across the windows.

Unfortunately, the carriage's exterior was a very different story: it had been painted in the same gaudy pastels the old regime had been so fond of using. What was it with them and this color palette? Mismanagement of the town aside, Evandria felt she had done a service in killing them for their aesthetic alone. She had been meaning to have the carriage repainted, and now all her favorites had been mercilessly destroyed. It was mortifying to be seen in this thing, but Louis had argued it would give the people a sense of familiarity.

The carriage was pulled by a pair of black stallions. Evandria preferred living animals to reanimated ones. For some reason, they never seemed to come back quite right, which was slightly unsettling. Part of it was rigor mortis, which couldn't be helped, but there was also a strange twitchiness to them. It was like looking at a puppet with its strings tied together, which Evandria thought was just creepy. Besides, living animals were much more pleasing to the eye, and she had to add some personal touches to this horrendous thing she rode in.

"I'm certain today's excursion will help improve the public's opinion of you, Mistress Evandria."

Maria sat opposite her in the carriage, a slender figure in a sapphire blue dress. Maria was pale, with golden blonde hair and eyes that glimmered like rubies. She was young, barely an adult, though she carried herself like one. Maria had been pale before she was turned, but now her skin was the same porcelain white as Evandria's teapot.

Evandria tried to think for a moment: who was it that the teapot had belonged to again? She thought it had belonged to Maria's *uncle* ... she could never quite remember. They had all been so obsessed with familial titles and wealth that she honestly couldn't tell them apart at this point. For Maria's sake, she had left them to rest in the family mausoleum instead of resurrecting them. That, and there was a small chance they'd become snobbish and annoying in undeath, which Evandria desperately wanted to avoid. She had decided to keep that last part to herself.

But Maria deserved better. She was a kind girl, totally different from the obnoxious barons who had previously reigned over the town. And the townspeople liked her for it. She listened to them, and they seemed to listen in turn. Evandria was lucky there'd been someone in town who knew how things actually worked. She couldn't imagine how much work she'd been saved just by having Maria around.

It was also nice to have someone who could talk to the townspeople without them raising pitchforks and torches.

"I appreciate your optimism, Maria, I really do," Evandria said, peering out the window at the overcast sky. "I just find it difficult to look forward to these sorts of things. I'm well aware of my reputation in this town. Rumors that I eat babies or something like that. I mean, who would do such a thing?"

Maria simply flashed her trademark aristocrat's smile, the one she used when she was trying to be polite.

"I remember similar rumors about myself when you first had me turned. It was an adjustment, to say the least, but I was able to show them that I was still the same person as I was before. What matters is that you go out there and show you don't bear them any ill will."

Evandria grimaced a slight bit. "I do bear them *some* ill will, really, but it's more out of frustration than anything."

She sat there in embarrassed silence as Maria took a long, deep inhale. *Comments like these are why the townspeople don't like me*, Evandria reminded herself.

"Just try to be as amicable as possible," Maria said. She had put on a forced smile that showed off the sharp points of her fangs. "Remind them that you and they share the same interests in the town's wellbeing."

Evandria hesitated before asking, "And no talking about necromancy?"

"*Especially* no talking about necromancy," Maria emphasized with a glare.

Evandria slumped back in her seat. *Well, there went half my conversation points.*

She turned her gaze back to the window as the carriage rode into the northern quarter, where the destruction had been heaviest. Most of the buildings had been scorched black by the fires of the insurrection, with many of them in varying states of collapse. Already, reconstruction was underway, but there were people gathered about, gawking as Evandria's undead laborers worked at rebuilding the town. She supposed they were searching for some hint that their dead loved ones were still in there. She couldn't blame them, though that really wasn't how it worked. Zombies were more like vague impressions in clay, but the townspeople didn't seem too interested in the finer details of raising the dead.

As the carriage rode past, the people seemed suddenly more reserved, some of them even turning away as if cowering in fear. She genuinely hated when they did that. It made her seem like some tyrannical despot, ready to execute someone for even the slightest offense. Evandria was no stranger to death, but that description was hardly appropriate.

Then again, perhaps that was part of the problem. Evandria simply felt more at ease around the undead, so it's not as if she ever made much of an effort to assuage their distrust. Truth be told, she was actually a little intimidated by the living, so excursions like these didn't happen very often. She probably wouldn't even be doing this if Louis hadn't suggested it.

"Do you think I'm doing a good job?" Evandria asked.

Maria's expression turned more sympathetic. "I think you're doing the best anyone could do in a situation like this."

Evandria frowned. "That's political speak for 'no,' isn't it?"

"Mistress Evandria," Maria said, leaning forward in her seat. "In the time you've been in power, public health and wellbeing have drastically improved. There was a time when beggars sat on the streets with festering wounds as they slowly died of starvation."

"Don't forget how awful the roads were," Evandria added.

"My point is that the people are discontent because they're *alive* to be so." Maria shook her head thoughtfully. "They may not fully know it, but I think they're, on some level, grateful for everything you've given them. What scares them, I think, is how different things are from what they'd grown used to."

What they'd grown used to. Evandria turned the thought over in her mind. She supposed they'd grown used to hating her, so maybe they were *scared* to like her? Evandria had been told she was scary, but this was a new one for her. It would definitely take some getting used to.

The carriage came to a halt. "*Gruuuuuuh,*" Louis said from the front.

Evandria peered out the window at the street. They had stopped in front of a long row of houses, newly under construction. This street had been where the fires first broke out, and most of the homes here had been reduced to cinders and ash. They had already been in severe disrepair, a fire hazard just waiting to happen. The insurrection had just been the metaphorical and *literal* spark that set it all ablaze.

Still, Evandria considered it a slight blessing. It meant she finally had a reason to renovate this section into something more hospitable. No one could complain about the changes if there was nothing left of the original. Granted, it meant that many of the townspeople living here were now either homeless or dead, and charred corpses were a real hassle to work with.

A large crowd had gathered outside, their attention turned on the carriage as they waited for someone to step out. Evandria pulled back from the window. "I don't suppose you have any last words of advice," she asked, looking over at Maria.

"Try not to be too tense," Maria answered. "Believe it or not, the people can sense when you're being disingenuous."

Don't be too tense? Evandria bristled a bit. What kind

of advice was that? That was like telling her not to stress over how she was stressed.

Evandria sighed. *Better to get the hell on with it,* she thought, knocking on the carriage door. Within a moment, the door swung open onto the street, a sound passing through the people in the crowd. Louis extended an arm as he helped Evandria down from the carriage.

The crowd stared at her with expressions ranging from fear to disgust as she stepped onto the street. Evandria felt deeply uncomfortable. It was because of moments like these that she tried to leave this sort of thing to Maria.

A small elderly woman emerged from the crowd. She wore simple brown clothing and walked with a slight hunch. This woman was one of the community leaders. Evandria struggled to remember her name. Gladys? Griselda? She knew it was something starting with G. Whatever her name was, the woman was a tough one. She peered up at Evandria with a stern expression which gave off the distinct impression that *she* ran the town and not the other way around.

"Mistress Evandria," the G-named woman said in a harsh tone. "To what do we owe the pleasure of your visit?"

"I'm ... simply here to observe the reconstruction," Evandria nervously answered. Already, this was off to a bad start. She desperately tried to think of something to break the tension. *Don't talk about necromancy. Don't talk about necromancy. Don't talk about necromancy.* "It's wonderful weather outside today, isn't it?"

"It's overcast," the woman replied.

"Yes, I find it perfectly gloomy."

Damn it. Nobody enjoys talking about the weather.

She had to do better. "I see there's already been some good progress made on this section," Evandria said. "I think that, with the right renovations and a few architectural flourishes, we could really usher in a new era for this town."

The woman merely scoffed. "Most people liked the way things were before."

The way they were before? Evandria struggled with that. Wasn't the consensus that things were overwhelmingly *bad* before she showed up? Hadn't Maria mentioned something about people dying on the streets? No, perhaps this woman was just trying to be difficult. She was certainly doing a good job of it, if she was.

Evandria looked over to Maria, who offered another one of her polite smiles in response. Evandria took a deep breath and tried her best to emulate her. "I'm sure many people feel that way, but there's no point in dwelling on the past. Let's try not to let one little skirmish distract us from focusing on our future, shall we?"

The small woman's face turned from an unpleasant scowl to an open sneer of disgust. "My son died fighting in that 'little skirmish,' as you call it," she said.

Evandria's forced smile quickly flattened into a stiff line. This was definitely not what she was hoping for. "I'm sorry for your loss," she managed to get out.

The woman simply nodded as she continued to sneer. "I believe you even resurrected him as one of your unholy servants."

"I promise to put him to good use."

Well, shit, Evandria thought. This was falling apart quickly. She glanced over at Maria, whose normally pristine facade was starting to crumble as she struggled to maintain calm. *We need to wrap this up quickly.*

"Well, this has been a lovely conversation," Evandria scrambled. "But I think it's time we got going. Maria, carriage. Now."

They moved hastily, rushing back up the steps of the carriage. As soon as the door shut behind them, the carriage lurched into motion as Louis drove the horses through the street and back toward the manor. Evandria noted that, as the carriage moved, there were no sounds of shouting or rioting or anything typical of an angry mob behind them. It seemed as though the crowd had just *let* them leave.

"That could have gone a lot worse," Evandria observed.

Maria simply stared back at her with wide eyes and a stiff expression. "It could also have gone a hell of a lot better."

Evandria squirmed in her seat under Maria's stern glare. "Be honest: how bad do you think it is?"

Maria took a deep breath as she regained her composure. "I think, at this point, they're coming to learn what they can expect from you. The fact that Galina was able to speak to you publicly in that manner means they're probably less scared of you now."

Evandria nodded. *That* was her name. *Galina.* She had been right, it had started with a G. "So, this is ... a good thing?"

Maria let out a sigh of frustration. "I think Louis and I will have to run damage control once we get back to the manor. But, at the very least, it's a sign we may be getting through to them."

Evandria leaned back. This wasn't the worst thing that could have happened. After all, no one had started any new fires, which she decided to take as a win. And open defiance was a welcome change from the terror they usually showed her. Still, Evandria couldn't help but feel guilty. Louis and Maria had both put in the effort to arrange today's outing, and it all ended miserably because of her.

"Maria, I don't pay you enough," Evandria mused.

Maria gave her a slight smile. "Do you even remember how much you currently pay me?"

"No, which means it's definitely not enough."

Both of them gave a tired laugh at that. It was something they both needed. As the carriage rode on, Evandria could feel a weariness in her bones. The whole encounter had really taken a lot out of her, and the little bit of laughter eased some of her tension.

"When we get back," Evandria started, "I'll have to get to work on the next batch of undead."

"Are you sure that's a wise idea?" Maria asked. "Wouldn't you prefer to rest a bit before throwing yourself into work?"

Evandria merely shrugged. "What can I say? Necromancy relaxes me."

Maria scoffed, and they rode the rest of the way in silence. Evandria thought about what she would make next. Perhaps a draugr. It had been a long time since she had made one of those. They were big and strong, and she had plenty of material. Perhaps she'd even treat herself by conjuring a few wraiths.

Evandria smiled. Already, her head was racing with ideas, and she was looking forward to testing each one. She didn't care what other people thought about her, so long as she could do what she loved.

Sometimes, a necromancer's only reprieve came from making the undead.

The End

Robin Talamas is a trans woman and aspiring author focusing primarily on fantasy writing. Based in Los Angeles, Robin is a graduate of USC and holds a Master's degree in pharmaceutical sciences. She is a fan of high fantasy stories with complex worlds and unique magic systems. In her free time, Robin enjoys baking and playing Dungeons and Dragons with her friends.

UNDERMIND

BY JONATHAN MABERRY

The man with the head of a honey badger looked up, adjusted his reading glasses, and asked, "I assume Killer Klown is a professional name, miss?"

"Well, I mean ... sure," the Killer Klown replied, biting the inside of her lip to cover up her nervousness. "It's not like my parents named me that."

"Of course not."

"Preschool would have been weird. Weird-er, I mean. We had a metahuman in there."

"Oh? Which side of the line?"

"Sulk, son of Bulk. His dad was that big rage freak who ran with that super team ...?"

"I *know* who the Bulk is," said the honey badger. His name tag read KEVIN. "My uncle was hurled into orbit by him. Twice."

"Your uncle?"

"Big Bad Badger."

The clown's eyes went wide, and she squeaked a little tin horn. "You're three-B's nephew? That must have been awesome growing up with him. Wait … wait … is your mom his sister? Sugar Slaughter?"

"She's retired," said the badger. "Gone back to using her maiden name. Debbie."

"Cool, cool."

The moment stalled. There was a long line behind the clown, all of them with their resumes in hand, all of them fidgeting. The guy ten back from the Killer Klown kept exploding into green flame and then getting blasted by halon sprays. There were nine other tables exactly like the one manned by Kevin—aka Hungry Badge, and with equally long lines.

Kevin banged a rubber stamp on all the right spots on the form the clown had filled out with nervous care.

"Everything seems in order, Ms. Klown—"

"It's Darla."

"Darla. The program begins in forty minutes. Feel free to look around, network a bit. There are snacks in the back of the hall, and be sure to check out the literature for upcoming programs and services provided by our associates. Welcome to Undermind!"

Feeling a bit dazed, Darla wandered away from the registration table and looked around. From outside the place looked like just another abandoned warehouse on the docks, but now she knew that was window dressing. Mood setting, really. Inside it was all bright lights, neon, glittering chandeliers, crisscrossing red carpets, and vendor tables.

It all made her want to run away. Ideally, she mused, into heavy traffic.

Coming here was a risk. Darla spent her very last bit of optimism to talk herself into it.

Maybe I can actually become a real super villain. Like everyone else at home. Like everyone I know.

Imposter syndrome dogged her, as it had since she took on the mantle of the Killer Klown. Darla had never killed anyone and didn't know that she actually wanted to. Not that she liked people—they mostly scared the crap out of her—but she wasn't innately murderous. Not like Aunt Alicia, Klown Katastrophe, who once destroyed the entire New York Philharmonic because they wouldn't include her theme song during their latest—and last—concert. Katastrophe was a legend, and she cast a big and intimidating shadow over the younger members of her family. Her niece most of all.

The plain truth was that Darla was raised to be a super villain, but she never felt the actual *calling*. She didn't want to fight, didn't want to battle superheroes. She feared she never could and that made her not want to. Failure would shine a spotlight on what a nothing she was.

Maybe nothing *is what I should be.*

The stress of that chewed at her. But being normal wasn't ever going to happen. Not with the relatives she had and the community around them. It was all pressure. It was all junk.

If this doesn't work out …

She had that partial thought ten thousand times and never finished it. Not actually articulating it in her thoughts. Those five words said enough.

So, Darla took a break and forced herself to at least *try* to have some enthusiasm. If she had any faith left, she'd pray. But faith, like hope, seemed to be covered in oil—there was no way to hold onto either. And, maybe no real reason to try.

"You're here, dumbass," she told herself. "So *be* here. Loser."

She nodded and looked around. Trying. At least doing that much.

All of the walls in the hotel's big ballroom were hung with banners showing the most famous super villains going back to World War II. There was Roman the Sea Conqueror with his pointy ears and iridescent scales. There were the Dreadful Duo in their pre-code not-there-at-all costumes. There was the Sneaky Six standing back-to-back with the Devil's Half Dozen. And legends like Dr. Raptor, Dr. Nefarious, Dr. Sinister, and—of course—Dr. Madbrain. All the greats.

Darla drifted aimlessly, a bit awestruck despite her depression, because there were some real heavy hitters in the room, too. Villains who'd made the cover of *Time*, *Rolling Stone*, and *Mad Science*. Some of the others, though, were third and even fourth generation—either legacy holders of costumes and powers, or newcomers trying to jump the celebrity line by suiting up as classic villains who'd either retired due to injuries, aged out, or were killed in big, splashy battles.

Everyone in the hall wanted to see Undermind. The waiters and greeters all dressed in Undermind's distinctive blue and shiny gold, form-fitting spandex, boots and gauntlets, billowing cape, and golden Egyptian death-mask with its fixed, beatific smile. They were all over the place, maybe a dozen or more, each with buttons on their chest that read:

IF YOU WANT TO BE MORE THAN YOU ARE
ASK ME HOW!

The thought of approaching any of them, even aware that none of them were the *real* Undermind, intimidated the hell out of Darla, and so she did not ask '*How*' of any of them. Instead, she drifted solo, keeping her head down and offering nothing that could be construed as a challenge. Especially around the more sociopathic and thin-skinned bad guys who were always looking for a reason to throw down.

It was her school friend, Nick Nitro—actual name, which was the universe being funny—who first told her about Undermind. Darla had already begun to notice how much more confident Nick was lately. His costume was way better, and he even lost a few pounds because an Undermind clip on Instagram said that "core strength was pure strength." And, best of all, Nick actually beat Arachnid-Boy in a fight. Didn't kill him, but handed the web-monger his narrow ass.

Nick had given Darla a brochure:

CORE-STRENGTH for that KILLER BOD: Spandex is unforgiving, and sprayed-on abs won't cut the mustard when a superhero is giving you a gut punch. Undermind's personal trainers will get you ripped and flexible, build your endurance, and help you max out your strength. (Disclaimer: side effects are generally mild and rarely cause mutagenic changes.)

In a last-ditch effort to fit in, Darla enrolled, and over the next few weeks she received a series of self-deleting powerhouse messages from Undermind's organization. Every now and then one of them would hint at a live event where Undermind himself would take the stage and give one of the massively popular motivational speeches.

Darla was both excited and filled with dread.

Now, all around her, was cutting edge empowerment in all of its aspects. And, if she attended the whole series of seminars and earned her Clenched Fist Pin, she would then have access to the Net's healthcare benefits, legal counsel, career guidance, and therapy for 'criminals of distinction.'

I want all that stuff, she thought, then corrected her assessment. *I need it.*

One of the biggest tables in the hall was there to promote the

INTERNATIONAL FEDERATION OF ALTERNATIVE ENTEPRENEURS, a registered union that did collective bargaining for wages and benefits, provided advisors to help launder money through their taxes, and offered a variety of benefits including healthcare—magical & nonmagical wound repair, gene therapy, dental, a prescription drug plan, and even a retirement package.

Darla took the brochure, though she was so down that she could not imagine ever living long enough to retire. She had a bottle of sleeping pills she'd filched from another of her aunts, Celia, who was doing twenty-to-life for kidnapping the last three former presidents. That bottle was enough to send Darla off without having to go down after a beating by some version of Captain Wonderful. Lately, she'd been sleeping with that bottle in her closed fist, knowing one day she'd take that night train.

Maybe tonight, if this motivational stuff didn't work

out. She felt that low. That useless. That much of a no-one-gives-a-shit.

As she turned away from that table, she was accosted by a serpent man in an excellent Tom Ford suit.

"You look like a menace to society, young lady," said the man, grinning to show too many rows of expensively-capped fangs. "Have you ever been in legal trouble?"

"Me? Well, I—"

"Of *course* you have, but even if you haven't, you *will*." The serpent man pressed a pamphlet into Darla's hand. "If some costumed do-gooder hands you over to the police, call us. We specialize in those kinds of vigilante civil crimes. And all of your other legal needs."

Before Darla could reply the salesman walked off and could be heard making the exact same pitch to someone else. Darla looked at the pamphlet. It was the standard legal stuff, though there was something on the back she found mildly interesting.

ANTISOCIALARBITRATION: If any two super beings are in dispute—whether it's over splitting the take on a heist or staking a claim over being the first person to be bitten by a radioactive insect, our arbitration team will guide them to a final and binding solution. Time allowing, the arbitrator will attempt to find a solution that everyone can *live* with. And if not, we offer a variety of clean-up services.

And that was how it went. Darla could barely go five steps before another sales rep got in her face to give a pitch for their services, leaving her with a glossy brochure each time. She got one from ...

GEAR UP with THE LAB RATS: Every metahuman needs a cool costume (one that won't split a seam at the wrong time) as well as great weapons and other equipment. The Lab Rats will create a special ensemble that fits your style, your power and your needs.

A real fancy one from ...

MASTER PLANS: Being superhuman doesn't mean that you know how to plan a bank heist or steal a nuclear reactor—or take over all of Manhattan. That takes careful planning, our team of experienced and innovative masterminds will construct a fool-resistant caper just for you.

And dozens of others. Some of the sales reps were well-known criminals, including a few who were constantly talked about on the Mass Murderer subreddit. Darla was too timid to say no, so she took all of the literature.

But not everyone who accosted her was selling things Darla didn't need. A very pretty young Asian woman in some kind of anime costume handed her a brochure that held a flicker of appeal.

HIT SCHOOL: If you're going to go toe-to-toe with a superhero you'd better know every dirty trick in the book. Well, at the Hit School we wrote that book, and our team of martial arts masters, disgraced special operators, and psychopathic killers will teach you how to hit first and—most importantly—hit last.

Darla folded that one and put it in her pocket,

knowing she would look into that if survival yelled louder in her head than the sleeping pills. After all, she was, at best, a mediocre fighter. An unskilled wannabe brawler who only did well in melees where so many folks were embroiled that no one could tell she wasn't pulling her weight. She was sure she gave one of the Teen Tornados a black eye once, and another time she accidentally stepped on Kid Legend's foot, making the hero have to sit out the battle with the Sky Rats. That was something, but it was an accident. Darla had no idea how to really *fight*.

A hand landed hard on her shoulder and Darla *yeeped* and nearly dropped to her knees. But it was only Nick Nitro. Her friend was grinning ear-to-ear and he wore a T-shirt advertising someplace called *The Yard*. He was a living brochure. He held up a finger for silence, then pointed at his chest.

"First ... read!" he ordered.

Darla read the shirt.

THE YARD: Tired from a long day of trying to overthrow democracy? Need somewhere to spend your ill-gotten gains? Come to the Yard, take off your power gauntlets, settle back with a criminally cool iced latte or a deviously delicious dark chocolate brownie. Kick back, relax, and unwind at the Yard! (Location changes daily! Subscribe to get today's address!)

"Um," said Darla, "cool. I'll, ah, look into it."

"Only if you want to be cool and hang with the big dogs," laughed Nick.

"Right. Sure. Absolutely. Who doesn't?"

Nick gave her a fake gut punch and Darla pretended to wince. "Glad you finally got your head outta your butt and came to see Undermind. Wait'll you hear what he has to say. It'll change your life, Dar. Not joking."

"I could maybe use a change."

"Exactly. And don't listen to the haters online. They just try to tear Undermind down with fake news. But tell me this, if Undermind wasn't one-hundred-and-fifty percent saying the real truth, then explain to me how the Antelope and his Battling Bovide kicked the living feces outta the Great Lakes Protectors?"

"I—"

"And how did the Runt—who was never more than fifth string—hand Colonel United States his star-spangled ass? Explain that."

"I have no—"

"No, Dar, Undermind is everything the hype says and ten times more."

Darla managed a weak smile. "Well, that's why I'm here."

They paused as an advert-bot trundled by, its head rotating to show each of the three ad screens. Because the bot was advertising clubs, Darla and Nick paused to read.

SECRET LAIR: The biggest and most accessible Nightclub in the Underworld. Great live music! Lousy food! High prices! This is where metahumans go to do a little evil with one another.

Then ...

THE HIDEOUT: The most exclusive and glamorous club in town. We cater to the Underworld elite. (No henchmen allowed!)

And ...

STASH: A diner where a lot of earthshaking deals are made.

Bottomless coffee and five separate escape exits!

"I was at the Stash once," said Darla. "The goat cheese and mushroom omelet was okay."

Nick appeared not to notice or care. He leaned close, dropped his voice and said, "Look, Dar, off the record and all, I started coming to Undermind's motivational talks because I don't always feel ... you know ... all that super-villainy."

It was a shocking confession, but it made Darla feel new affection for her friend. This was behind-the-mask stuff.

"Yeah," she said. "I can relate."

Nick nodded. "So, even though we both have some real ass-kickers in our families, given the actual power *levels* we're at, we got like two choices." He paused and glanced around nervously before adding, "Maybe three."

Darla brightened. "Yeah ...?"

"Yeah, I mean we could buddy up to do what I already started doing."

"The core training stuff?"

"Absolutely. Option two is riskier. I'm talking about some of that wild stuff they're doing—CRISPR gene editing and chemical baths."

"I don't know, Nick. You saw what happened to Allison and her mom, right? They had the CRISPR stuff and now they're lawn flamingoes. I mean real ones. Actual flamingoes and all they do is stand out in front of their house and squawk at people. I was so sad."

Nick's face was pale. He nodded. "Yeah. Damn. And Ralphie McGuire's uncle did a chemical bath and he got super strength, and you know what happened there."

Everyone knew about that. Once Big Al McGuire became indestructible, he began wasting away because the cell walls of his stomach were too strong to allow nutrients to enter. He couldn't even breathe because his lungs were as dense as Kevlar. He didn't die exactly, but what was left of him was taken away and put into cryogenic storage until the genetics guys figured out how to make what they called 'minor adjustments to form and function.'

"What's option three?" asked Darla listlessly.

"We could become acolytes."

"What's an acolyte?"

"Oh, c'mon Dar, they're the most devoted followers of Undermind. I mean *real*. Sworn to secrecy, blood oaths, midnight ceremonies, the works. Anyone who gets into his inner circle is *made*. Absolutely made." He paused. "The downside is that it's total commitment. Once you swear the oath there's no take-backs. You're in it to win it, or out all the way to the boneyard."

"Jesus." But to herself she said, *I have a bottle of pills that says I can get to the boneyard all by myself.*

"But think about it, Darla. You get the training, the seminars, and personal sessions. Undermind isn't just motivational lectures and shit ... he's *above* above, you know?"

Darla didn't know but didn't want to push it. What she said was, "I want to hear what he says before I make any life choices."

A voice behind her said, "And that is the smartest thing I've heard all day."

They both turned to see one of the greeters in his *faux* Undermind uniform. The man wasn't tall or massively built, but he exuded a great deal of personal power. The golden mask was disturbing because it had only that one secretive, contented smile permanently fixed. The eyes, though, were a bright green and filled with energy and mischief.

"Hope you don't mind," said the greeter, "but I overheard some of your conversation. It seems to me that you both have doubts."

"No," said Nick quickly, "we think Undermind is awesome, cool, and—"

The greeter waved it off. "No, no, son, not that. Besides, Undermind doesn't need people to fawn over him. Needing praise is a weakness."

"Yeah," said Darla, seeing the value of that insight.

"What I heard," continued the greeter, "was two young people engaged in a conversation about their purpose. Not destiny, but true purpose born of choice. Purpose born in the fires of doubt but refined, purified, made stronger beneath the hammer blows of understanding, of knowledge, of shared awareness. I heard the two of you express your doubts about whether you are, or are not, meant to be villains. To make statements like that, to speak truth as deep as that may feel like confessions of weakness, but I am here to tell you, my friends, that it takes *courage* to admit to weakness. It takes depth of character to admit that you *don't* know, and it requires a measure of nascent nobility to come here—here of all places—and speak of those doubts." He smiled. "I am honored to have shared that moment, however accidental. Truly honored."

Nick and Darla stood gaping at him, mouths open,

eyes unblinking, brains sputtering as they tried to put all of that into some shape that made sense.

"No," said Darla.

"Ah, *no* is not a word Undermind believes in. *No* is a shield raised against the arrows of truth."

"No ... I mean ... what I meant was that I don't think I'm cut out for super villainy."

"I might be," said Nick, but the greeter seemed not to hear.

"Doubt is not certainty," said the greeter, "and in that gap lies potential and choice."

Nick's eyes were glazing a bit. He nodded at everything the greeter said, but Darla was pretty sure her friend didn't actually *understand* it. But she thought *she* did. Or, at least Darla felt something shift inside her chest. Inside her head, too.

"So," she said, feeling her way through what she wanted to say, "it's not wrong to question whether the whole superhero/supervillain thing is for me?"

"Wrong?" The greeter shook his head and patted Darla's shoulder. "If we never question, we can never understand."

"Wow," breathed Nick.

Darla said, "My uncle said he knew even before he got to preschool."

"Perhaps he did," said the greeter, "but what of it? Some people know from the first time they open their eyes who and *what* they are. Some are born heroes, others are born villains. Just as some are born to be poets, dancers, politicians, users, soldiers, slackers ... the good and bad among us, the dimmest and brightest lights are often those folks who are *sure* they are on the right path, and by god and thunder, they won't veer right or left by half an inch."

He took a small step closer, effectively closing Nick out of the conversation.

"But Undermind was not like them. Did you know that?"

All Darla could do was shake her head.

"It's true. Undermind was a nobody for most of his life. No powers, no inner storms pushing him one way or another, no compelling sense of purpose."

"But he's *Undermind*."

The greeter shook his head. "Not at first. He was plagued with self-doubt, with confusion, with insecurities, all of which became magnified by social pressure to *be* someone, to *do* something. The more pressure that was applied to him, the more he crumbled under its weight."

Darla listened, transfixed.

"It was only after a series of personal calamities, losses, heartbreaks, and frustrations that he realized he was falling. Plummeting, really. And that the ground was reaching for him, begging him to hit hard and lose it all. But *as* he fell, Undermind had a moment of clarity. Call it an epiphany. He realized that he was as low as he could possibly get. The fall was not merely from grace but from existence. He had failed at being himself and that fall was inevitable."

He leaned forward and lowered his voice.

"But here's the secret, my young friend. Here's the truth, and it's so simple that once I tell you, you'll understand. You'll *get* it. Shall I tell you?"

Darla licked her lips. "I'm not sure. It sounds scary. Maybe I'm not ready to hear it."

Those green eyes seemed almost glassy, as if wet with

sympathetic tears. "There," he said. "That is exactly why you *should* hear it. Anyone who thinks they're ready hasn't fallen far enough down. So ... listen to me and I will tell you the thing that Undermind discovered."

Darla stood there, trembling but transfixed. She felt herself nod.

"Undermind realized during that long fall that life—everything he was, everything that defined him, and all of his heart and soul—was crystalized into a simple truth about what would happen when he truly hit rock bottom.

"Can you guess what that is?"

Darla said nothing, but she felt as if she *might* know.

The greeter said, "When all else is stripped away, when there is nothing but the truth of falling and the inevitability of hitting bottom, there are only two possible outcomes. First, you *splat* and, in that immolation you cease to be. Oh, you might live past it, but there's nothing left of you. You're broken beyond repair and broken beyond anyone caring. It is *The End* writ large. Nothing, gone, erased from mattering to the world. Or ..." said the greeter, his eyes glittering like polished emeralds, "instead of smashing, you hit bottom and *bounce*."

"What?" said Nick.

Darla said, "Ohhh."

And meant it.

Her eyes went wide and she *got* the message. To hit the lowest point and rebound meant that the fall was one thing, but what happened at the moment of impact was something entirely different. Something potentially ...

Darla fished for the right words.

"You have nothing left to lose," she murmured, and the greeter nodded.

"And ...?"

"Everything after that is different. You already fell. You already hit bottom," said Darla, surprising herself at her own ability to articulate it. "You can go up …"

"Oh yes," said the greeter. "There is nowhere to go *but* up. And the deeper truth is that it is entirely up to you to decide how far up." He straightened. "You can return to your life, tear it down and rebuild it in an entirely new and possibly unknown shape. You hit the ground with legs bent, muscles tight, feet springy, and embrace the potential in Newton's Third Law of Motion. And I quote, '*To every action, there is always opposed an equal reaction.*' Now, tell me how that applies to falling."

"If you hit rock bottom," said Darla slowly, "you bounce as high up as you fell down."

"Or higher," said the greeter. "As high as you want."

The lights in the hall flickered—the signal for everyone to file into the lecture hall. The greeter placed his hand once more on Darla's shoulder.

"Come on," he said, "I'll walk you in. Though … I think you might already be on the point of understanding the message. I think you have actual promise. I think you are about to hit rock bottom. I wonder … will you splat or bounce?"

"I … I d-don't know …" Darla tripped over the words, but she let herself be ushered inside. In the dark she lost contact with the greeter as she found a seat. Then she saw the man—at least she thought it was the same greeter—walk all the way down the aisle to the foot of the stage, where the other Undermind impersonators stood. All of them clustered around, looking identical. And yet Darla was sure that she could tell which one had said those amazing words to her.

She was certain.

Then she felt herself freeze as the greeters all turned to form a corridor down which that one greeter walked. Moving with stately elegance and great confidence, the greeter mounted the steps to the stage. He turned and held his arms out wide.

"Now," said the greeter, "who here wants to be amazing?"

The crowd shot to its feet, and they all went absolutely wild.

Darla watched as the greeter looked out over the assembled crowd of thugs, villains, evil geniuses, madmen, killers, and monsters. He stood there, arms wide, as the applause rose like thunder, loud enough to shake the whole building.

And all that time the man looked directly at Darla.

She could feel the bottom rushing up toward her. As she looked at the man on the stage, at *Undermind*, Darla felt her body begin to tighten, to crouch, to tense for the impact ... and the great leap upward.

She smiled.

Perhaps the first and truest smile of her entire life.

The End

Jonathan Maberry is a NYTimes bestselling author, 5-time Bram Stoker Award-winner, 4-time Scribe Award winner, Inkpot Award winner, editor, writing teacher, poet, playwright, and comic book writer. He writes in multiple genres including thriller, horror, sci-fi, mystery, and fantasy. V-WARS (Netflix) was based on his books/comics; Alcon is developing his Rot & Ruin novels for film; and Chad Stahelski, director of JOHN WICK, is developing his Joe Ledger thrillers for TV. Marvel's BLACK PANTHER: WAKANDA FOREVER was partly based on his work. He's written more than 50 novels, 200 short stories, 30 graphic novels, 1200 feature articles, and two dozen nonfiction books. Jonathan has also edited 30 anthologies, including Aliens, The X-Files, the official tribute to Scary Stories to Tell in the Dark, and many others. He's the president of the International Association of Media Tie-in Writers, and the editor of Weird Tales Magazine. www.jonathanmaberry.com

FANGS

BY E. M. NOLLER AND JANINA SCARLET

September 3, 2022

Luna Duskbane

███████████

Portland, OR 97200

Admissions Committee
Northbridge School of Orthodontic Medicine
███████████

Portland, OR 97500

Most Illustrious and Respected Members of the Northbridge Admissions Committee,

I am entreating upon your wise and noble countenances to heed, with a compassionate ear, my entreaty to be accepted as the very first Vampire student to attend your august and venerable institution.

I am desperately hopeful that you will hear my plea, because not only am I an excellent student,[1] I am, in fact, also a recipient of the treatment developed by the esteemed, prestigious practitioners of your distinguished profession.

However, my initial experience with the ingenious contraption that is the mark of your profession was, indeed, quite humiliating. The first time I saw my reflection with braces glinting across my fangs, I recoiled in horror.[2]

You see, in my family, perfection is paramount, and crooked fangs are considered a mark of failure. My mother taught me that, because we come from a long line of proud Vampires, our gloriously symmetrical denticular projections are a symbol of our prestigious prowess.

Mother is an immigrant from Eastern Europe, where she and others of our kind were hunted mercilessly for centuries, victims of ancient superstitions and prejudicial, provincial attitudes.[3]

---

1. Although I have only attended Vampiric institutions, based on my understanding of the academic achievement evaluation in the United States, my calculations indicate that I have always earned what's colloquially known as "straight As." In Vampire culture, we categorize academic achievement using the VESS (or Vampiric Edge Sharpness Scale), whereas the sharpness of our teeth is used as a metaphor for how keen our intellect is proven to be. My VESS is currently a 50, which I assure you is the sharpest.

2. Yes, we Vampires can see our own reflections. How else would we know if there's something stuck in our teeth?

3. Vampires do not "turn" their blood providers—a ridiculous supposition which ignores the fact that we are a different species altogether. Vampires must be born from other Vampires, evidenced by the fact that I come from Vampire parents, just like all my ancestors before me. We

My parents came to the United States to escape the oppressive and dangerous society of their birth. Once they arrived, mother created a baroque antique chain (catering exclusively to humans), Nightfall Curiosities, staffed by our loyal human contractors, which began in Portland and has expanded all over the U.S. and throughout Europe, and has therefore enabled many of my people to immigrate to the United States. She is the first of her kind to achieve such a spectacular feat of modern capitalism.[4] Mother even showed me an advert for her boutique, which played inside a box with tiny humans inside of it. I believe she called this box a *Telle Vision*.[5]

In response to my unignorable, increasingly asymmetrical visage, my mother advised me to become so feared that no one would ever question the shape of my fangs. A suggestion worthy of her fearsome reputation.

But, desiring to emulate my maternal progenitor's unorthodox and revolutionary approach to problem-solving, I decided to try something unconventional—and like my revered and terrifying matriarch, something none of my kind had ever done before. I went to see a human orthodontist.[6]

---

meet our need for sustenance through the employment of contractors who are well-compensated for their regular donations.

4. My father mostly golfs. At night. He is less ambitious than Mother.

5. This was the first time I had ever seen a *Telle Vision*. At first, I was a bit distressed that these tiny humans had been trapped in such a cruel way, but Mother assured me they were safe, and it was more like a moving painting. Having spent all my life thus far only among my own kind, I still have much to learn about human society and culture.

6. I first became aware of the miracle via the *Telle Vision*, which is where I was first blessed to gaze upon Dr. Payneless's beatific visage. She was much larger in person than I expected. When I expressed this

Your esteemed colleague, Dr. Imogene Marigold Payneless, was the best doctor I have ever seen. She made me feel at ease and explained my options. She fitted me for braces, which transformed more than my bite—they reshaped my confidence, my empathy, and ultimately, my future.

Even though the idea of silver threads entwining and restricting my canines made me lose my thirst, Dr. Payneless found creative ways to ease my embarrassment and discomfort.[7]

Over time, I have become more accustomed to the metallic shimmer embedded in my grimace, and to my eventual maxillary metamorphosis. Even though Mother was initially skeptical and apprehensive, she has come to support my decision to see an orthodontist and even helped me market my bracket invention. Father also nodded in approval.

It is thanks to Dr. Payneless that I first imagined myself becoming an orthodontist, specializing in Vampire health. To the best of my knowledge, no such practice exists yet. This is a problem, because unlike Dr.

---

observation to Mother, she speculated that we, perhaps, needed to invest in a slightly larger *Telle Vision*.

7. Dr. Payneless first encouraged me to pause and gaze at the braces in my reflection several times per day, without judgement, as a way of honoring my transformation process. When I felt self-conscious about revealing my braces to my adolescent peers, she showed me images of human teenagers showing off their braces via a small hand-held *Telle Vision* containing additional moving paintings and explained that metal braces had recently become "cool." She even demonstrated how to decorate my braces with crimson rubber bands, although I didn't quite understand the point. My fangs are already tinted red due to my diet. But I appreciated the empathetic nature of the gesture.

Payneless, many human orthodontists do not know how to accommodate Vampire clients.

For example, Vampire fangs are crucial when penetrating the skin (even the skin of a blood bag), and my braces often got in my way. I was constantly struggling with feedings until I, with Dr. Payneless's help, designed a modified bracket[8] and wire combination that did not impede my bite strength. There are other such accommodations Vampires will need, such as late-night appointments.[9]

I vowed to myself that one day, I would become a Vampiric orthodontic paragon of smile beautification beyond compare.

I've chosen Northbridge School of Orthodontic Medicine because of its unmatched education in dental arts and orthodontics, with a "strong focus on building empathy and cultural awareness and a commitment to diversity."

As the first Vampire student admitted to your school, not only will I learn everything I need in order to one day become an orthodontist specializing in Vampire braces, but my unique cultural and ethnic background would certainly enrich the experience of your human students.[10]

---

8. Which I ingeniously plan to market and sell through my office as VampBrackets™. The name of the device was Mother's idea.

9. Another myth we Vampires must often dispel is that we burst into ash when struck with even the smallest beam of sunlight. This is inaccurate. We're just not morning people. Dark glasses and an extra pint of O negative are usually enough to tempt us into the sun. I simply desire that all my clients be especially comfortable.

10. If you are worried about me being in the same school with human students, I want to put your fears at ease. Just as some humans have dietary restrictions, such as eating a vegetarian or gluten-free diet, so do Vampires. My diet consists strictly of locally sourced O negative blood,

As you will see in my transcript and attached letter of recommendation, I care deeply about my studies and believe that my experience, ambition, and my strong sense of empathy will make me an ideal student to attend the Northbridge School of Orthodontic Medicine.

Thank you very much for your time and consideration.

I remain, with humblest and proudest reverence, your dutiful servant,

Luna Duskbane

~

February 12, 2023
Admissions Committee
Northbridge School of Orthodontic Medicine
█████████████
Portland, OR 97500

Luna Duskbane
█████████████
Portland, OR 97200

Dear Ms. Duskbane,

We are writing to inform you that your request to

---

that is freely given and entirely GF (garlic-free). Thus, you do not have to worry about the safety of your students. In fact, I'm sure my fellow students will welcome me with open arms (if not open veins—many humans are eager for Vampiric employment).

attend Northbridge School of Orthodontic Medicine has been denied.

While we were quite impressed with your story, and your passion for orthodontics, we have a strict "humans only" policy at our institution to ensure student safety. For questions regarding this policy, you may contact our Department of Campus Security Office at the following number ███████████████.

Best,

Hugh M. Bean

Director of Admissions, Northbridge School of Orthodontic Medicine

~

Local Vamp Teen Sues School for Orthodontists

By M. Raker, Southwest Portland Responder

April 8, 2023

A local teen is challenging student safety policies regarding Human/Vampire interactions by taking on the Northbridge School of Orthodontic Medicine (NOM)'s policy against the admission of non-human students. The youth, Luna Duskbane, is a member of the Hematomic-Deficient Community, or HDC (colloquially known as "Vampires"), who are not considered human according to both state and federal law.

Her lawyer, Hope Bytesmore, Esq., gave the following statement: "NOM's antiquated and exclusionary policies are long overdue for an update. My client has never bitten a human without their express written consent, and she deserves the same opportunities as any passionate devotee of orthodontic treatment."

Officials at the school could not be reached for comment. However, parents of current students have expressed concern. One local parent, who asked to remain anonymous, told our reporters, "I'm all for equality and stuff, I'm just kind of worried my kid will get bitten by one of those bloodsucking fiends."

The court date is scheduled for later this month.

~

April 28, 2023
Dr. I. M. Payneless, D.M.D.
BrightLine Orthodontics
████████████
Portland, OR 97200

Portland Superior Courts
████████████
Portland, OR 97500

Dear Judge Masterson and the members of the jury,

I am writing this character witness letter on behalf of my patient and intern, **Luna Duskbane**. I had the opportunity to mentor Luna during her internship at my orthodontic practice, and I can truly say that I have never worked with someone as kind and motivated as she.

I would like to speak directly to an incident introduced by the defense, during which several staff members were said to have witnessed Luna attack me physically. This was a simple misunderstanding. A few moments prior to the incident in question, I had donned a surgical mask and face shield at the request of a current patient, a ten-year-old boy, who is immunosuppressed. Luna had never seen me in a mask before and didn't recognize me. When I came into the room, the boy began crying, and Luna knocked me over. I was startled, but uninjured. Once I removed the mask Luna recognized me and immediately apologized. Later, she mentioned something about me resembling "a Templar Knight in a plastic helmet," and I came to understand that the mask and face shield appeared similar to headgear worn by ancient human aggressors who performed mass executions of her people. Her intention was a gut reaction to protect the child, not to injure me, who she initially believed might attack him. We laughed about the mix-up and it never happened again.

Other than this one isolated incident, Luna has been nothing but professional and caring to all my patients. For example, when a shy teen was too anxious to open her mouth for a procedure, Luna used gentle encouragement and humor to put her at ease. To be fair, at first, Luna hypnotized the girl to calm her, but Luna also responded well to my feedback that hypnosis is not an ethical approach to calming a patient's fears, and she never did it again. This demonstrates that Luna is coachable, responds well to feedback, and is a quick learner.

Thanks to her courage to try braces, Luna has been able to use her experience to encourage several other Vampire teens at her school to explore their dental options as well. I realize that Luna's passion is to someday set up her own orthodontics practice specializing in working with Vampires, and I know that it is something that she will succeed in.

I believe that Luna deserves to be admitted to the Northbridge School of Orthodontic Medicine and believe that she should not be discriminated against simply due to her heritage. I believe she will make an excellent student and will excel in her studies. Please feel free to contact me at impayneless@brightlineorthodontics.com should you require any additional information.

Sincerely,

Dr. I. M. Payneless, D.M.D.

∼

Hugh M. Bean <hugh.bean@nom.edu>
May 22. 2023, 9:42AM
To: Faculty and Staff
Subject: Update Regarding Student Safety Protocols

Dear NOM Faculty,

Pursuant to the recent decision of the state court, the Northbridge School of Orthodontic Medicine will be admitting one student from the Hematomic-Deficient Community (HDC), also referred to as a "Vampire," effective immediately.

In response, updates to the Student Safety Handbook are currently in development and will be distributed upon completion. Attendance at the upcoming Friday staff meeting is mandatory for all faculty and staff to review revised protocols and appropriate procedures. Additional details regarding the meeting schedule will follow.

The school has also received a generous donation from Nightfall Curiosities to support the future construction of an HDC Student Center. Please note that, at this time, the HDC population within our student body will remain limited to one individual.

Thank you for your continued professionalism and cooperation.

Sincerely,

Hugh M. Bean

Director of Admissions, Northbridge School of Orthodontic Medicine

~

Local Teen Accidentally Murders at Orthodontic School

By M. Raker, Southwest Portland Responder

October 31, 2023

Tragedy struck at a local school of Orthodontics today when a misunderstanding involving an HDC (AKA *Vampire*) teen and her classmates resulted in bloody mayhem. Ms. Duskbane, who earlier this year sued the Northbridge School of Orthodontic Medicine due to their discriminatory policies against non-human applicants, was subsequently granted admission to the university, along with an apology for the school's actions.

Last Friday evening, Ms. Duskbane was attending a university performance of "Van Helsing: The Musical." Witnesses say that during the scene in which Troy Kingsley Sterling the 3rd (the actor portraying the role of

Van Helsing) "slayed" the vampire family, Ms. Duskbane jumped onto the stage and proceeded to bite Mr. Sterling.

"She flew onto the stage like a wicked witch, or something, and drained poor Troy dry," said 19-year-old Lulu Anne Bean, daughter of NOM's director of admissions, who was in the audience at the time. She then added, "I knew they shouldn't have let her kind in here. My father didn't want to admit her in the first place. Clearly, he was right."

One of Luna's professors, who asked to remain anonymous in fear of retaliation by the school's administration, confessed that she had encouraged Luna to attend the musical because she worried that Luna hadn't yet made any human friends. "Luna had never even seen a play before becoming a student here, or a smartphone for that matter, so even though she clearly overreacted, I'm not sure she completely understood what was happening. Although in retrospect, maybe a dramatization depicting the brutal murder of her ancestors wasn't the best choice for Luna's first theater experience."

Ms. Duskbane was arrested on a homicide charge following the incident and is being held at the Southwest County Sheriff's Office without bail. Her lawyer could not be reached for comment.

An official communication from the college states that Ms. Duskbane "is expelled effective immediately and the school will be pressing charges."

～

NOVEMBER 11, 2023

Federal **A**gency for **N**onhuman **G**overnance and **S**ecurity

Portland, OR 97200
Subject: ███████████

Today, on ███████████, F.A.N.G.S. Agency has officially recruited the HDC subject, LUNA DUSKBANE to ████████ ████ ██████ █████████ for our mission titled ██ ████████████.

As a part of this mission, Ms. DUSKBANE has agreed to ████████████████████████, which would require that she complete government-operated orthodontics program AKA ██████████ ████████ ████████ ████████ ████████████████ in exchange for four years of service and ████████████ █████ ████████.

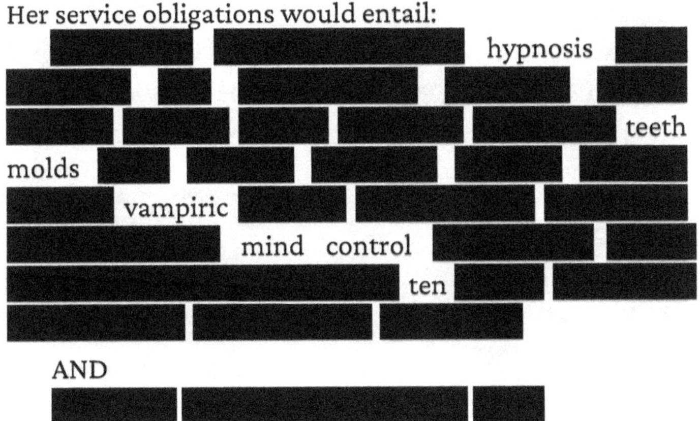

Her service obligations would entail: ████████ ████████████ hypnosis ██ ████████ ████ ████████ ████ ████ teeth molds ████ ████████ ████ vampiric ████████ ████ mind control ████████ ████ ten ████ ████ ████████ ████████ ████████

AND

████████ ████████████ ████

Morana Malum
  Deputy Director of Supernatural Operations

~

December 27, 2023
  Dearest Mother,
  I must keep this short because we are about to ███████ ██████ ████████████ ████ ████ ████████████ and other vampires. I am writing to tell you that I miss you and that ████████████████ ███████████. Even though I know Orthodontics was not your preferred choice of profession for your sole progeny, you have nevertheless provided me with stalwart loyalty and unwavering support. I could never have made it this far without your undying devotion to my success.
  School is going well. Today we learned that ██████████████████████████████ ███████████████████████████, anguished and distressed ████████████ quite harrowing. In fact, ███████████ █████ ████████████. You were right. About every-thing. Humans are so much worse than I realized when I began my pursuit of their odontogenic doctrine, but at least I will get to ████████ ████████ ████████ including, but not limited to, ████████ ████████ ███ ████ ████████ ████ ███ ████ ████████, and soon. Give Father my love, and tell him I wish him many cloudy days on the golf course.

I remain, with humblest and proudest reverence, your dutiful daughter,

Luna Duskbane

Vampire Weekly – Classifieds / Announcements Section
January 5, 2026

Introducing: Duskbane Orthodontics – Most Illustrious Vampyric Orthodontist For Fangs That Impress

Are your fangs crooked, uneven, or awkward?

You have nothing to be embarrassed about!

Dr. Luna Duskbane, Certified Orthodontist, is proud to announce the opening of her exclusive orthodontics practice for Vampires.

Services Include:

VampBrackets™ designed specifically for your unique fang shape

Private, after-dark appointments

Custom retainers and fittings for all fang types

Refreshments provided, all blood types available on tap

Why Choose Duskbane Orthodontics?

Empathy born from personal, lived experience

Precision, artistry, and discretion guaranteed

Safe, modern techniques tailored for children of the night

Location: ███████████████ Suite 13, Portland, OR 97200

Appointments: After moonrise only, please call to schedule

Contact: (555) █████████

DISCLAIMER: NO HUMANS ALLOWED ON PREMISES or signed waiver allowing the use of hypnosis and absolving this institution of any liability if any of the following should occur: severe blood loss, anemia, iron deficiency, scarring, maiming, dismemberment, and/or death. Please note that at this clinic, Vampire Privacy under HIPAA *or* VIPAA is not guaranteed. Proceed at your own risk.

~

SEPTEMBER 15, 2026

Federal **A**gency for **N**onhuman **G**overnance and **S**ecurity

███████████

Portland, OR 97200

Subject: ██████████████

The HDC subject, LUNA DUSKBANE continues to provide F.A.N.G.S. Agents with much needed intel on ████ ██████ ██████ ███████ ████████ ██████ ████ ███ for our mission titled ████ ███ ██████ ███.

Our agents have learned that:

██████████████████████████████

██████████████████████████

varying fang shapes  areas of the brain, as well as exsanguination, but not

Our next steps will entail:

- the attorney general and ambassadors to , and

- Additionally, the CEOs of , and .

In exchange for additional, agency-funded education of HDC individuals in the areas of:

- phlebotomy 

- woodworking,

- I

- fire science

AND

- ███████████████ mind control.

Until such time as we are able to guarantee success in our pursuit of ███████████ ████████████ and to ensure the United States dominates the fields of ██████ ███████████ █████████.

Morana Malum
Deputy Director of Supernatural Operations

~

Message intercepted on the Vampyric International Telegram Agency (VITA) as follows:

DEC 31, 2026
DEAREST MOTHER -[STOP]- ALL PAWNS IN PLACE -[STOP]- OUR UTOPIA AWAITS -[STOP]-LOVE, LUNA

~

JUNE 2, 2027
Federal **A**gency for **N**onhuman **G**overnance and **S**ecurity
INTERNAL MEMO:

ALL OPERATIONS INVOLVING AGENT DUSKBANE ARE TERMINATED EFFECTIVE IMMEDIATELY. ALL

RECORDS PERTAINING TO OPERATION ███████████████ MUST BE DESTROYED WITH UTMOST PRIORITY.

~

West Coast Declares Sovereignty as an HDC Haven

By M. Raker, Southwest Portland Responder

October 31, 2027

In a shocking and historically unprecedented move, the entire west coast of the United States, including Washington, Oregon, and California, has seceded from the United States, with the full permission of the U.S. government, and several of its allies, and declared itself as a haven for the HDC community and its human employees/contractors.

The announcement was made this morning via a three-hour-long televised statement delivered by the CEO of Nightfall Consortium, Luna Duskbane (who is well-known in odontological circles for her many scientific advances in the field of vampyric orthodonture, and for her legal battles with Northbridge School of Orthodontic Medicine, resulting in controversies that eventually led to the school's permanent closure), who has declared herself the president of the newly founded country, which will be known as Nyx Corvina.

None of the current governors of any of the three states could be reached for comment. More details to follow on this story as it develops.

The End

E. M. Noller is a neurodivergent writer of horror stories and weird fiction, and the acquisitions editor at Divine Feminine Publishing. Her work has been published in several journals and anthologies, including the short story, "What the Tide Brings," forthcoming in 2026 from Twenty Bellows Press. She is currently working on a novel that examines the narcissistic cycle of abuse through the lens of speculative body horror. E. M. Noller lives with her family (including a few feral animals, an absent-minded engineer, and various offspring) in Longmont, Colorado. To learn more about her, visit emnoller.com.

Dr. Janina Scarlet is a psychologist, author of 18 books, and a TEDx speaker. She is also the Founding Director of Divine Feminine Publishing. A Ukrainian-born refugee, she survived Chernobyl radiation and persecution. She immigrated to the United States at the age of 12 with her family and later, inspired by the X-Men, developed Superhero Therapy to help patients with anxiety, depression, and PTSD. Dr. Scarlet is the recipient of the Eleanor Roosevelt Human Rights Award by the United Nations Association for her work on Superhero Therapy. Her work has been featured on Yahoo, BBC, NPR, Sunday Times, The New York Times, Forbes, and many other outlets. She regularly consults on books and television shows, including HBO's The Young Justice. She was also interviewed for Marvel's MPower series and was portrayed as a comic book character in Gail Simone's Seven Days graphic novel.

SEEKING GRAY
BY BRIANNA ALERS

By the time she found herself dangling from the spire on the Empire State Building, Francesca Perez had begun to wonder whether she was really cut out for this villain business after all. Her cape began to tear as she wriggled to escape. Staring at the sheer drop below her, she could almost see all of her accomplishments falling away. The delicious screams of a city cowering in fear. The many dramatic speeches filled with extravagant imagery and sesquipedalia. Her grand display of magic lightning arcing over even the city's tallest skyscrapers. None of it had mattered in the face of her enemy.

The only thing worse than the full body bruise beginning to form was the pressure of thousands of gawking eyes and cameras reveling in her defeat. She was almost relieved when she saw the fireball headed straight toward her. Francesca found herself sweeping through the sky like the world's saddest star to wish upon. The plunge into the East River was nearly refreshing.

Slinking off in despair, she returned to her secret lair

in the sewers and changed from her sopping robes. She stretched her aching muscles and performed the cleaning spell she was beginning to know a little too well. Francesca avoided turning on the television, knowing from experience that her embarrassing failure would be plastered across every network. There would be general outcry that the Gray Witch of Manhattan had struck again, laments about the property damage, and worst of all, praise for the city's hero, Sunburst.

Francesca's glossy hair, which was enchanted to float around her head like lively serpents, stroked her cheek in what she supposed was intended as a comforting gesture. The action felt hollow without the warmth of a real hand behind it. With all the time she had sunk into her villainous pursuits, she was just as alone as she had been back home in North Dakota. When the phone rang, she jumped, still on edge from the fight. She didn't have to look to know it was her mother, as it was after every failure.

A deep breath was required for this phone call. A deep breath and comfort food. Popcorn? She pulled a packet out of the pantry, placed it on the kitchen table in front of her, and set it popping with a flick of her wrist. Her phone floated into her hand, and she smacked her writhing hair out of the way in order to bring it up to her ear.

"I saw you on television, Fran."

Francesca's nose wrinkled at the nickname. "I wish you wouldn't watch that stuff, Mom."

"Why is your dress so ragged? You could have fixed it up after your last fight." Francesca could almost see her mother now, phone held up to her ear with her shoulder as she ironed an already pristinely crisp article of clothing.

Francesca sighed, suppressing an eye roll. "Mom, we've talked about this. That's the style. The robes are supposed to look that way. It's meant to terrify onlookers and remind them I'm not to be trifled with."

"But that color? Why would you choose gray? You need to shine bright on the TV, not blend into the background."

"It's not gray! It's more of an olive green. I don't know what they were thinking calling me the Gray Witch of Manhattan when I specifically introduced myself as Madame Mesmer. It's not my fault the press is as stubborn as they are lacking in creativity. At least the color is as dignified as I am. I'm not trying to look like a clown, like *Sunburst.*" She said the name with a venom she hadn't intended. Bitterness was difficult to avoid post-ass-kicking, especially when said kicker wore spangly spandex. Francesca ripped open the bag of popcorn, though the spell hadn't quite finished. A kernel flew from the bag and popped midair, almost hitting her in the eye.

"But, honey, people love Sunburst. Don't you want to be more like her?"

Bouncing the steaming bag between her hands, Francesca crunched on her popcorn and said nothing. It burned her tongue, but at least this heat didn't send her face-first into a dirty river with a cannonball of fire. An image of Sunburst's glowing, golden eyes flashed in Francesca's mind unbidden. Those eyes were to blame for it all. That and Sunburst's perfectly springy curls. Just one look during the fight had caused Francesca's heart to stutter and her normally nimble hands to falter mid-spell.

"Fran?"

With her jaw clenched, she said, "No. I don't need to

be loved. I'm here for me. I'm here for power, respect, and a city, if not the world, at my mercy."

"Sunburst has all of those things, though. And I think you're selling love a little short, Fran. People love her for more than just her heroics. Sunburst is interesting. She doesn't peddle the same gloomy messages every time she appears to the public. She actually has something to say, and you can tell her heart is in it." Though her voice was gentle, it felt like a stab wound right in the ribs. Betrayal from her own mother.

Francesca's gut curdled with the uncomfortable truth of it all, churning around the mountain of popcorn she had just consumed. How long had it been since Francesca had enjoyed her work? Part of her was starting to wonder if there was another reason she kept putting herself in the way of Sunburst's flames, but Francesca extinguished that thought before it could run wild.

Her mother was still speaking, and as Francesca attempted to refocus on the rambling words, she discovered the well-intentioned insults were not finished. "I heard from Judy last week, you remember Judy, right? From the block party? She was saying that the Striking Viper was having some trouble taking over Denver, but she—"

"Hey, Mom? I'm actually really busy right now, so I have to let you go. Okay?"

"Okay, Fran, but you know you work too much. You could use a vacation. Maybe come visit your poor, lonely mother sometime, huh?"

"Yeah, maybe," Francesca replied around a mouthful of popcorn. She hung up before her mother had a chance to launch into another round of advice from Judy from the block party, a block party Francesca had never actually attended, by the way. She didn't know who Judy was, but Francesca wished the woman would stop talking to her mother about the Striking Viper's successes. It was hard enough hearing her mother's feedback without additional contributions from neighbors and friends.

As Francesca attempted to shake clear of lingering irritation, her mother's final piece of advice held steady in her mind like a burr on cotton. Francesca was in desperate need of a break. She had been planning and failing to implement them for a solid three months, longer if you counted childhood daydreams. People like Judy from the block party simply didn't understand the kind of toll this work took. From the time she was six, Francesca had pushed against society's conventionality. She had brainstormed a list of ways to dramatically enter a room, taught herself how to make even the toughest people cry with only a few devastating words, and discovered the magic that would later catapult her to fame (and into the East River). In all that time, she had never once considered taking a vacation. Villainy was a lifestyle, as she was fond of saying. Only people with a constitution as strong as her own could handle the heavy burden, whereas the average mortal would have crumbled beneath the pressure by now.

After her mother's needling remarks had shaken an already vulnerable foundation, Francesca decided that even someone as strong and talented as herself could require some time away from the pressure. A trip home would certainly be the opposite of a restful vacation, but Francesca figured it was worth finding some way to relax right here in the city.

After a quick internet search, she settled upon a spa treatment at a top-rated place on the Upper East Side.

Pulling on a hoodie and sweatpants, Francesca sneaked out from beneath a manhole and joined the throng of people cascading down the sidewalks.

She did her best to hurry. Even though she had changed into more casual garb, it was impossible for Francesca to travel around the city truly incognito. The enchantment on her hair was essentially permanent, as were the other modifications she had made, from her claw-like nails to eyes that glowed when the lights were low. As helpful as the enchantments were for building up her terrifying persona, they also unintentionally caught the attention of passersby when she was off-duty, on days like today.

One businessperson was so engaged in a phone call that they stumbled right into her writhing nest of hair. They fell to the ground with a scream, and Francesca was yanked down with them.

"Not again," she muttered as she fought the hair's grip with strategically placed karate chops.

The businessperson wasn't making things easy, swinging their limbs around in distress. Once they were freed, they scrambled away and fled across the street, ignoring the honking of inconvenienced vehicles. Their phone call took a bit more of a "911" vibe after that, so Francesca ascended from the crowded sidewalks and flew instead.

She landed in front of the doors of the facility and stopped for a moment to recenter the hate brewing within. Then, she thrust her hands outward and blew the doors open in a theatrical whoosh. The receptionist flinched and peered around his computer.

"Can I ... help you?"

"The Gray Witch of Manhattan has need of your services. I will require a full treatment."

"Um, so, our spa is appointment only. I might be able to find an opening for the salt pool in an hour, but most treatments are booked out unti—"

"Silence! Did you not hear me? I am the Gray Witch of Manhattan! I will be treated here today, or this business will face the consequences." She raised one hand with a practiced flourish and balanced a plume of fire on the tip of her pointer finger. The receptionist's eyes widened. His hand crept to the side for what was clearly a panic button, but Francesca wagged the flaming finger at him.

"None of that. All I require is a nice, relaxing spa day. If you can provide me with that, I will leave this building untouched by flames or any other magic."

The door opened behind her with a pleasant chime. A young woman with a Prada handbag and a leopard-print coat took a step in and froze, her eyes locked on the fireball Francesca had begun to juggle. She stood there for a moment longer before jumping backwards and slamming the door behind her. Francesca could see the shadow of her fleeing form through the opaque windows.

"I think a spot just opened up in your schedule."

The receptionist gulped and looked down at his computer again. "I ... believe you're right. It looks like I can fit you in for a massage first, then a manicure, and you can finish with either the sauna or the salt pool. Which would you prefer?"

"Both."

"Of—of course. We'll get you back right away. You can take a seat in the chairs to the right while you wait."

Instead of following his instructions, Francesca leaned

casually against the receptionist's desk, to keep an eye on him. His hands hovered over the keyboard, clearly waiting for her to walk away before continuing his work. When he realized she wasn't going anywhere, his jaw clenched, and he leaned back in his seat. He pasted on a smile.

"Anything in particular bringing you in today?"

"Just my mother," she said, rolling her eyes.

"Oh?" he murmured, noncommittally.

"She doesn't think I make a very good villain, and sometimes I agree with her. I used to think if I could only earn her attention, I would be satisfied, happy even. But her attention tends to hurt just as much as the disinterest I grew up with." Francesca had no idea why she was spilling her soul to this random peasant. It must have been some innate magic of receptionists that unlocked little secrets and tragic backstories. The receptionist fidgeted in his seat, wary but somehow unsurprised at his truth serum effect.

A crease formed between his eyebrows. "You're really doing this for *attention*?"

"Oh, yes. It's a bit more complicated than that, of course. I really do think I'd do a better job running this city than your current overlords, but who else launches an entire career based on villainy if not for us attention-seekers? I'll be happy to get back to blowing up buildings, but I just needed a break today, you know?" The receptionist's face grew pale at her final statement, and she hurried to follow it up. "But not this building, of course. This one will last the day, at the very least."

Her ill-advised monologue was interrupted by the entrance of the masseuse, whose eyes grew wide when she caught a glimpse of her latest client. Without moving her head, her eyes traveled slowly to the receptionist whose face was again caught in a customer service grimace.

"There was a *slight* change of plans, but your next appointment is right on time."

Francesca rolled her eyes at their tight movements as both employees attempted a complicated series of nonverbal communications. She strode past her masseuse and through the swinging doors, concealing a small smile. Relaxation awaited her. She had forgotten how pleasant small evils could be. After months of show-stoppers, it was nice to be among the people again. It was so easy to get caught up in the grand scale of things. She missed watching the sweat bead on people's foreheads or listening to the way they tried to slow their shallow breaths. This was what had drawn her to villainy in the first place. All eyes on her, waiting with bated breath for her next move.

Her masseuse scuttled after her and directed Francesca to a small room emanating calming harmonies of notes that reverberated a few seconds too long. A pleased sigh escaped her as she settled onto the table for her massage. Sure, it could have been a better experience. The masseuse's hands shook the entire time, and she had to take frequent breaks to battle with Francesca's enchanted hair. A few curls even attacked Francesca's own face, but she was used to that by now and didn't let it disrupt the calm. And, boy, was she calm.

Too soon, Francesca was transported to the next room for her manicure. This proved to be a tricky endeavor. She hadn't poured some of her strongest magic into her claw nails for nothing. They resisted the mani-curist's every effort, shattering three nail clippers and an entire pack of nail files. The woman became increasingly distressed as she scrambled for the next technique with which to tackle Francesca's nails. Francesca just closed her eyes with a small smile on her lips and lay back into the cushy seat.

"What are you doing?"

Francesca startled. She knew that voice, though they had rarely spoken. Their relationship up to this point had been a bit ... punchier.

"I could ask the same of you," she intoned in response. She kept her eyes closed and her face blank to conceal how unprepared she was for this interaction. Those little snitches in the lobby! Or was it the pedestrian her hair had assaulted earlier?

"Obviously, I was called here to stop you ... from whatever it is you're doing."

Francesca's eyes flashed open to find the manicurist had disappeared. In her place stood Sunburst, in full battle armor, complete with the obligatory sun logo. Heat radiated from her and began to turn the room into the sauna Francesca had been scheduled for. "I'm relaxing. Is that illegal?"

"It is when you hold spa workers hostage."

Francesca yawned, removing her fingers from the manicure bowl to inspect them. They looked the same. What a waste of time. "That's a bit dramatic. It was just a little intimidation. I would hardly call this a hostage situation. And anyway, don't you ever get tired? You can't blame me for needing a break every once in a while."

"When I take a break, I don't 'intimidate' people into serving my every whim. Now, get up. I've let this go on for too long. I need to arrest you."

"You don't need to intimidate people into serving your whims because they'll do it anyway. You have this whole city eating out of the palm of your hand. They adore you and your cute little button nose."

Sunburst reached up a hand to her nose self-consciously and gave it a small tap. She shook her head and refocused her attention. "Maybe people would do the same for you if you stopped destroying their livelihoods."

"I doubt it. I don't have your golden eyes or perfect hair." Francesca stretched out her arms, reveling in her loosened muscles after such a fabulous massage. Though she feigned nonchalance, her heart was beginning to patter. This was the longest they had ever held a conversation and Sunburst's voice was making her skin buzz. Clearly, she shouldn't have trusted herself to speak so openly if such cheesy lines were all she could summon.

"If you're implying that I have only gotten this far because I'm conventionally attractive, then—"

"The only thing I'm *implying* is that I think you're beautiful. And if you're about to cart me off to super-prison then you deserve to know." They both stopped short at that statement, each blinking in surprise. Francesca shrank back a bit, already regretting her boldness. "It seems that massage loosened my tongue as well as my other muscles. Just ignore—"

"Have you even seen your hair?" Sunburst's eyes suddenly slammed shut, her face scrunched.

"I—what?"

When Sunburst responded, her voice was a bit shaky. "You called my hair perfect before. But yours? It seems pretty perfect to me."

Francesca reached up to her hair and her fingers were immediately strangled by a lock on the prowl. As she worked to disentangle her hand, she kept her eyes on Sunburst in wonder. She couldn't tell if her hand was going numb because of the death grip from her hair or if it was just the nerves. Finally, she pulled free. She cocked her head, allowing herself to consider possibilities she had worked so hard to lock away.

"You know, all this villain work has really worn me out. I can't seem to catch a break as long as you're around. I have to imagine that you're getting tired of dealing with me too. Would you like to take the afternoon off? Maybe we can get that manicurist back in here, so you get a turn."

Sunburst's eyebrows rose. "Have you lost your mind? I'm here to free them, not subjugate them further!"

"Ooo, 'subjugate'. Now there's a fancy word. You should know those are my weakness."

"Be serious!"

Francesca gave a wry smile. "I am. I'm a sucker for grandiloquence."

"No, I mean serious about this situation."

"I wasn't lying before about this city loving you. If you just ask, I think they would be happy to come back and give you a manicure. They'll probably even do it for free."

"I'm no villain." Sunburst pushed back a lock of dark, coiled hair and kept her hand on her face, massaging her temple.

Francesca faltered. When she spoke again, her voice was softer, a little kinder. Normally, she would have been mortified to show anyone kindness, let alone her supposed enemy, but by now, she was far too relaxed to care. For some bizarre, unknown reason, she wanted Sunburst to stay. After all her efforts to keep that fact buried, the tranquility of sitting here with Sunburst allowed her to push past her lingering hesitations and speak vulnerably. "I know. I'm not asking you to be. I just thought you might like to be a little less than perfect, for once." She stopped short for a moment, considering how to explain it. "Take a little bit of the light and a little bit of darkness and we'll have our own personal gray area. It's even in my name."

Sunburst paused for a moment, considering. "You're more of an olive green."

Francesca beamed. "Yes! You get it!"

Sunburst examined her nails before heaving a sigh. "Alright. If I get a manicure, do you promise to leave the spa in peace afterwards?"

"Scout's honor." She gave a little salute and then inclined her head conspiratorially. "I *might* even pay for my services."

"No, you will absolutely pay. As will I."

"Are you sure you don't want to step a little further into this gray area?"

"Yes, I'm sure." Sunburst rolled her eyes before stepping back into the hallway. She disappeared for a moment, but Francesca could hear her request for two manicurists and a second chair. Sunburst was immediately peppered with murmured questions, but her response was confident and echoed clearly down the hall. "Look, I want this building to stay in one piece. If we start a fight, that won't happen. This is the only way I can think of to get her out of here with your business and employees still safe. I'll keep an eye on her and I won't let anything bad happen. I promise."

When she stepped back into the room, Francesca suppressed a smile. "That sounded an awful lot like a threat. What has gotten into you, Sunburst, if that *is* your real name?"

Sunburst sputtered. "What are you talking about? Of course that's not my real name. And that wasn't a threat."

"If you don't give me special treatment, we will burn your building down? Sound familiar?"

"That's not what I said!"

Francesca was appalled to hear a giggle pass her lips, but the room suddenly warmed as Sunburst observed her reaction. Maybe this could work.

Maybe they weren't as different as Francesca had imagined. Francesca's failures at besting Sunburst might not have been failures at all, but the start of something new and hopeful, if a little unconventional.

"Welcome to the gray area, Sunburst."

The End

Brianna is a fiction writer, aspiring physician, and voracious reader. When she isn't working on her first novel, she can be found obsessing over Star Wars and spending lazy mornings with her cat.

MY BONNIE GIRL
BY ALEXIS WRIGHT

That morning, extended on smooth steel, Harry Mater offered My Bonnie Girl a morsel of her favorite meal. High in protein. Great texture. No pesticides or parasites.

My Bonnie Girl thought often of the warmth of his skin and the softly haired texture of his long arms. The hairs were springy and tickled whenever he held her. At first it made all of her senses spasm and crawl, but she grew to tolerate it over time. After her first year in captivity, she learned that she didn't need to run and hide when she heard the latch and saw the shape of his hand reaching for her.

Eyesight wasn't one of My Bonnie Girl's stronger senses. She smelled and tasted Harry Mater more than she clearly saw him, but she knew that he wore some of his longest and thickest hairs on either side of his beakish nose. My Bonnie Girl found them impressive and intimidating and believed that if he showed any desire to dance with her, she would be inclined to accept. He never asked, though. He just showed up regularly with her meals on metal.

That morning, My Bonnie Girl smelled meat on his breath. It was tinged with a touch of aluminum, smeared with something fatty, and mixed with a pale planty crunch she couldn't quite place. The tang of a yellow seed puffed through his lips as he watched her eat. He didn't panic when she used her teeth. In spite of restricting her movements, Harry honored her survival. She couldn't conceive of a more radical act of love. Gentle and punctual, never forgetting about how sensitive she was to perfumes and chemicals, his greatest compassion came from what he chose not to do.

This was how she knew he always thought of her. This was why she suspected Harry Mater was actually obsessed with her and would ask her to dance if he only knew she wanted him to. For all her yearning, though, My Bonnie Girl had no clear way of telling him what she wanted.

He did all right with what she needed, generally speaking. Her living conditions were comfortable, even ideal. Water was always available. Food wasn't, so when he did bring it, it was the high point of My Bonnie Girl's week. She was always hungry enough to eat, but never fully satisfied. Harry measured her carefully with his eyes before feeding her, judging whether or not she risked becoming obese.

My Bonnie Girl saw nothing wrong with the prospect of obesity. It sounded wonderful to her, even aspirational. She hoped to someday eat enough to achieve it and believed that she absolutely could if Harry Mater was just a little less withholding. It was his most frustrating flaw, if not the largest thing standing in the way of the attraction she was sure she felt for him.

She waited all afternoon, spending her time sipping water and rearranging the decor in her living space. She knew he had returned when she saw a shadow fall across the door outside one of her home's clear walls. A ruffle of motion occurred as he pulled back the comforter on his bed. When she could feel the vibrations of his snoring gently rocking and rattling her floor, My Bonnie Girl settled in for a long, pleasant night.

Her limbs jerked at a movement in the corner of her enclosure. She froze, tensing as the stillness of the air made her hairs stand up and prickle. Wings! It had been the buzz and flit and thrum of something alive. For the moment she forgot her contentment, the sleep that might have taken her, and even her dearest Harry Mater. She rushed the creature down, gathered it with her front legs, effortlessly overpowering it, her fangs poised to pierce its soft flesh.

The kicking little-boned thing tangled in My Bonnie Girl's legs shrieked, sending a cringing ripple through her setae. She dropped the creature and its heel painfully struck her small cluster of eyes. She scurried back, but all she could see was a blinding flash that didn't recede back into shadow. Shapes cut their outlines into her limited vision, and instead of vague shadows and shades of gray, her dullest sense showed her the bright eyes, vivid colors, and crystal rendering of a little winged woman who glowed. She was much smaller than My Bonnie Girl and cowered behind the enclosure's cork bark hide.

"Please," the creature begged. Unlike Harry Mater's booming drone, her voice was tiny and high enough that

My Bonnie Girl could reliably decipher it. "Please don't kill me, My Bonnie Girl!"

"BUG," My Bonnie Girl said. "BUG. MINE. KILL." The sound of her speech was clicking and guttural, not a tiny strand of gossamer string, but the creature seemed to understand.

"I understand," the little winged creature squeaked, watching My Bonnie Girl anxiously.

"You're wondering how I knew your name. It's written on a label on your enclosure, along with your species. Grammostola rosea, commonly called the Chilean Rosehair Tarantula. You're very beautiful."

"KILL BUG," My Bonnie Girl said. "FOOD." She wondered how the creature tasted and moved a little closer.

The creature cast off violent ripples of vibrations as she trembled. "Don't kill! Not food! Listen, there must be something you want, My Bonnie Girl. Something wonderful."

"HUNGRY," My Bonnie Girl said, thinking warmly of her dream of obesity. Harry Mater thought she needed to cut back and let her abdomen shrink down smaller than her carapace over the next few months. She would be ravenous and cranky the whole time, when she had the potential to become gloriously enormous.

"Of course you're hungry!" the glowing creature said quickly, her little voice full of sympathy. "I completely understand. But surely there's something else you want? Something I could give you? I was called here, you see, by the purity of the deep desire in your heart. I am Rainblossom, guardian of unrequited love, and you drew my attention and my pity. What can I do to ease your yearning?"

"CRICKET," My Bonnie Girl suggested, grooming her fangs excitedly with her pedipalps.

"My Bonnie Girl," Rainblossom sighed, "I would urge you, if I may, to think … bigger. Use your imagination."

My Bonnie Girl's pedipalps groomed more quickly. "HORNWORM." She thought of the fat, bright blue delicacies she remembered from the pet store. She used to perceive the vibrations with envy as the pretentious bearded dragons next to her enclosure chowed down. Hornworms were never wasted on the midsize terrestrial inverts like Chilean Rosehair Tarantulas, but she would dearly love to liquefy a hornworm's hemolymph.

"Oh, honey." Rainblossom stepped up onto the cork bark hide, beckoning. "Think even bigger! More huge."

"OBESE," My Bonnie Girl said thoughtfully.

The fairy stared pointedly, pressing a hand against one of the acrylic walls. My Bonnie Girl trundled after her. Harry Mater slumbered in his bed a few feet away. "You love Harry, don't you? Would you like to be with him? Truly with him?"

My Bonnie Girl watched Harry scratch at the impressive, curling twin pedipalps under his nose.

Rainblossom clasped her hands. "I knew it. The purity of your love was like a clarion call in the night. How glad I am to have answered it!" The fairy stood on the tips of her toes, pushing her little arms against the lid of the tarantula enclosure until the magnets released.

"Go on, My Bonnie Girl! Run free!" Rainblossom urged. The tarantula stared dumbly atop the cork bark for a few moments, unsure what the fairy meant.

"SCARED," she said uneasily, planting a foot on the enclosure's side.

"No need, my silly! Trust me. You are so close to

achieving your most passionate dream!" The fairy flitted beneath My Bonnie Girl, wings whirring as she hefted the heavy-bodied tarantula by the rump. Many legs scrambled to gain footing at the top, and Rainblossom gave a little yelp and scrambled backward as a bouquet of urticating hairs exploded in her face. "Oh, my dear, you itch!" she exclaimed. "That simply won't do when you go to embrace your love! Let me see ..."

My Bonnie Girl carefully crawled over the lip and down the outside of her open enclosure, but the warm glow of Rainblossom's spell extended to the claws of her foremost tarsi. She scrambled to catch herself, because suddenly she was falling. Her body met the floor, but she wasn't ruptured. She had half as many limbs. Her hair was almost completely gone, except for a pale pink fall past her shoulders.

Rainblossom suddenly looked many times smaller, but she seemed delighted, flitting level with the tarantula's face, her clear blue eyes brimming with delighted tears. "You make a beautiful human, My Bonnie Girl! Most spiders would, I think, but you simply take my breath away!"

Everything about My Bonnie Girl's current form was new and alien. She stood, only to trip and fall face-first onto the bed with Harry Mater. He grunted in his sleep; his voice seemed softer, now that they were on the same scale. He smelled like gentle, powdery soap, and My Bonnie Girl realized that he must have showered at the end of the day to keep the scent from bothering her.

"It's like a fairytale," Rainblossom sighed, pearly tears streaming down her tiny, rosy cheeks. "Wake him, my dear, but gently!"

My Bonnie Girl's eyes swiveled to rest on Harry

Mater's bushy pedipalps. He hadn't danced for her or drummed the correct rhythm, but with a human's vision, she could see reproductive potential. She moved to align her epigynum with the wiry, hairy arms on his face, but forgot, in the moment, that humans needed to breathe. Harry spluttered and woke, shoving her off of him.

"What the hell? Who are you and how did you get into my house?" he demanded. Rainblossom flitted hurriedly out of sight.

My Bonnie Girl reached for his bedside table, pawing at his phone and smiling in what she hoped was an enchanting, seductive way. Her teeth weren't very sharp anymore, but there were many more of them.

"My phone? Oh ... Wait ... Carly? Kylie? From Halloween? With the pink hair? Did I give you my number?"

"DANCE," My Bonnie Girl said.

He furrowed his eyebrows. "That's right, I guess we danced at the club."

"FEED."

"And got some food at the bar? Yeah, that's right, it's coming back to me now," he said, still sounding far from certain. "I must have given you my address too, huh? I don't usually do that ... or wake up to this kind of surprise." He grinned nervously.

"SURPRISE," said My Bonnie Girl, showing more of her teeth.

Harry Mater swallowed. "So, do you want to have some fun, uh ... Carly?"

Altogether, My Bonnie Girl found the experience satisfying, though it didn't quite go as she expected. She didn't know that male humans had only one spinneret, or that they kept their pedipalps there. It seemed to get the job done. Rainblossom sighed and arced dreamily out the window, leaving the lovers to their clasped hands and shallow breathing.

The next morning, My Bonnie Girl basked in the sunrise, still half-tangled in bedding. Rainblossom flitted through the curtains of the open window, beaming as a sparkling many-colored band of light trailed in her wake.

"My Bonnie Girl!" she trilled, lighting delicately on the bedpost. "Have all of your dearest dreams come—"

My Bonnie Girl clapped her hands over her human ears. Because though the fairy had started out quietly and pleasantly, now she was just screaming, for some reason.

"What have you done?!" The fairy doubled over, puking a thin, sparkling stream onto one of Harry Mater's pillows.

"FOOD," My Bonnie Girl admitted. She leaned over for another bite of Harry Mater, but Rainblossom flew in, smacking her open mouth away from his gaping chest cavity.

"This is terrible! Just terrible!" Rainblossom wailed. "My Bonnie Girl, this is not how love works! Bad tarantula! Love is like the gentle wind among the water lilies, the laughter of a delighted child! Love is pure! Love is—"

"OBESE."

"What?"

"OBESE!" My Bonnie Girl threw herself back happily and patted her stomach.

Rainblossom took one last look at the scene, covered her eyes with her tiny, manicured hands, and started to rush out the window. In an explosion of glitter, My Bonnie Girl snatched her out of the air and stuffed her in her mouth, where she burst like an ortolan.

Thinking of eggs with legs and the squirming

triumph of new life, My Bonnie Girl was distracted momentarily by something sinewy stuck between her teeth. Unfortunately, the spiny rib she broke off of Harry was too large and blunt to use as a pick.

My Bonnie Girl's eye caught a flash of smooth steel near her open enclosure. She used the tweezers to dig out a morsel of her new favorite meal before sucking the tongs clean. High in protein. Great texture. No pesticides or parasites.

The End

Alexis Wright has a BA in linguistics and has spent the last five years working as a freelance ghostwriter and editor. She attended the Clarion Young Author's Conference hosted by Michigan State University in January of 2006. The next year at the same conference, she won multiple awards for her submission in the Infinite Pen writing contest. Her short story "Papercut" appeared in Hillsdale College's literary magazine, The Towerlight, in Fall of 2007. Alexis publishes weekly on her Substack, "Alexis Writes Fiction."

BEFORE I CROAK
BY JOCELYN WALLEN

"I'll wait as long as it takes for your answer, Tibia," says Auricle in her looking-down-my-nose-at-you-iest therapist voice, crossing one leg over the other and leaning back against the sleek leather chair. Her assignment to my case was probably extra punishment, given how we'd picked at each other all through school.

"Are my answers mandated too?" My mouth is dry around the words. "I thought it was just the sessions." Twelve whole hours of impulse management therapy. All for one *teensy* little broom incident. The council was fully overreacting. Unsurprising though, given that they'd never much liked Lothrum or his followers.

Auricle simply stares, waiting for an answer. Why is everyone always asking why I do things? As if Witchhood isn't mostly the same for all of us. As if the pursuit of magic is something less than connection with power, the divine light of our Gods. That's the rub though, isn't it? As a follower of Yvaine, she'll never have it as good as me.

Still, Auricle's face is a mastery of open blankness.

Tapping my tongue against the back of my teeth, I roll my eyes. The silence isn't *that* awkward to sit in.

And yet, I still open my mouth and blurt, "Nothing feels the same anymore." *Fuck.* "With my magic, I mean," I say, waving a nonchalant hand to cover my fill-the-silence admission. The bruises on my arms ache from going through the store window, a firm reminder of my failure to land even though the cuts are gone.

Auricle's pen twitches as if she wants to scribble on the pad in her lap. Not surprising after three previous sessions of unanswered prodding questions, but she doesn't take the bait of the impulse, so I let the moment linger between us a second longer.

"It used to feel so good." It was an unreachable high, my magic. The first time Lothrum's light found my fingers was so overwhelming, I cried on the spot. Lothrum's Will was a blessing that so few received, I devoted myself to serving in His image. But now, after so many years, it's hard to keep the same gusto when every day it feels as though He's a little farther away.

Auricle's eyes track the circular rub of my fingers across my sternum like she can see the ache I'm trying to relieve. I snatch my hand away in a fist. Followers of Yvaine are too gentle to understand the true embrace. It was stupid to have said anything.

"It hurts to feel alone," she offers. "I understand."

Lonely little Auricle, still the same girl sitting in the library during school lunch, nose tucked into a book to hide the wide rims of her glasses. I bite back the urge to say how sure I am that she knows what it's like to be alone. It used to feel so good to put her there, to pluck away her friends like flowers from a garden, to revel in the power of Will, of changing reality to suit myself. But here in therapy, no matter how good it might feel, plucking at her won't help me.

It strikes me how long it's been since I gave Him something like that, how much I've been seeking His light without really giving an appropriate offering. No wonder He's looked away. How didn't I see it sooner? I've been failing Him in the simplest of ways.

Auricle scribbles on her pad, looking between her notes and my face. I don't care what she sees.

"Have you tried the support group yet?" The card was abandoned at the bottom of my bag somewhere—*By Witches for Witches! Find Community, Coven, and Recovery!*—useless. I'm not some junkie or gambler; it had been more proof that Auricle never really understood the situation at all.

She ends the session with her usual disclaimers of who to call during an emergency and a few pleasantries that I promptly tune out, and I lie about checking out the group as I leave.

Outside, the city bustles with midday business, and I join the current of bodies, going west toward the shadow of skyscrapers. It feels nice to leave therapy with a positive purpose for once. It had seemed like the whole point of therapy was to make you feel ashamed of who you were and what you'd done, but I don't.

I just need a spark, something to bring back Lothrum's favoring eyes. An offering will be just the thing.

I scurry down the block to the next alley, cutting over and making my way to the door of my walk-up. With a wave of my hand, it unlocks, and I slip inside the portal.

Nestled deep into the growth of my swamp, cradled in the arms of my stone God, rests the hut my foremothers have tended for generations. His feet are below the water, the legs of His visage growing thick as trunks from the dark up to the bare beauty of His torso, covered only by the thatching of the shabby hut. His hands link in front of the door, making a stoop of His palms decorated with potted plants—a nod to my late mother's garden from before I moved to the city.

My skin settles immediately as the swamp air caresses my cheeks. The sun filters in through the overhanging trees in golden waves, setting the swamp aglow to a cacophony of frogs and flies and cicadas. I kick off my kitten heels, wading into the water on smooth stones. I could just as easily use my magic to whisk myself inside, but that isn't the point. This is how He would approach.

I make my way to the altar at the base of Him and smudge away some of the accumulated moss. I reach for Him and press His Will out from me like a bubble. The closest frogs hop over to my station, lining up in front of me, one short, one fat, one yellow. A cab driver who charged me double fare, a bad first date, and the hairdresser that insulted me and messed up my bangs. I opt for the hairdresser.

Her skin is slimy in my grip—*who has a bad skincare regimen now, Stacy?*—but she doesn't fight the Will of magic as I lay her across the altar and flay her, arranging her froggy limbs into Lothrum's mark and smearing her blood around the symbol. It really is beautiful. I should've handed over one of my frogs to Him much sooner.

The sacrifice eases something in me, but as I lean against the table, I don't feel the elation of light, the sparkle of His touch. More is required.

I'm in my hut the next instant, off for a bath and to curl my hair. If a frog wasn't quite enough, I'll offer him some flesh–I know just how to do it. I'm His favorite for a reason.

I take my time with it, painting on a face that I know He will love–red bow lips and swooping raven's wings of eyeliner, over a milk-white base to smooth out my smile lines. With a swish, I squeeze my hips into a cute little black and white number with a zip up the ribs, and I'm out the door in six-inch heels with plenty of night to burn.

The bar down the street is dim but busy, the pulsating music attracting bodies to dance like flies to meat. The bartender is cute, with a blonde buzz cut and an eyebrow ring. She makes an okay Cosmo but ignores my first few attempts to catch her in conversation, giving short answers past the pink glob of gum smacking around her mouth. A bubble of envy pops in my throat as she throws a smile to an ugly little goth girl at the end of the bar whose makeup is caked onto her face to cover her acne, so I turn from the sticky wood of the bar to easier pickings.

Balancing my drink, I weave between bodies out into the pond of the dance floor, stopping with my back to a school of young men toting beers and shoving at each other to see who is brave enough to attempt to join the throng. I sway back and forth and raise my hands above my head, careful not to spill as I swing my skirt across the tops of my hamstrings and bounce my curls to the techno-rhythm.

It isn't long before one of them snags on my lure, large, warm hands settling on my hips and grinding closer to the beat. I can feel the itch of his five o' clock shadow as he leans close to speak into my ear.

"Hey," he says, the courage of his drink still fresh on his breath.

I continue to spin a spider's web with my hips, bringing one hand down behind me to stroke his cheek. We align to the beat of the music, strangers illuminated in neon and strobe, until I swear I can feel the hum of His Will in my hands, my hips, and as a light buzzing in my head. I pull the stranger toward the door, and he follows the string of my hand past the bartender who smirks as we pass.

Outside, I get a better view of my catch. He is handsome in a generic-blonde-man kind of way, sure of himself for no reason that I can see. When we lock eyes for the first time, he stutters.

"Oh," he says, running a hand down the back of his hair and stumbling a step to keep up with my clicking pace. "You're older than I thought."

I freeze.

"No!" He tries to recover, caressing my arm, but my skin has gone cold. "It's totally cool, I just meant—"

His pathetic sentence ends in a croak, his voice box shifting and changing with the rest of him into a stout green and brown frog. He tries to hop, but is too discombobulated and I snag him, digging my fingernails into his sides.

"I guess neither of us is what the other thought," I spit in his face. I blink and he is gone, hopefully drowning in the deepest part of my swamp.

I'm walking before I have any idea where to go, wishing like hell for my broom, or another drink, or both. I can feel every passing glance oozing across my outfit, my shoes, the lines in my face, and it makes me want to claw at my skin, rip and rip until I am naked and wild and free. The next street is blissfully dark, and my mood cools a fraction as I slow.

The only sign on this block is a red neon crucifix, blinking to show three drops of spilled blood falling from Jesus's heart. Below the sign, a slash of moony yellow illuminates the street from an open window.

Inside, a gaggle of witches sit in a circle, colorful clothes and eccentric styles at odds with the gray of the space. Some are knitting, or dancing, or listening to each other speak. The church's altar is covered in black cloth, and a shabby A-frame sign standing in front of it reads: *Be Your Own Magic.*

I swallow around my dry tongue. This is the group Auricle nagged me about, but I don't see her. A witch near the front catches my eye and perks up, waving me inside, but I'm gone the second our eyes meet, stewing in my sour mood the rest of my walk home.

The swamp is alight with lantern glow and fireflies, if a bit muggy. I whisk myself into my hut and kick off my shoes on the porch, wobbling with the change, annoyed at my buzz until I realize that even as I stand flatfooted, everything is crooked.

My heartbeat is in a frenzy as I search for the cause, finding a crack in Lothrum's legs forming below His perfect knees. How could I have let this happen? I stare up at the bottom of my sagging hut in His hands. I have too much, it is all becoming too heavy.

Inside, I slam the front door to ease the swampy buzz of insects and frogs and give myself a second to think. I need to get rid of everything that isn't necessary, to bail the water from my sinking ship.

I begin with things I have a lot of, dishes mostly. Scratched with use and worn in like old friends, but heavy and easily moved. I toss them out the window from the cupboards, following up with the tarnished silver my mother bought. It was always too much upkeep anyway.

I focus on useless comforts next, tossing bulky blankets and bottles of lotions and perfumes. I toss shoes and sweatpants and lounge shirts, and all of the half full bottles from my shower to make the space lighter for Him.

The croaking outside is a scalpel to my skin, slicing under the sweat and grime, straight to the nerves underneath the flesh. I wish for the frogs to be crushed under the weight of everything I've tossed from the windows. I want them to suffer for all the ways they've tortured and wronged me, including this one, for the sound of their small army made with my own two hands.

I rip open the door, ready to go on a warpath, but am interrupted by a witch, fist poised to knock. She smiles at me like it's normal, like it hasn't been a hundred years since someone knocked on my door. Her emerald-green hair is cropped short, accentuating the gold circular glasses she wears over her bright brown eyes.

"I saw you earlier," she says, voice deeper than I expected. She holds out a card with a date and time inked on one side. "I wanted to invite you to the next meeting personally."

I take the card with numb fingers and she nods.

"I hope you can make it," she offers, turning to leave. "I won't keep you, it seems like you have work to do." Then she's gone, and I'm alone again, in my crooked house, surrounded by nothing but croaking and broken dishes.

The meeting is a week from the witch's visit, and I spend most of it skipping therapy, digging through everything I have ever owned, and making a mess of my lawn. In front of the altar sits a soggy pile of items that the frogs are making into their new home, topped with my late mother's curtains and my grandmother's false teeth. The sacrificial symbol is still there as well, along with about a hundred flies, which surely only entice the frogs.

I leave for the meeting in no small part just to escape the incessant buzzing.

I'm earlier than I intended, and most of the chairs are still empty, so I distract myself by nibbling on cookies from the snack table and sipping from my tiny plastic cup of water. The cookies are soft and sweet, definitely home-made, and someone has taken the extra care to add ice cubes to the water pitcher, so my glass sweats in my hand.

As the other witches arrive, we all make little nametags and I learn a few names. Vena is the one who came to my house, and Auricle is here this week too. We sit in a circle, a hilarious cacophony of styles and colors, and the meeting begins as Vena speaks.

"Welcome, dear community, and thank you as always for coming," she says. I watch the other witches, trying to catch them staring at me while I'm not looking, and trying to see what they think of Vena, who is going over some kind of list of community happenings.

Everyone is engrossed in her words, and when they do catch my eyes, most just smile or nod. I tap my fingers against my thighs as I sit, ready to jump out of my skin, regretting having come to try to fill the growing pit at the bottom of my stomach. The only thing that has ever filled that void is His light. I was stupid to have tried this.

I zone back in as Vena continues, "So, that's why this week our healing theme is Recovery of Self." I'm plotting my swift exit when she catches my gaze and smiles, offering her story to the group.

An alcoholic and magic abuser, she lost everything in an endless search for Cerrum's Love—her job, her wife and daughter, even her home. She catches my eyes more than once as she explains, casts her web of self to the group. "That's why I'm so grateful to be here with all of you, to hear your stories," she says. "To see that I was wrong, there is no perfect effigy to the Gods. We are all a perfect version of ourselves already and they only share in the light that we give them."

She has more to say but I'm no longer listening. I scan the crowd, seeing true their flaws. A man with too large of a nose, a woman with huge eyebrows, others with bad style or thinning hair or rotten teeth. Of course they would be the kind to misbelieve in their Gods' light, if they were ever deserving in the first place.

I slip out of the meeting early, guilty and riled, during the space for others to share about their experiences with their Gods. Only Auricle watches me go.

I spark a cigarette, sucking on it to ease the roiling inside me. *Abandoned.* I can't be abandoned, not after how much I've given, how devoted I've been. I flick the cigarette butt to the gutter, rubbing my shirt against my teeth to clean them and smoothing my hands through my hair as I round the corner onto the next street.

"Dear Lothrum," I say. "Please allow me a single taste of your Light, a glimpse of your love." My voice cracks as I continue, "It's been so long." I stop in the center of the sidewalk and wait, gazing up at the distant stars, the moon nowhere to be found. The seconds bleed into minutes as I beg and beg, first silently then through hiccupping sobs, as I carve his symbol into my forearm with a clawed fingernail, spilling my blood to prove my sincerity. A flash of light cuts across my chest.

"Ma'am, are you alright?"

I squint into the light at the silhouette of Him, and fall to my knees, prayers finally answered.

He has come to me, a man in blue. His badge shining bright on His chest as He puts away the flashlight He was holding and leans closer.

I scrabble for His hands and He rears back, pushing me away.

"What happened to you? Why are you bleeding?" The disgust in His voice is sharp.

"For you, my Love," I try to explain. Surely if I just explain, He will see that this is why He has come, to offer His Will and save me.

"Disgusting," He spits. "You're feral." He tries to back away but I'm fully crying now and crawling after Him. My hands are slick with blood as I clutch at His sleeve and extend my forearm to show Him the symbol. I've seen His face so many times in life, in every city and every light, but it's as if He has never seen me before.

He yanks away from me, yelling at my tears, and cracks me in the mouth with the baton from His belt, two of my teeth spraying out onto the sidewalk. He is shouting still, as I stare down at the teeth, a canine and an incisor, broken and red against the cold of the concrete, abandoned. After everything.

My sorrow spears me, flays me, and crystalizes into rage. My fingers shake, then my arms, still slick with blood, then my shoulders as my cries turn to madness, to laughing and sobbing, then I reach into that dark cauldron at the bottom of Me and *yank*.

I clutch the writhing glimmers of His Will, smothering them in my darkness, eating the sparks and setting them free anew. My Will. My Anger. My Turn.

He tries to grab my wrist, cuff it, but with a flick he is a swatted fly, laid out prone on the sidewalk, his golden hair a mess over his terrified eyes. Before me, I make him small, and green, and sticky, unable to escape the hold of me, the force of Will that is completely mine. I lift my shoe and bring it down again and again, until he is no more than pulp on the sidewalk next to my teeth. I leave it all behind.

Home is exactly as I left it, crooked and shabby, surrounded by unpleasant creatures. I wade closer, letting the ick run off of me in rivulets until I'm nearly upon the altar of discarded things. From the top, I pluck the crown of my grandmother's iron teeth, pulling two from the dentures and pressing them into my broken gums. It stings like no truth I've known before, and I set to work, once again pulling the threads of My Will.

I break Lothrum's shrine at his knees, forcing the statue to topple forward, my hut falling in his cold arms into the swamp below. I batter the stone until it falls to pieces, each bit of rubble revealing a little more of my sagging hut until it sits freely, leaning to the left and dripping with muck.

The frogs have gone silent, but I can see their eyes shining in the dark, an audience to my misery, to my fall. I refuse them the pleasure of it, pressing My Will toward my home, the home of my foremothers, and watch it rise from the water on long green legs.

I whisk myself inside, along with the frog-ridden pile of my belongings that have been rotting on my lawn, and my house takes its first leap away from the swamp. I light a fire as it leads me away and catch several of the little green intruders in my biggest pot to set over it. For the first time in an age, my hut is quiet, save the bubbling of my sustenance. Once the meat is tender and my house is warm, I lean against the windowsill to feast under the cackling gaze of the full harvest moon as she watches me, and my house, embark on a path unknown.

The End

Jocelyn Wallen is a queer speculative fiction writer from Denver, Colorado. She completed her Bachelor's at the University of Colorado Boulder before earning an MFA in Popular Fiction and Publishing from Emerson College. She spends her human hours running a restaurant, and her vampire hours at home with her wife, AJ, and their three pet gremlins. A lifelong reader of fantasy, romance, and horror, she is working on her own queer novel, tentatively titled Below the Bloody Sea. She loves late nights, the color burgundy, and you, for no particular reason at all.

ORIGIN STORY
BY DAVE BEAUDRIE

I began my morning on the roof of my loft, the smell of burning metal wafting into my nostrils as I lit multiple chemicals and materials ablaze. I patiently molded the materials into a structure of twisted, colored steel. It would take the mortals of this world weeks to envision such a creation, let alone complete it. This ritual had become my tradition in recent times, and I took great comfort in both the regularity of my routine and in the sometimes surprising results. An internal weight temporarily lifted, and I contemplated what to call this latest effort.

Unfortunately, my moment of peace was ruined when I noticed that the billboard facing the opposite side of my building (blocking my view of the cityscape, no less) had been changed to advertise a new summer film showing heroes and villains battling under a giant portal in the sky. I felt my face twist into a scowl.

Multiverses.

The term was foreign to me in my past life and home. For all the many millennia since my creation, I'd never even heard of the concept of multiple realities all existing simultaneously while stacked atop one another, let alone there being a word to describe it. How ironic then that not only would the word become the key to my undoing back home, but also that my new reality would eventually embrace the concept of multiverses so whole-heartedly that I couldn't go a day without seeing references to it in pop-culture, science articles, or the occasional conspiracy website.

Putting the offensive reminder out of my mind, I closed my eyes and instead focused on what I felt had just been temporarily purged from me and put into this construct, giving me its name.

Solitude of the Void.

I encountered my Billboard Nemesis up close a few minutes later as I walked down Broadway toward Library Street and Cafe Caffeinated, as I'd done almost daily for the past eight solar cycles. The same advertisement, featuring heroes battling villains in some sort of interdimensional warfare, was displayed on the side of a passing bus.

Yet another reminder of my complete and total failure.

My noble "steed" Eater of Worlds was by my side (she's an all-white Italian Greyhound/Chihuahua mix puppy—a far cry from the three-ton carnelian dragon/actual steed I had in my home world—more on her in a moment), and she yipped next to me in apparent agreement with my annoyance. Or maybe she saw a squirrel.

I've never seen any of the entertainments these billboards and buses advertise. They mocked me enough just by existing without me wasting time or currency to view them in their entirety. While I have had to adapt in many ways in the 4,392 days since my banishment, succumbing to constructs like "blockbuster movies," "reality television" or "social media" has not been part of that process.

At least, not until today.

YIP!

My reverie was broken by Eater of Worlds demanding my attention with a high-pitched bark. She had stopped sharply and tried to prevent me from walking farther by pulling against her lead. While her meager seven-pound frame would be no match for my dominating strength, I stopped and regarded her curiously. My dragon, Destroyer of Realms, in all our centuries together, had never altered course mid-flight or questioned my judgment, so this little one's temerity was both amusing and oddly fascinating.

As it turned out, I had been so distracted by my own thoughts that I'd nearly walked right by the coffee shop I was seeking. In my brief time with her, Eater (as others called her) had grown accustomed to getting treats from the employees there, and she was not about to let me go ambling by such a treasure trove of puppy delight without gaining her due reward.

"Well done," I acknowledged. I placed my hand under her little belly to lift her up under my armpit as I continued, "You must never forget to collect tithings from those that worship you. You are learning well."

We entered Cafe Caffeinated, the subtle *ding* of the bell on the door announcing our arrival. The humid summer air was forcibly shoved back outside by the stubborn onslaught of an overworked air-conditioner as I closed the door. Several familiar voices cheered upon my entrance. (I acknowledge that the cheers might have been for Eater, but a cheer for her is a cheer for me.)

"Dom! You're right on time!"

Grace came bounding from behind the coffee counter with her laptop tucked neatly under her arm. I could feel Eater's tail vibrating against my ribs as she approached. The pup whimpered and squirmed out of my grip and leapt up at Grace, who caught her expertly with her free hand. Eater began devouring Grace's nose with licks (in the most loving way possible) and Grace laughed as she handed me the laptop.

"I'll take the puppy. You take the computer. I just got on break, so we've got some time."

One adaptation I'd had to make almost immediately upon my arrival was the taking of a new name. I had been known as The Dominating God of Oblivion in my home world (a world I'd taken to calling "Origin" for both brevity and clarity.) Upon my arrival to this dimension, I discovered that not only were my powers not living up to such an awesome Moniker of Doom, but also, once I was starving and in need of economic sustenance, putting such a name on a job application was a sure-fire way of being soundly laughed out of whatever job site I was hoping to conquer.

Nowadays, I had shortened my Created Name to simply "Dom." Even then, people here were initially resistant to accept the shortened name-form, arguing that I needed a "last name" as well. I then discovered that if I referred to myself as an "artist," my singular name was immediately accepted, and no further conversation was required.

Such an odd world.

A few minutes later, we were set up in the back corner of the coffee shop. Grace sat opposite me, staring intently into her computer screen, while Eater sat in my lap, happily chomping away at a doggy biscuit.

Grace has always mystified me. One of the first people I'd encountered upon my arrival in the city, she began working at Cafe Caffeinated as a teen and had been very close to the original owner, Susan, whom Grace described as a mother-figure to her. Once Susan had gotten older and passed away, Grace had left college and gotten a loan to buy the shop and keep it open. (It took me a while to figure out what a "college" and a "loan" were, but I'd learned a lot in my subsequent time here about how this society functioned.)

Grace was the shop's only employee for those first few years, even sleeping in the back room at times in her struggles to stay afloat. Business had turned around as of late, thanks to good word-of-mouth and the introduction of social events like board game nights, live music, and open mic comedy. But the true deciding factor through it all had been the sheer force of Grace's persistence. Nowadays, the shop earned enough to support a small staff in addition to her. A picture of a teenage Grace embracing Susan hung proudly above the entrance as a tribute to what had once been.

When I'd first met Grace, I thought I'd found this world's version of my nemesis from Origin, known as Tranquility's Soldier. They looked strikingly similar in appearance, though Grace was missing the scars, battle armor, and world-weariness of my enemy. Since this world loves shortening names, I'd found myself referring to Tranquility's Soldier as "Sol" in my mind recently.

Back in Origin, we were equals who fought each other for generations. I'd commanded the power of Fire, and I could bend most minds to my will. Sol could manipulate both Water and Ice, and she was not only immune to my powers of manipulation, but she could also undo the effects of my Mind Magic on others. What I didn't know then (and I'm not sure Sol was aware either until it happened) was that Sol could also open gateways to other realities.

Like this one.

It took a while for me to get my bearings after being forcibly thrown into this plane of existence. Once I realized I'd somehow crash-landed in a new world (New York City, to be specific) with no Sol to oppose me, I was overjoyed. How perfect! I could simply take over this world as its undisputed ruler! However, I soon realized there were a few problems with this plan.

First off, the citizens of New York could not care less about my arrival, even though I tried loudly proclaiming my dominance over them. They just walked by as if I didn't exist, making me wonder if I'd gained the power of invisibility when falling through the portal. (I had not. They treated everyone that way.)

My powers, while still extraordinary by Earth standards, were greatly diminished from what they'd been in Origin. My mighty flames had become meager sparks. My Mind Magic was reduced to mere persuasive suggestion. My immortality faded completely, and I found myself aging at the same pace as my would-be worshipers.

While I had assumed that the city would immediately fall, without question, at the sight of my awe-inspiring presence, I instead discovered that I would need to actually put some sort of plan together and earn people's acknowledgment of my undeniable superiority.

My disappointment was immeasurable.

While I did discover an existing path to power in this

world—a system called "politics"—it sounded long, boring, and convoluted. Plus, the ones worthy of ruling almost never ascended, as far as I could tell, so I ruled out that strategy. Instead, I would wow them into submission!

I'd initially found some success in Times Square, as my sparks and flames grabbed people's attention and even earned me money for sustenance, which I now knew I needed. I was referred to as a "magician," so I'd leaned into that persona and planned on taking over Times Square before branching out to the entire city, state, and then world.

Instead, I got asked by authorities if I had a permit for pyrotechnics and thrown into a jail cell when I indignantly tried to punish their insolence. (I'd never heard of a stun gun before, but I'd rather not make its acquaintance again.) Much difficulty followed, and I decided afterward to start with a smaller, more docile city to dominate before moving to other targets.

I chose Detroit.

The theory was sound. In its heyday, Detroit had been a large, pioneering city, but had fallen on hard economic times and seen its population dwindle greatly. Surely it would be ripe with takeover opportunity!

My error was that the people of Detroit were anything but docile. They were also not about to be ruled by anyone, let alone a magician with a criminal record. These people were survivors, and I found myself quickly trying to survive alongside them instead of dominating them.

I tried using my remaining Mind Magic abilities to work in sales, but while I had some success at it even in my diminished state, I felt a pain inside of me that I later learned was called "guilt." I had not previously known this sensation, and I did not like it. There was no guilt in Origin. There was only conquest. (Or failed conquest, as the case may be. Let's not dwell on that.)

When I first saw Grace, her uncanny resemblance to Sol made me feel apprehensive out of habit, but Grace had looked up at me with a big smile and asked if I was in the mood for a hot chocolate.

I had come in to ask for directions as I was still getting my bearings in this new land, but I surprised myself by saying that yes, I would accept one. It turned out her espresso machine had broken and hot chocolate was all she had left until it could be fixed later that day, so she was being proactive in directing customers' orders before they could decide differently. But I quite enjoyed the beverage, and I'd gotten a hot chocolate nearly every day in the time since.

It was Grace who directed me toward the loft in which I currently live, as she was friends with the building owner. It was Grace who found Eater while taking the trash out to the alley a few weeks ago, cleaned up the crying pup and fed her. Grace's apartment had a strict "no pets" policy, and since she'd heard me bemoaning the loss of my beloved Destroyer of Realms, she hinted/suggested/ recommended/demanded that I give the little one a home. Much like with the hot chocolate on the day our paths had first crossed, I couldn't say no.

Perhaps Grace had some Mind Magic of her own?

Nonsense.

I could never succumb to such sorcery.

"Okay," she stated matter-of-factly, snapping me

again out of my own mind. "Pretend I don't know you. Tell me about yourself."

I found myself at a loss for words. Grace let the silence linger for a moment.

"Let's try this," she suggested. "First thing that comes to mind. What are some goals? What do you want in life?"

"World domination."

Grace chuckled. She assumed it was a joke, which was probably for the best. I was so used to that answer internally that I spoke it before considering whether or not it was still true.

"Nice. A little 'crypto bro' for my tastes though. That'll probably scare people away."

"Is that not a good thing?" I asked, genuinely confused. There was still a lot about how this society functioned that I had yet to decipher.

"Sometimes yes, sometimes no. If you're about to be mugged, yes. If you're creating a dating profile, not typically."

Dating profile. Two words that, when paired, sounded more ridiculous than "multiverses."

What was I thinking?

To answer that, I had to acknowledge that I wasn't thinking at all. Not really. I was feeling, which was a weakness this world had also bestowed upon me in addition to aging and knees that hurt when it rained.

A week ago, I had been sitting in this very spot when Grace had sat down at the table next to me and started working on her laptop while we chatted. I glanced at her screen and asked about the website she was on. She'd misinterpreted my question to mean that I hadn't known about that specific site as opposed to the concept of "online dating" in general, but her description of the site and how it functioned allowed me to grasp the larger context and meaning. Grace was attempting to socialize outside of her daily interactions. Apparently, she had been using this website for some time with limited to no "success." Despite this, she'd then offered to help me set up my own profile on the site, which I'd originally dismissed but had then reconsidered. That brought us to today.

I owned no computer and possessed no ability to use one, which I'd long recognized as something to correct. My original thought of teaching Eater to use computers for me proved foolhardy after spending some time with her and realizing that training efforts were better spent teaching her not to defecate on the floor. Grace, shocked at my lack of technological prowess, had offered her assistance.

"Earth to Dom?" Grace's voice pulled me back to the current moment. "What do you want out of life?"

I was not used to talking about myself in this world.

My activities here were largely solo and therefore most dialogue was transactional in nature, with Grace being an exception. I thought of how to reword my stated goal in a way that sounded less ... crypto- bro-ey?

"I would like to realize my greatest possible potential in the limited time we are given here," I finally stated. Grace raised her eyebrows.

"Cool. A little dark, but we can work with that."

She silently typed for a moment.

"What would you say is your biggest weakness as a person?"

"Weakness?" I asked, almost laughing at the concept.

"Yeah. We're defined by our flaws and failures more

than we are most successes, especially in how we deal with them. That's what makes us interesting."

I gave this some thought.

"First thing that comes to your mind. Name a weakness," Grace encouraged.

"Wormholes and dimensional rifts, apparently."

Her expression let me know my answer left much to be desired.

"Okay, second thing that comes to your mind."

As she requested, I spoke without contemplation. "I don't understand this world we live in. I don't understand my place in it. I feel ... lost ... much of the time."

My answer seemed to surprise her as much as it did me.

"Is that why you became an artist?"

Her question was less about filling out a profile and instead genuine curiosity, as we had never discussed this before.

"No. I just wanted to be called by a singular name and someone suggested it."

She laughed again. Grace laughed often, which I found remarkable given her struggles.

It was definitely a sound I'd never heard escape Sol's mouth.

"I've seen your stuff, though. It's incredible. How did you learn that?"

She was talking about my use of fire to weld various materials together and how I utilized both fire and smoke to transfer images onto metal canvases. People trade currency for these artifacts in a primitive system of tribute. It's how I have been able to survive in a city of survivors and carve out my own little nook in a world I don't understand.

I still didn't know what a "crypto bro" was, though. It sounded like a label to be avoided, like "out of work magician." Back to her question.

"I guess I was just ... born with it? I don't know how else to describe it," I answered truthfully.

Eater had finished her biscuit. She climbed up onto my chest and nuzzled into my shoulder, sighing heavily. Grace cooed at her and then pulled her phone out.

"We're gonna need a pic of you. This is as good an opportunity as any."

Click.

She turned the phone around and I saw the visage of a god with a tiny animal drooling on him.

"People find such images attractive?"

"Sure!" she replied. "It's cute. You're a bigger dude with a deep voice, so the vulnerability and contrast with itty-bitty Eater is endearing."

We continued our collaboration for a bit before Grace had to get back to work. Even as the owner, she was never one to abuse her break time when someone else was relieving her. I found such dedication admirable.

What was left of my hot chocolate had grown tepid in my neglect, so I subtly heated the cup between my hands to make the last few swallows enjoyable. I then pulled out my telecommunications device to see the fruits of our labor for myself. Even though I was not technologically inclined, I could navigate the Internet, though my device was considered archaic by today's standards.

I found the dating site in question, entered the login credentials Grace had provided for me, and there I was in all my godly, puppy-drooling glory.

So far, there were no matches.

I went to the search bar and entered in the name

"CaffeinatedHopper." Grace was named after Grace Hopper, a computer programming pioneer and naval officer from generations past that Grace's mother had admired. As such, Grace was fond of using variations of the word "hopper" in her online pseudonyms.

She also found the word amusing.

A photo came up, and I found myself looking at the same profile Grace had been tweaking the other day, her smile as bright as ever.

I now had a decision to make.

I had been created to conquer, or so I'd always believed. It has recently occurred to me that maybe I wasn't created to defeat Sol, but rather to maintain a balance with her as my competing other half. I don't know what became of Origin's balance, or Sol herself, since my abrupt absence, but what if I was somehow meant to maintain balance in this world as well? In which way were the scales currently tipping? Earth didn't need more beings trying to dominate it, and my early attempts to do so had fallen woefully flat. I couldn't even conquer Detroit.

But when Eater needed a home, I provided one. Balance. Grace and I both needed a friend. Balance. And yet, there was still a feeling of loss, of imbalance, that only dissipated briefly when Eater did something silly, or when Grace smiled and said something profound or amusing.

If I couldn't change this world, perhaps I could still bring balance to my little corner of it. I hadn't wanted to subconsciously influence Grace in any way with my persuasive Mind Magic, even in its weakened state. Therefore, my solution was to meet her where she was in such a way as to grant her easy exit if desired, which cyberspace seemed ideal for.

Once I navigated to Grace's profile, I had three choices. I could do nothing, swipe the screen left to say, "not interested," or swipe it right for "interested."

I chose "right" and put the device down before I could second-guess myself. Eater yawned against my chest and started snoring.

There is a saying in this world that everyone is the hero of their own story. But for me, fate or destiny had always cast Sol as the Hero, and me as the Agent of Chaos.

But Sol was gone. My world was gone. And I was alone.

Eater sneezed, showering me in puppy mist.

Okay, I was *almost* alone.

Across the cafe, Grace's phone beeped. She pulled it out and glanced at the notification. There was a pause, and then she looked up and raised an eyebrow at me.

Then she smiled.

And swiped right.

The End

Dave Beaudrie has written articles, entertainment pieces, comedic lists and creative content for a wide array of companies in business and entertainment, including Cracked, About, The Spruce and Geeks Have Game. He holds a BA in Advertising from Michigan State University and graduated as Valedictorian. He is also a produced screenwriter.

MARGOT GOES ON VACATION

BY JANINA SCARLET

I thrive in chaos. It's when I feel most alive. Like a great white shark, pausing for too long feels like certain death.

Unfortunately, stopping is my only option now. My doctor gives me one of her trademark head tilts—the same one she uses whenever I show up with another broken limb or bullet hole, and she reminds me to be "more careful."

Bitch!

I run my fingers over the shark tooth necklace I've worn for over a decade now. The black cord is old and frayed, but the shark tooth is as sharp as ever, reminding me of my true nature. Reminding me of how I've survived.

The doctor tilts her head to the side and pauses, as if weighing out her words more cautiously than ever.

"What is it?" I snap.

She bites her lip and takes a step closer. "Look, Margot. Your test results came back."

I'm guessing the results aren't good. I'm not

surprised. At twenty-seven, I've already lived ten years longer than I thought I would.

"How bad is it? How much time do I have left?" I ask.

She sits down and motions for me to sit as well. "That depends on you."

"The fuck is that supposed to mean?"

"You are severely burned out."

I stare at her. *Is she serious?* "Burnout? That's all you got?"

She shakes her head. "It's not just that you're burnt out, Margot. Your vitals are off the charts. Your blood pressure is high, your cholesterol is through the roof, your resting pulse is 158, and the rest of your biomarkers are that of someone at least 60 years older than you. You're anemic, your vitamin D is low, your white blood cell count is high despite you having no evidence of cancer, and—"

"I get the picture."

"What I'm saying is, if you don't take a minimum of four weeks off—effective immediately—your body will make the choice for you. And it won't be sunny shores on a tropical island. It'll be a hospital bed. Tubes everywhere. Machines beeping every few seconds."

That makes me pause.

Trapped. Unable to leave. The tubes. The beeping.

I don't want that. I don't want to be like her.

I'm NOT like her.

I thought I made sure of that.

"I don't think they'll let me off for a whole month," I finally manage to respond.

"I'm sure they'd rather let you off work for four weeks than lose their top assassin permanently. I'll write you a note."

Two days later, I board the plane to the Islands.

First class. Courtesy of workers comp.

The flight attendant approaches—a cute blonde with a perky smile and a neck scarf. Easy to choke someone with.

No, I'm off duty.

"Champagne?" she chirps.

I frown at her and shake my head.

"We also have wine—white and red—"

I run my finger over the shark tooth and press the tip against its sharp edge.

I could rip off the necklace and jab it into her throat. I could smash a champagne flute over her skull. I could—

No. The doctor said absolutely no work.

"I don't drink," I mutter.

"OK then, I'll bring you some juice," she coos and vanishes behind the curtain before I can object.

"First time flying first class?" asks the man sitting beside me.

Mid-fifties, white hair, suit and tie. A briefcase tucked under his seat.

I shake my head.

"Michael," he says, extending a sweaty hand. Gold cufflinks. Diamond studs.

I shake it, even though it's the last thing I want to be doing. "Margot."

"Nice to meet you, Margot," Michael says. "You traveling for work or pleasure?"

I still stare at him, willing him to shut it.

No luck.

"Me, I'm flying for work." He pats his briefcase. "The

banks don't sleep. No, ma'am. And what do you do for a living?"

"Contract killing," I manage with gritted teeth.

"Orange juice?" the perky flight attendant asks, and hands me a champagne glass full.

"Is it true—you're really a contract killer?" she asks once I take a sip.

I nod.

"That's amazing!" Her eyes shine. "I've always had this great idea for a legendary kill. Maybe you could do it —we could split the credit!"

"I'm on vacation," I grunt.

"Yes, of course, so sorry," she mumbles and disappears again.

I sip my juice, fighting the urge to bite through the glass.

"You know, I could've been a contract killer," Michael says.

I turn and glare.

He drones for the next hour about how his parents talked him out of it, how he has no regrets, how being a banker is noble work.

I fight every urge, squirming in my seat. If I stop moving, I will die. When I stop moving, the images flash before me like a vicious horror film I'm forced to watch over and over again. Either I will kill him or the images will kill me.

I am off the clock, I remind myself, again.

"Where are you headed, miss?" the cab driver asks me.

"The Four Seasons."

"Business or pleasure?"

I stare, hoping my silence will be enough to indicate in the politest way possible for him to shut the fuck up.

"So, what do you do for a living?"

"I kill people," I deadpan, pressing my fingers against the shark tooth and wearing what I hope is the queen of resting bitch faces.

Wrong again, because he does not seem deterred. "Ah, that's nice."

I grunt, hoping that it will be the end of our conversation.

"Thought about going into the killing business myself," he adds. "Hard to break into. Only 1% really make it. The rest gotta keep our day jobs. You know how it is."

I nod, just to shut him up.

"Thought about killing my uncle Marv though. He's a real piece of work."

I nod again. Will he *ever* shut up?

"You know how I'd do it?"

Twenty minutes later, I escape the cab after hearing every detail of how the driver would kill Uncle Marv, his neighbor, and half of his family—if he ever got into the business. He still hopes to, maybe when he retires.

I step into the luxurious lobby of the Four Seasons and my fingers reach for the necklace.

It's gone.

Shit!

It must have fallen off in the cab.

I run out the door, but the cab is nowhere in sight. I didn't even get his name or license number.

What is wrong with me?

Oh, that's right! The stupid bitch doctor said that I'm not allowed to work when I'm on vacation. When I get back, I'll deal with her.

I'll have to find another necklace while I'm here.

"Checking in," I say to the concierge and hand her my ID and the company credit card.

"You have a massage at 3:15 today," she tells me after checking my ID.

"I didn't book it."

She stares at the screen. "Says here that it was booked by Kill-R-Us."

Translation: not optional.

"Wow, you're her aren't you?" the concierge asks, pointing to the cover of *30 Under 30 Assassins* magazine on her desk.

I give her the obligatory nod, though I hate how I look in that picture.

"You know, I always thought about becoming a contract killer too."

I snatch my room keys and the itinerary and head straight for the elevators.

～

Week 1

"Take off your clothes and cover yourself with this sheet," the masseuse tells me.

Her tone is firm, but not unkind.

I scan the room the second she steps out.

A massage table stands in the center of the room with thick white foam on it, and a fresh sheet draped over it.

Dim lights glow in all four corners of the room.

A cheesy painting of a sleeping tiger with the caption, *Even predators need to rest,* hangs on one of the walls.

Twelve candles flicker, evenly split between the two nightstands on either side of the massage table. Massage oils. Hot stones.

I can use the candles if I need to start a fire.

I can squirt massage oil into her eyes or use it to make the floor slippery behind me in case I need to get away.

I can throw one of the hot stones at her.

The masseuse returns. "Ready?" she asks as I lie down.

I grunt. My fingers squeeze into tight fists under the sheet.

If she asks me about what I do for a living I'll break her jaw.

"I'm going to pull the sheet down to your waist now, is that alright?"

The consent-seeking throws me off. "Do whatever you need to do," I mumble. "I'm only here because my work made me."

"Try not to think about work right now," she says. "This hour is all about you. And about letting go."

"The hell is that supposed to mean?"

She pulls the sheet down, gently, tucking it at my sides.

I don't like this. I'm too exposed.

"I'm going to apply a little pressure," she says, tapping on my trapezius muscles. "When I do, I want you to focus on exhaling."

She presses into my shoulders. Pain radiates, and with it—memories.

Her. Drunk on the floor again. Me, begging her to wake up. My mother, too far gone to protect me.

"Exhale," the masseuse says. "Let go."

I do. And tears slip out before I can stop them.

Week 2

The masseuse presses lower, into my spine, and another ghost rises.

My first girlfriend. Her smile, the way it shattered me when she left. The sharp ache of abandonment.

I reach for the shark tooth, but it is long gone. Only the tiger sleeps in the painting on the wall.

"Exhale. Let go."

I breathe out—ragged, broken. The ache loosens, just enough for me to notice the release.

Week 3

She works into my hips, thighs. My body stiffens.

Him.

The stepbrother who taught me about sex. The one who stole more than childhood.

Rage claws inside my pelvis like a sharp blade.

"Exhale. Let go."

My fists shake, nails digging into the sheet, but I force the air out. For the first time, I feel the weight ease. Not gone. But lighter.

Week 4

She presses along the length of my back, slow, steady.

This time, the memories come softer. Not screams—whispers. Loneliness. Fear. Faces I've buried under blood and work.

"Exhale. Let go."

I release the breath, and it's like something unclenches in my chest. For the first time in years, my body feels ... mine.

"How are you feeling?" the masseuse asks me softly at the end of my last session.

My eyes are still wet, but my voice is softer than it has been in years. "Do you have time tomorrow?"

She nods. "Same time."

I walk out lighter, still exhaling. Four weeks ago, I thought stillness would be the death of me. But perhaps I am no longer a shark. Perhaps, just like the tiger, I might be able to rest tonight.

The End

DEATH AND THE MAIDEN
BY JASMINE GRIFFIN

B efore the arrival of Death, the entity, there had been some discussion of death, the concept. Though, when one works at a funeral home, one seldom discusses anything else.

Brianna Crosley had spent the better part of the morning going over obituaries with her father. "Mrs. Osborne passed away this morning. Was a sweet woman. Always inviting me over for tea."

She'd spent the afternoon putting makeup on the dead. "Do you believe this is a good shade of lipstick for Ms. Clayton? I'm not sure it fits her coloring. You know she was very particular about that sort of thing."

Brianna's own appearance often struck those upon first sight. She was a slender thing, tall and formidable, with skin pitched black and eyes that glinted brown and gold like those of a cat. She kept her hair cropped close to her head, the tight black coils reflecting an odd array of colors in the light of the funeral parlor's glass chandeliers. Most said that, though her beauty was undeniable, her appearance was in fact, very fitting for her occupation.

At nightfall, Death knocked on their door, cloaked and pale and ever so sullen, coming to join Brianna and her father for dinner. It was his normal quarterly visit to see how their business was fairing. But tonight, he was also there to get their opinion on how he might improve his own state of affairs.

"No one fears me anymore," he bemoaned. "I come for all and yet no one recognizes my power."

Brianna's father, Timothy, huffed out a sound, deep voice echoing as he spoke. "If you already have power," her father asked, "what need do you have of recognition?" His brown balding head was a nice match for the baked potato on his plate.

Death pondered Timothy's question, picking at the brown lettuce and molded bread in front of him. (Because Death mostly ate the food in the fridge that had molded or turned sour, they found his visits rather useful in more ways than one.) Brianna was already certain of Death's answer even before he spoke it out loud.

She was well aware that when it came to Death himself, humans had not only grown comfortable with the concept of death, but with the entity. It was an inevitability. Starting with cartoons like *The Grim Adventures of Billy & Mandy*, even children began to view Death as more friend than foe. Death wasn't something to be feared any longer. He was simply last in the long line of chaos that was their lives. Some, poor souls, even sought Death out before their time.

Crosley Funeral Home had been partnered with Death for some twenty years now, practically all of Brianna's life. Death had propositioned her father when Timothy's business began to fail, and they had been in the business of collecting souls from Death's contracts ever since. Due to their unique partnership with the entity, Brianna's father was always one of the first responders to the scene when someone died, and he inevitably gained the business of the deceased.

It had been working very well, until Brianna had entered their family business. Through no fault of her own, Brianna, even with her formidable figure, had a very calming effect on people. She was soft-spoken, had a heart-shaped face, and the only thing less threatening than her constant smile was her demeanor. Whenever she collected souls, they were at peace. Ordinarily, this would not be a problem; however, there were too many souls going peacefully into the night, and as a result, even more people were unafraid to die, which meant that Brianna became one of the many reasons Death was losing his notoriety.

By dessert, Death and Timothy were locked in an immortal squabble over the last slice of sweet potato pie, Brianna's mother's recipe. Death, having placed his scythe over his lap as a means of intimidation, glared at Timothy, who was armed with nothing but a funeral urn and stubby ash-stained fingers.

"It isn't precisely fear that I want." Death frowned. "Or recognition. It is, perhaps, respect."

Timothy's bulging brown eyes rolled at the answer. "Power is better than both."

"The thing of it is," Death pressed, "fear breeds respect. And power, or rather showcasing it, should be enough to breed fear and respect alike."

Timothy still looked unimpressed. "Isn't that what your Omens are for?"

"Hellhounds," Death declared, bony finger wagging, as Timothy indulged in the tumbler of brandy in the hand that wasn't occupied by the urn. "They're the most fearsome, my claim to fame, if you will. I even considered using them for an emblem when my dear brother, Sleep, created the app for us deities to stay in touch and such."

Timothy snorted so hard brandy almost came out his nose. "An Emblem? More like an avatar. Or perhaps, you can create a GIF of them pissing in my shoes, Death. If they can't breed fear, at least the implication would be as good as a 'Screw you!' I know the smell usually is."

Death huffed in a way that told Brianna his eyes would have rolled were his eye sockets not empty. "Please spare me your theatrics, Timothy," he said, setting his scythe aside and acquiescing to a slice of pie as a peace offering. "Your penny loafers were unfashionable long before the Hounds got to them."

Timothy grumbled but set down the urn in favor of the pie in question.

"What about the Banshees?" Death pressed. "Their wails can make a man's ears bleed!"

"In the words of Kendrick Lamar, 'Be humble, sit down'," Timothy spat, crumbs sputtering from his open mouth. "They can barely hit a high C. One of them sounds like a cat in heat." Brianna snickered a bit despite herself, coughing to cover it as her father next spoke. "What about the Deathwatch Beetles?"

"Now when anyone hears them, they think of Sandra Bullock and *Practical Magic*," Death muttered angrily. "If the Owens sisters were real, I would have cursed them again thrice times over. I petitioned to take Alice Hoffman before her time. You know, set an example. Writers have been too comfortable commenting on our world since

Stoker and the *Dracula* exposé. But The Fates shot me down. Old hags."

Brianna threaded a needle at the side table, quietly mending Death's cloak while the two men puffed up like rival roosters. She cleared her throat. "Gentlemen, perhaps there's a middle ground."

Neither of them paid her any attention as they had now moved on to sitting by the fire in overstuffed antique chairs, facing each other and ignoring Brianna as they were wont to do when they were both up in arms.

Brianna cleared her throat and shook Death's cloak out pointedly. "I have spent much time in the company of the Omens the last few days," she said, once she finally had their attention. "I do believe that I may have some insight."

The Omens, upset by their Master's suffering, had been tormenting the Crosley family for weeks. The Deathwatch Beetles ate holes in all of Brianna's clothes. The Hellhounds had indeed pissed in all her father's shoes, and the acrid smell became quite unbearable. The Banshees, who were in charge of the washing, made threats beyond shrill screams, waving her father's bloodied work clothes around in the laundry room whenever Brianna entered, and commenting on her lingerie, screeching loud enough for the neighbors to hear when they hung the laundry out to dry.

Brianna had, however, found a way to placate each of the Omens. She offered to do the Banshees' makeup to hide the moles and scars on their faces, fed the Hellhounds fresh meat to distract them anytime they appeared, and offered the Deathwatch Beetles fresh dung out of the cat's litter box. They were all quite softened toward Brianna, which incidentally made it harder for them to do their jobs effectively.

Brianna, not wanting to be the one who ruined the family business, imagined she could leave collections to the Omens and help the funeral home in other ways as a form of meeting in the middle. "Perhaps my presence is making things harder for you and the others. I am the only one collecting souls now that the Omens are satisfied and finding it hard to dredge up the anger to inspire fear. It seems as if your reputation suffers due to me, and you know how much I hate to inconvenience you, Death." She could be just as effective doing makeup for the open caskets and cause a lot less trouble in the process, she reasoned.

Death, after considering this for some time, shook his skeletal head and said, "You're good at what you do, just perhaps too good. We'll need some peaceful deaths, but we must have some go in fear as well."

As an alternative solution, Brianna's father suggested that the collections be split between Brianna and a few of Death's Omens. Sending the Omens in hoards was no longer effective now that they weren't as murderous as they once were. Death agreed. Where they began to disagree again was on which Omens to send out and which would serve Death better by managing souls down in the Underneath.

The debate lasted long and was rather ridiculous to witness, Death gesturing wildly with his bony hands and her father yelling with bits of crumb and sweet potato stuck in his mustache. Eventually, they both agreed the Deathwatch Beetles were a must-have. The ominous *click, click, click,* brought about the most delicious bouts of anxiety and apprehension. Those could stay.

The disagreeing points were the Banshees and the Hellhounds. The Hellhounds would inspire the most fear, it was determined, but Timothy wanted them to stay in the Underneath. Aside from the danger they brought to his poor penny loafers, he believed they would serve Death better guarding souls there. Not to mention, cleaning up after a Hellhound mauling was never pleasant, so keeping them confined to the Underneath would save Timothy and Brianna the time and energy they spent washing all the blood stains out of their clothes.

Death disagreed. "The Banshees are as good a guard as any for the Underneath," he said. "And while the Hellhounds can provide companionship, they cannot provide conversation. The Banshees should stay in the Underneath with me and the Hellhounds will remain here."

"But the Banshees' screams can be only so lethal to those that are already dead, dear Death," Brianna said, smiling, the gears in her head turning. "Then again, Father's points on Hellhounds are fairly made as well." She looked between the two men who doted on her as she began to realize that fear was as subjective as Death himself. "I have an idea, but you may not like it."

Death sighed a heavy sigh that sounded hollow and rattled his skeletal form as he leaned back in his chair and the fire in the hearth danced off the white pallor of his bones. "I trust your counsel, Brianna. Tell us what you think."

"I believe you need both Banshees and Hounds in the Underneath," she said. "Beetles too. At different times and in different ways, that is. They will need to be able to move from one realm to the other freely. I, however, am of the surface and if I were to collect the souls, you needn't bother distributing the Omens as much."

Death cut her off. "We've been over this," he said with a frown. "We cannot have all souls going in peace."

"I know, my dearest Death." Brianna grinned. "I can inspire fear all on my own. You're thinking like a deity. But I know humans, and human fear is something that doesn't always require a supernatural touch. Who is better to inspire fear in a human than one who shares a human's mind? I will need but one Hellhound, one Banshee, and a handful of Beetles. They are fond of me now and obey me as they do you. I can work a bit of power on my own. If I can inspire fear with just these beings, then I will take charge of collecting souls, and those above will once again respect and fear what lies below."

Death studied Brianna's tall frame and looked at her now stony face in the shadow of the flames from the fireplace. He could envision it. The monster just beneath her skin. Something darker than what she ever allowed to surface. "You seem awfully sure of yourself," he said, despite appearing to be somewhat swayed.

Brianna glanced between Death and her father once more. "You know what Momma always said," she stated. "Never send a man to do a woman's job."

Death glanced at Timothy and could see that Brianna's father was skeptical. But Death was willing to give it a try, and so, Death and Brianna shook hands on the matter.

Just then, the clock struck twelve and it was time to collect the soul of another.

Harry Waters, who lived three doors down, had a contract that was up. He was a contemptible and angry man who didn't have an agreeable bone in his body. He was set to die a fearful death and would be just the right test for Brianna.

Death, along with the Omens that Brianna requested, accompanied her to the Waters' residence. They went in through the back door without much preamble and found Harry in the kitchen. Harry stared, wide-eyed, as Brianna offered to make tea.

Harry had, just that morning during church service, lifted a twenty-dollar bill from the collection plate, stole Deacon Johnson's parking spot, and pestered Widow Jones for a butterscotch candy during prayer. Now, he fell to his knees and clasped his hands together, suddenly pious at the sight of a sharp-toothed Hellhound.

"Oh no, Mr. Waters," Brianna said, flicking on the kettle like she was about to host a garden party. "You've made quite enough bargains with higher powers, don't you think? You've got decisions to make, and I'll need your undivided attention."

She tsked while pulling out his wife's floral China set, frowning at the delicate little roses circling each saucer, as if she were offended that he owned nothing more befitting the moment. One by one, she placed teacups in front of Death, the Banshee, and Harry, the Hellhound waiting like a well-trained lapdog at her feet.

"Y-you've always been such a sweet girl," Harry stammered.

Brianna poured boiling water into the cups with a smile as pleasant as thorns on roses. "Sweetness is for molasses, Mr. Waters. I'm here because your contract has come due." She picked up his sugar dish and turned to him, one eyebrow raised. "The first question will be an easy one," she said. "Would you like one lump or two?"

Harry looked for a moment like he might implode—

an angry retort on the tip of his tongue. He sobered quickly as the Hellhound at Brianna's feet growled in his direction. "Two please," he answered, a strained sort of manic smile forming on his lips.

"There's those manners I know your momma raised you up with." Her tone was so calm that it unnerved Harry more than comforted him.

The bite returned to Harry's voice as she put sugar in his tea. "Manners?" he sniped. "You're one to talk about manners, showing up here with the likes of these creatures?"

Brianna smiled as she stirred the liquid in his cup. "We are here so that you can choose how you would like to die, Mr. Waters," she said sweetly. "We figured it'd be the polite thing to do. You don't have choice in much else, you see, for death, I'm afraid, is an inevitability, and Death has come for you."

Harry's face paled as he looked between the room's inhabitants. His eyes narrowed and he began to sweat. "I've heard rumors," he said. "I know you take folks calm and peaceful like. I choose you."

Brianna looked almost sad as she shook her head. Death heard Harry's pulse increase and his breath hitch.

"Oh no, Mr. Waters." Brianna frowned. "I'm afraid I am not an option tonight. But since you've left the choice up to me, I suppose I'll have to do a coin toss. I couldn't possibly bring myself to decide your fate on my own. So, heads, mauled by the Hellhound, and tails, the Banshee's scream."

Harry let out a slew of curses, his eyes blown out wide. "You wouldn't dare you crazed little bi—"

Brianna held up one finger and shook her head

slowly. "Language, Mr. Waters," she warned, "there are ladies present."

Brianna calmly studied the horror on Harry's face as she took a coin from her dress pocket. It was a penny she had snagged from one of her father's loafers, blessedly free of Hellhound urine. The beetles clicked and clicked as she flipped the coin, and as it sailed through the air, Harry's fear reached its peak. Brianna turned to Death and he smiled at her, all bony and hollow. Brianna knew, no matter how the coin landed, she would be the one that came out on top.

"You were right, Brianna," Death mused aloud as the coin hit the ground and Harry pissed his pants. "I just needed a woman's touch."

The End

Jasmine C. Griffin (she/they) is a writer and arts educator whose work blends the speculative, the Southern Gothic, and the deeply human. They hold an MA in Creative Writing from Wilkes University and are the author of Strange Religion, a poetry chapbook released by Amused Moon in 2024, and TRUTH & LORE, a poetry collection published by Alien Buddha in 2025. Their fiction, poetry, and essays have appeared in Coffin Bell, Vast Chasm, Eunoia Review, Cleaning Up Glitter, and other literary journals. A Cincinnati native, Jasmine currently resides in New Orleans.

THE SISTERS SWITHIN
BY DEWEY L. YEATTS

Early one morning, the master detective donned a starched white shirt, a smartly tailored blue jacket with matching trousers, and a complimentary blue tie.

She walked out of her patio, through her garden, continued to the greenhouse, and, amongst her beautiful flowers, she added the final touch she was known for—a cream-colored gardenia flower, as her boutonniere. Eccentric geniuses can dress as they wish.

Jane Swithin was a trim, athletic woman in her early fifties with white hair. Not white-blonde. Bone white. Her dark brown locks began to go grey when she was just a teenager, and by the time she was forty, her hair had been leached of all color. She never dyed it. It was still thick and soft. She kept it short and impeccably coiffed.

Usually, Jane was reclusive, drawn out only to take on cases, the most *difficult* cases, when the police needed her assistance. But today, Jane was going to visit her twin sister.

Jane and Eve were identical, and Eve had also gone

grey on a similar timeline. The sisters not only had identical features, but the same strengths and frailties that genetics had given them. They were genius-level intellects, with strong athletic bodies, and keen senses. They excelled in everything they took on, from academics to sports, and they had inherited a substantial family fortune. However, their roads diverged sharply after university.

Jane had used her comfortable wealth to ensconce herself in this country manor, tend to her garden, indulge her voracious academic pursuits, and, ultimately, to lend her keen mind to helping the police. The first case had been happenstance—a man was murdered nearby, and she grew intrigued with the case, and found herself first at loggerheads, then in lockstep, with the man assigned to the crime, one Inspector Jasper Cardinale. They ended up solving the crime together. After that case, Cardinale and other law enforcement sought Jane out and her reputation grew, even as her tendency toward isolation increased.

Eve, however, took her money and ran off to parts unknown. When the sisters made contact years later, Jane was horrified to learn that Eve had turned her intelligence to the other side of the law—she had become a criminal mastermind. Jane had thought such an appellation was that of cheap fiction, but no other word encompassed the web of evil that Eve had spun. She ran a clandestine operation—always one step ahead of the law —that spanned the globe.

With Jane's contacts, and her ability to focus on the details, to see connections others could not, she had mapped out her sister's criminal empire; had seen Eve's hands in many nefarious deeds.

How had they both taken such different paths in life?

Jane straightened her flower, made another pass at smoothing her hair. She was ready to visit her sister at the facility.

About ten months ago, Cardinale had come to Jane with a crime committed in the heart of London. A man had been killed in a locked room. Suicide had been ruled out, but there was no evidence of how the murderer managed to shoot the victim and escape without being detected.

Jane saw the telltale signs of her sister in the crime. She knew Eve's organization had been a hub for assassins, and suspected that her sister had personally seen to several deaths, including this one.

Still, Eve was her sister, and no one had asked her directly—before now—to investigate a crime in which her sister could be part. And while she loathed her sister's lifestyle, Jane was not inclined to see Eve jailed. Solving crimes, for Jane, was an intellectual pursuit, not a moral one. Jane wondered if her reticence indicated that her own moral compass was skewed, and if, perhaps, the ethical line between her and her sister's life paths was not as defined as she had always believed.

Jane considered refusing Cardinale, but it would have been the first time she'd ever done so, which might arouse suspicion as to where Jane's loyalties lay.

But in the end, the prospect of matching wits with her sister was the deciding factor. The girls had been fiercely competitive as children—in their schoolwork, puzzles, games, and feats of strength, speed, or agility— and their victories were almost always evenly split. Crime solving, however, was an arena in which Jane was confident her experience lent her the upper hand. Additionally, this competition would be for much higher stakes, which would render Jane's inevitable victory that much sweeter.

She agreed to help Cardinale with his impossible murder.

The M25 was murderous as usual, and Jane was getting to the facility later than she had wished. It was a surprisingly nice day in the English countryside, very fair, and sunny. The staff tended to bring patients out to the garden in fair weather, which meant Jane would be able to see her sister outside, the warm sun on their faces.

The facility was a specialized care house with meticulously maintained grounds. It housed people with severe cognitive deficits, including dementia, Alzheimer's, and those with severe brain damage. To a casual observer, it resembled any other country estate, but to someone like Jane, it was impossible to miss the formidably high walls, tastefully camouflaged security cameras capable of recording every angle, and the complicated locks on the heavy wooden doors that separated each ward.

In any given room in the world, Jane could walk in, secure in the knowledge that she was likely the smartest person in the room. Most of the time, it didn't take long for someone to open their mouth and immediately confirm the fact that she was a mental giant amongst dwarves. Even Cardinale, a sharp and intuitive Inspector, was a rube compared to Jane Swithin.

But here, as Jane walked toward the terrace, she

noted that the men and women milling about or sitting slumped in their chairs were even further compromised, and Jane did not delight in her intelligence. *There but for the grace of God, go I,* she thought (even though Jane was an atheist, as any rational person would be, she understood the spirit of the idiom). The loss of mental faculty due to age or illness could happen to anyone. Jane, quite reasonably, feared the loss of that which made her unique.

Jane spotted Eve, staring blankly to her left, sitting in a chair by a small patio table, an open chair across from her.

For all the genetic similarities between the twins, their eventual divergence did not rest solely on which side of the law they ultimately aligned with, but rather in the genetic lottery that doomed one sister and not the other.

Jane walked over to Eve and waited for her sister to notice her arrival. Slowly, Eve turned her head and stared at Jane without comprehension. Jane sat down.

Alzheimer's does not only impact the brain's cognitive functions. Its pernicious effects can spread to other parts of the body as well. Certainly, the decrease in cognitive abilities had given her sister's face a drawn look, so unlike the energetic and bright-eyed visage that had illuminated her in the past, but the physical effects of the disease appeared to have drained her as well. Jane was looking at herself aged decades, even though the sisters were only minutes apart in taking their first breaths. Jane knew the disease would also begin to compromise Eve's autonomic functions, like eating and swallowing properly. The doctors had told her Eve was very close to requiring a strictly pureed diet, as she tended to choke on, and nearly aspirate, her food. Choking, or pneumonia resulting from food in the airways, would likely be the thing to eventually kill her.

"Hello, sister."

No response.

Jane was not usually one to give in to sentimentalities but seeing her twin brought low, betrayed by her own genetic wiring, was heartbreaking.

Eve continued to stare at Jane without any recognition. Jane forced herself to look at this face that had once been a mirror, now dimmed. In less than a year, Eve had withered like an apple left in the sun to rot.

And Jane feared that the same fate lurked in her own genetic code.

Ten months prior, when Cardinale asked Jane to help him solve an unsolvable murder, he brought her to a hotel room in Chelsea. The room had been locked from the inside—they had to kick the door down, as the security latch was engaged. The window was also secure—no sign of tampering—and it, too, was locked from the inside. The body was positioned face-up on the bed; cause of death appeared to be one bullet through the heart. The bullet had passed through the body and was lodged in the bedding. The angle of the entry and exit wounds suggested the shooter was just a few feet away, facing the man as he reclined on the bed. The pattern of bleeding suggested the victim had not been moved after he was killed.

And yet, there was no evidence of entry or exit on the window or door. The security latch on the door was of a newer design, a metal U-shape instead of a chain, impossible to latch or unlatch from outside the door once it was closed. The only two signs of violence were the dead body, perforated by a single shot, and the door that had been forced open by the police to discover said body.

Jane had examined the room with Cardinale and the forensic team, and later reviewed all the files and evidence that had been collected. Something nagged at her, but from that initial inspection, she had been unable to form a coherent theory. Just a feeling that eluded definition.

Two days later—after absorbing all the facts of the case—Jane returned, looked again at the hotel room, and tried to pry out the splinter in her mind's eye—the nagging feeling that she had missed something.

Against the wall, just to the left of the door upon entry, there was a high round table, presumably a place to put keys, wallet, or other personal items after entering the room. The table had a skirt around the bottom, and the hem brushed the floor. It was of a similar dark and woodsy print to the fabric of the drapes and bedspread, but there was something off about it.

Jane swept up the skirt and saw nothing at first glance, other than the table's legs. The forensic team had gone over the room well, but would they have looked closely under this skirt, if they had not initially seen anything untoward? The nagging feeling did not go away, and Jane was attempting to pull the skirt further back when she heard a slight clinking sound as a small metal object hit the tiled entryway.

It was a tack. She looked again at the skirt, and now it gapped a bit where the tack had fallen out. She peered closer and saw the skirt had been pinned to the table edge with tacks. It seemed a sloppy way to attach an unnecessary piece of design to the room, and had damaged the wood of the table, which looked old, perhaps even antique.

She held the skirt out further to examine the table's edge, and again, this bit of fluff did not appear to be functionally or aesthetically necessary, and had been attached in a sloppy, slightly destructive manner.

The space under the table was large enough, she gathered, to fit a decent-sized person, if they folded themselves up, knees to chin, back resting against the wall.

Certainly a woman, maybe her size, would fit handily in this spot.

Jane pulled on the fabric until more tacks fell and it was completely detached from the table. Jane tossed the skirt aside.

There was a hair on the floor. A white hair.

Taking out her tweezers, she picked up the hair, held it to the light. She plucked a hair from her own head, held it up for comparison. The hairs were very similar.

She took out an evidence bag, placed the hair inside, and placed her own plucked hair in her pocket with the tweezers, keeping the crime scene as pure as possible. After searching the skirt carefully, she found several more white hairs clinging to the fabric and placed them all in the evidence bag.

Jane imagined the scene, then—her sister enfolded under the table, behind the skirt she had hastily secured with tacks. Jane could not nail down a satisfactory timeline for the placement of the skirt, but no matter. The victim had been as unobservant of his room's décor as any average man and had not noticed anything different. A woman, and not even an extremely intelligent one like herself, would probably have noticed a change in the furnishings. But a man? Much less likely.

After the victim—a ranking government official in Belgium—had dozed off, her sister quietly unfolded herself from under the table and fired the fatal shot—a suppressed shot, as it had not been reported. Then she had engaged the security latch (or the victim had already done so) and crept back into her hiding place. The victim had not been reported missing, and therefore the body had not been discovered, until the following morning, when he failed to appear at an appointment. Eve had been determined enough to wait in her hiding place for quite a long time.

Then, somehow, in all of the hullabaloo when the hotel discovered the executed Belgian, Eve had slipped out and made her escape. Perhaps she'd been dressed as one of the staff. Or perhaps she'd just crept out the door silently, unnoticed. The sisters had always been nimble.

Jane could see it all laid out before her, and she held evidence (seven white hairs with follicles intact) that could prove this theory and finger her sister as the assassin.

What she could not figure out was *why*. There were certainly simpler ways to kill a man than with this bit of theater. The chance of being caught was high, and it lacked the airtight planning she associated with her sister's criminal enterprise to date. Was she slipping, or was it something else?

The only thing that made sense was that the act was intended to draw Jane into the case. A locked room mystery. A foreign official killed in London. It was likely that the master detective, Jane Swithin, would be consulted.

Was it simply to engage in a battle of wits? Or was some other motive at play?

Swithin reported her findings to Cardinale, and DNA confirmed it was her sister's hair. An arrest warrant was issued. Her sister was apprehended coming out of a theater in the West End, having just seen a play. Jane was immediately notified—Cardinale himself went straight to Jane's home to inform her in person that Eve had been arrested.

The trial had barely gotten under way before things began to go sideways. Far from a master criminal, Eve Swithin appeared to be confused, unsure even of her own name. She was angry and confrontational. Many thought it was an act, but Jane engaged the services of the best doctors, and they performed test after test. They found a diagnosis, and it was an impossible one to fake—Eve had early onset Alzheimer's, a particularly advanced case, proceeding rapidly.

She would not stand trial, as she was not competent to do so.

Due to Jane's service to the police, and the ironclad diagnosis, Jane had her sister transferred to this facility, watched over by the finest doctors and nurses.

What became of Eve's criminal empire? From all that Jane could tell, it ran cleanly after her arrest and placement in the facility. Nothing in the crime Eve had been arrested for had pointed back to her network of criminality. As far as anyone, including Jane, could tell, it appeared that the murder of the Belgian had been random. It served no purpose that would benefit any criminal enterprise, nor did it have any strategic, economic, or political gain that would have inspired someone to hire out the killing.

"Eve." Jane said her sister's name with true affection, and a hit of poignancy.

Her sister turned to her and slowly shook her head. "I'm not Eve."

"Of course you are, that is your disease talking. Oh, my dear sister."

Again, she shook her head. "You are a liar."

"That is not a nice thing to say." Jane knew Alzheimer's sufferers were not only deeply confused, often unable to recognize familiar people or recent events, but that they could also become rather obstreperous when contradicted. Jane had been counseled to go along with any delusions or confusion to avoid such upsets.

"Come on, old girl. It's me, Jane."

A sneer on the withered face. "You're not Jane."

Jane sighed. It was common for someone in this condition to not recognize their own kin. Sometimes they would recognize a picture of their relative taken in their youth. But faced with the contemporary version of a loved one—aged out of what memory they could recall—they would be unable to recognize the "old person" before them.

"I'm not Eve, I'm Jane, and you are a liar. You've always been a liar, Eve." The anger was clear now, and her sister gripped the chair as if to stand up, but was unable to, muscles betraying her.

Jane shook her head. "No, I'm Jane. You're Eve."

There was doubt on her sister's face, but only for a moment. Then her eyes glittered again, as sharp and intelligent as before the disease had taken hold of her.

"You put me in here."

"For your own good."

"No, you put me in here to hide what you had done. The switch."

The detective smiled then. These moments of clear memory were few and far between. But she relished them. It was a chance to play the game again, to dance on the thin edge. She leaned closer, conspiratorial.

"Yes, dear sister, I will admit it. You are indeed Jane. And I am Eve. But the world will never know. In a few minutes, that bright light in your eyes will fade, and you won't know it, either. But for now, let us talk for as long as this moment of lucidity allows."

"You bitch. It wasn't enough to be a criminal and a killer, to sully our family name. You did this to me."

Eve Swithin, criminal mastermind, now masquerading as her detective sister, shook her head sadly. "No, your own body did that to you. I just took advantage."

Jane snarled at her. "You are a madwoman and an awful sister."

"That stings, Jane. I've always loved you, no matter what side of the law either of us were on." She sighed. "But yes, I saw an opening. I had been observing you closely all these years, both out of a need to make sure you did not meddle in my affairs, and also because you are my sister and I care about you.

"Once I realized you were declining, I killed the Belgian to draw you out. I saw for myself that you were having issues and that they were proceeding rapidly. It took you far too long to figure out the trick with the fake table skirt, which only confirmed my suspicions. The only difficulty in the whole scheme was finding the best time and place to make the switch."

Jane was still angry, threatening to lift herself from the chair, but Eve could already see the glint in Jane's eyes beginning to dim. Not much time now.

"It was at the theater. I purchased the ticket in my name, but had it sent to you. You took the bait—you could not refuse a night at the theater—and went. You used the ticket, not even noticing it was in my name, not yours. The lines had truly blurred. I simply let myself into your home while you were out and waited there for Cardinale to arrive. Your state of mind had deteriorated to the point that no one questioned my identity as Jane and yours as Eve. I was able to guide the continuing investigation and legal proceedings, now on board not just as the detective who had solved the crime, but as the relative of the accused, soon to be her legal guardian."

Eve saw Jane's features begin to lose their tension, the light fading from her eyes. She was losing Jane. She had to talk faster.

"By the time you were in custody, your ravings and your confusion about your own identity were just further proof of your lack of mental capacity. When you were deemed unable to stand trial, I had you placed here, as I love you, whether you believe it or not, Jane. I wanted you taken care of." She paused. "And also, so that I could visit and play the game with you, on your best days, if I so desired."

Just before the light could dim completely, Eve continued, "It's mostly fun being you. I don't miss committing crimes as much as I thought I would. Building a criminal empire was more a game than a true calling, a challenge to see if I could do it. Everything else came so easily that being a criminal—and getting away with it—was a grand challenge.

"I truly mourned when I learned of your malady, but it presented an opportunity, a magic trick, if I could pull it off, which would allow me to see the world in a new light. And, in the process, my love, I am keeping *your* legacy and good name alive. For when the world thinks of Eve Swithin, it is as a criminal brought low by a dread disease. But Jane Swithin will always be the master detective, adored by the dull, teeming masses. I have solved many strange crimes since I took over from you. Dare I say, I might even be better at it than you were."

Eve took her sister's hand in hers. Very little comprehension was in Jane's eyes now. Still, Eve had to say the last of it, even if her sister did not understand the words.

"I must confess, though, I've considered that it could be fun to commit a crime as you. Just to see if I could get away with it again, but also because I might be asked to consult on my own dastardly deed. A leopard cannot really change her spots, as I am sure you have heard." She cocked her head. "Leopards. Cheetahs. Did you know that cheetahs are all descended from the same surviving cheetah? Their DNA is so similar that they can be acutely susceptible to disease in captivity.

"That thought fills me with dread, as I fear that maybe I also carry the genetic code for the disease that has robbed you. I am sure you felt as I do, that your intellect has always been what defined you, and to lose that is to lose life itself. I mourn you, sister—and I fear for myself."

Eve was a woman of logic, but emotionless she was not. She had tears in her eyes as she looked at her sister, and saw Jane no longer comprehended what Eve was saying. She patted her sister's hand, and then stood, wiping at her eyes.

"Goodbye, Jane. I hope to see you soon, on one of your good days. Then we can have this conversation again, like we have many times before. The spaces between grow longer, and I dread a world without my sister in it. You are a part of me. You always have been. If we have been at war, it is only because humankind is always at war with itself."

Eve leaned down and placed her hand on Jane's shoulder. Jane reached up and absentmindedly patted Eve's hand. Jane's hand was papery thin—parchment that would blow away in a breeze.

Then Jane's hand fell away and Eve sighed. She began the long walk back to the main house, where she would remind the doctors—even though they had standing orders—to call her when there was hope of a good day.

As "Jane" walked through security and on to the parking lot, her phone buzzed.

It was Cardinale.

Time to get back to work. Her sister's work, but also hers now, for as long as she could cheat her genetic destiny.

She would make her sister proud.

The End

Dewey L. Yeatts lives and works in Pennsylvania. He is married and is the proud dog dad to a wonderfully high-

strung Shetland Sheepdog. He has had stories published by Three Ravens, Hellbound Books, and Carnage House.

THE VILLAINS CLUB
BY JANINA SCARLET

Villains Anonymous—or the Villains Club, as we called it—met every Tuesday at 10 am. Unfortunately, it was also pudding delivery time. Tragic scheduling.

Dr. Rivera, the lavender-perfume-wearing assisted living psychologist, led the meetings in our media room. A tall, curvy brunette in an expensive periwinkle suit, she talked with her hands, making her gold bracelets jangle.

I was not only the newest member, but also the youngest at 87 years old, not counting Dr. Rivera, of course, who appeared to be in her late 30s.

"Would anyone like to share?" Dr. Rivera asked, her gaze darting around the room.

There were only four of us in the meeting this morning. The other residents were either at golf or at bingo.

Wusses.

Dr. Rivera's gaze landed on me. "Granny Grift, why don't you start us off today?"

I sighed. This was only my second meeting, so I was

still getting used to the process. "Fine. My name is Granny Grift, though I go by GG, and I am a villain in recovery."

"Hi, GG," Dr. Rivera and the other three chorused.

I fiddled with one of my bobby pins, before sticking it back into my silver bun, alongside the others that I'd sharpened into lockpicks. "I guess I can share. I didn't start conning and grifting until my late 60s. So, don't ever let anyone tell you that you can't teach an old dog new tricks."

The other three members chuckled as I went on, "I used to be a baker. Worked all my life. Was always a *good girl.* And then one day, after I retired, I accidentally stole a sweater in the mall. It was unintentional. I tried the sweater on, tucked it in my reusable shopping bag, then forgot to pay for it. When I went to leave and the alarm sounded, the security guard jumped on the teenager next to me and told me to 'go ahead, ma'am.' That was when I realized that no one ever suspects an old lady. After that, I was unstoppable. At the height of my career, I pulled off three heists in three days across three different countries."

"That sounds deliciously exciting," Madame Willow purred. In her scarlet low-cut dress, she looked like Jessica Rabbit, if Jessica was nearing a hundred. Glitter sparkled over her numerous wrinkles and her fake eyelashes clung on for dear life. "Tell us more, darling."

"Remember, no cross talk allowed while someone else is sharing," Dr. Rivera reminded her.

Willow wiggled in her scooter, clutching her boa to her chest, and gave Dr. Rivera a wide smile, red lipstick smudged over her three remaining teeth. "I'm sorry, sweetheart. I've been naughty. Are you going to spank me?"

Dr. Rivera blushed and shook her head at Willow before turning back to me. "Please continue, GG."

I nodded at her. "I am working on not stealing anymore. One day at a time, right?"

Everyone nodded solemnly.

"I can go next," Ashley, the dark-skinned, white-haired granny to my left, said. She removed her tinted goggles from her face and put them on top of her head, a stark contrast to the white scrubs she wore today. "I am Dr. Ashley Arkane, but you can just call me Ashley. I am an astrophysicist and also a villain in recovery."

"Hi, Ashley," we echoed.

"I am also working on the notion of one day at a time," Ashley said, scribbling something in her notebook, "although, according to my calculations, it's more like one thousand four hundred and forty minutes at a time, which seems excessive."

We all nodded like that made sense.

Ashley continued, "I like building things with my hands. Being a woman, and a woman of color at that, I got sick and tired of others stealing my ideas and passing them off as their own. So, to get my frustration out, I started pranking them. I reworked the sinks in corporate offices to splash water down people's sleeves. I engineered flour that made burgers fall apart on people's plates. And one time, I literally made it rain on the president's parade. Before you know it, I became *the* prankster villain. Top of my kind."

Note to self: I need to partner up with her. She knows things.

"Anyway," Ashley continued, "I am working on letting go of resentment and not pranking others."

"Thank you for sharing, Ashley," Dr. Rivera said, and then turned to the only man in the group. "Lord Bane, would you like to go next?"

He nodded. The man wore a purple velvet robe covered in skull designs. I think it was meant to look intimidating, but it screamed Halloween pajamas.

I swallowed a laugh as he introduced himself, "I am Lord Bane. I am a warlock. And a villain in recovery."

"Hi, Bane," we all recited.

He took a pump of his inhaler before continuing, "I was always the smallest kid in my school. My gym teacher was literally a retired army drill sergeant. He would yell at me and humiliate me for not being athletic. One day, I came home and started playing a record backwards because I heard that you could learn dark magick that way. And you know what? It worked! The very next day, in my gym class, I used the incantation I learned to turn the pommel horse into a real horse, completely under my command. After that, I would regularly use dark magick to cause chaos. I once cursed an entire city so that every time someone sneezed, their snot turned to glitter. Their economy still hasn't recovered from clean-up costs."

"That's diabolical!" Willow hooted.

"Again, please be mindful of the cross talk," Dr. Rivera said.

Willow blew her a kiss and nodded.

Bane continued, "I am working on not using my magick and also taking it one day at a time."

Just then, the door squeaked open and Gary, our

nurse, came into the room, wearing navy-blue scrubs that showed off his dark chiseled muscles. His gorgeous locs were tied together. He was pushing a cart in front of him. "Pardon the interruption, Dr. Rivera. It seems that someone reprogrammed all the TVs again to only play kitten videos on all channels."

We all stared at Ashley, who snorted from laughter.

"Ashley," Dr. Rivera scolded, "you know that making amends and changing your actions are both important parts of your recovery."

Ashley shrugged. "Fine. I'll change them back."

"Was there anything else?" Dr. Rivera asked Gary.

Gary shifted his feet. "Well, someone keeps stealing the pudding cups. So, I thought I'd bring some to everyone attending this meeting before they're all gone."

He handed me a butterscotch one, my favorite. He then gave Ashley and Bane a vanilla one each and handed the chocolate one to Willow.

"Mmm, that looks delicious," Willow purred while making eyes at Gary. "Want to rub it all over me, handsome?"

Gary gave an uncomfortable laugh. "As I've told you many times, ma'am, I'm gay. And I'm married. *Happily* married."

Willow batted her crooked eyelashes at him. "Oh, that doesn't matter, darling. I'm a modern woman. You can invite your husband to join us."

Gary laughed again and took a step back.

Willow grinned, lifted her boa, pulled the sides of her dress apart at her chest, and flashed her impressively creased breasts at him. "Do you want to know how I got these scars?"

"Willow!" Dr. Rivera chided.

Gary averted his eyes and stumbled out of the room, Willow cackling in his wake.

Dr. Rivera shook her head again and turned her attention back to the rest of us. "Where were we?"

"Ashley was about to make amends for reprogramming the TVs," I said, shoving the unopened pudding cup into my purse to join the four others I stole last night.

"Fine," Ashley said, finishing the rest of her pudding with a measuring spoon. "But if I have to apologize, then Bane has to stop summoning demons to do his dirty work for him. He says they're just drafting his official curse threats, but it's somehow turned into hours of arguing about tone, punctuation, and whether eternal doom needs more emphasis. And they are always eating pastries while they do it. There are literally crumbs everywhere."

"What?" Bane asked, adjusting his hearing aids, or what he thought were his hearing aids. I actually stole them before this meeting and replaced them with a pair of ear plugs.

"Never mind," Ashley said. "I take full responsibility for reprogramming the TVs, but I'm not sorry about the kitten videos. They're cute, damn it."

"That's not exactly an apology," Dr. Rivera said. "We'll work on that, but it's a step in the right direction." Then she turned to Willow. "Would you like to share today as well?"

Willow loosened her boa, exposing her wrinkled cleavage. "I thought you'd never ask, darling. My name is Willow Cruz, and I am also a villain in recovery."

"Hi, Willow."

She flashed us her lipsticked smile. "I know you all

have your trauma origin stories. And I respect that. I really do. But my case is different. I've lived a life full of adventures. If it was fun, then I did it. I guess you could say that I'm a bit of an adrenaline junkie. I once waltzed into a jewelry store in a full evening gown and convinced everyone that I was there for a fashion shoot. I walked out of there covered in their diamonds. Another time, I seduced my rival for his famous, top-secret dessert recipe and used it to bake a cake for a prince, just for the fun of it. And on another occasion, I poisoned an entire banquet by giving them severe indigestion, a perfect revenge for not letting me attend the previous year. Ah, those were the times."

"And are there any amends you'd like to make?" Dr. Rivera asked.

Willow shook her head. "I know we're all supposed to be sorry and whatnot. But as I look back at my life, I'm not sorry. My oncologist says that I have a few days left. So, there's no time to be sorry. I'm grateful for what I've got. I suppose it's a bit ironic that these babies—" she pointed to her breasts, "which used to be my biggest weapons, are now the reasons for my death."

We all sat in silence for a minute until I reached into my purse, pulled out my butterscotch pudding, and handed it to Willow. "Here. You need this more than me."

She smiled at me. "Thanks, love." She grabbed the pudding and wiped at the corner of her eye.

The four of us sat together at lunch, our moods fouler than Bane's demons.

"Willow, is there anything we can do?" Ashley asked.

"Maybe Bane can magick something for you? Or I can make it snow, even though it's September."

"Thanks, gorgeous," Willow replied. "Not unless you can turn back the clock. The only regret I have is that this is it for me. The thing is, I'd give anything for just one more job, you know? Just one more heist."

We all nodded back at her, except Bane, who asked, "What did she say?"

Willow patted Bane's hand and said, "Never mind, love," and wheeled her scooter to her room.

I rummaged around my purse and handed Bane his hearing aids. "Here. I ... found these."

"What?" Bane asked and then put his hearing aids in.

"We have to do something," Ashley said.

"What do you have in mind?" I asked.

Ashley motioned for Bane and me to lean closer and shared her plan.

At exactly 5:40 pm, just after a dinner of chipped beef on toast with a side of mushy peas, we set the plan in motion. Bane poured out the pepper from the shakers on the tables and magicked each little grain into a cockroach, creating a spectacular distraction. As the nurses hurried to help the frantic residents, I wheeled my own scooter toward Gary, who was in the process of arranging pills into small paper cups, and pointed to the wave of insects about to overtake his wheely tray. I snagged his employee ID, and two more puddings, while he was busy making a futile attempt to keep the roaches from crawling into the cups of pills.

"Follow me," Ashley said and the three of us wheeled our scooters after her.

"Where are we going, love?" Willow asked, bouncing in her scooter seat.

"It's a surprise," Ashley replied.

Willow clapped her hands. "Oooh, I LOVE surprises."

"Where do you think you are all going?" Gary asked, walking up to my scooter. "And give me back my ID, GG, I *know* you stole it."

"Get away!" I shouted, handing Gary's ID to Bane like it was an Olympic torch. "I'll distract him. Go!"

"No!" Bane shouted. "No man left behind! Or ... no person left behind, I mean."

Ashley gunned the joystick controller of her scooter. "C'mon, Bane! They're gaining on us!"

Gary folded his arms, strolling right next to Ashley. "You're joking, right? You're going like a mile an hour."

This was certainly not the *Fast and Furious* high-speed chase I envisioned in my mind. It was more like the *Slow and Slightly Irritated*.

"C'mon guys," Gary said. "If you crash into a potted plant or something, I'm the one who'll have to fill out incident reports. So, how about it? Huh? Please, stop."

"Nope!" Bane shouted and mumbled an incantation in a language I couldn't understand.

Seconds later, Gary's shoelaces tied themselves into a pretzel, and he almost faceplanted, steadying himself against a chair. "Get back here!" he shouted.

But we weren't listening. We followed Ashley toward the staff elevators, using Gary's ID to enter.

"Where are you going?" Dr. Rivera shouted, mere steps from the elevator.

"Catch," Willow shouted and threw her boa at the doctor.

It worked. In the second that it took Dr. Rivera to free herself from the feathered accessory, we managed to close the elevator doors.

"This is so exciting," Willow said, beaming at us.

Ashley smiled and pulled a screwdriver out of her pocket. She pried the elevator panel open and reprogrammed it. Within minutes, we were hurtling toward the top.

As we wheeled our scooters onto the roof, the sun had just begun to set, painting the horizon in shimmers of gold and bronze.

"Here," I said, opening my purse. "Take it." I handed each of them a pudding cup and took one for myself.

Just then, the staircase door burst open, and Gary and Dr. Rivera came rushing through, both panting.

"You want me to wheel them back to their rooms, Doctor?" Gary asked, still trying to catch his breath.

Dr. Rivera glanced at each of us holding our pudding cups, and a strange expression crossed her face. It was almost a look of recognition, like something she'd seen before, or experienced before, but I couldn't be sure. Finally, Dr. Rivera shook her head. "No. Let them have it." She then addressed us directly, her tone softened now, "Don't stay out too long, you hear?"

"Why don't you join us?" Willow asked.

Gary raised his eyebrows in question at Dr. Rivera.

She looked back at him and then at the rest of us and nodded. "Any more pudding?"

I pulled out the two remaining cups from my purse and handed them to our enforcers.

We ate in silence, savoring the bittersweet moment.

"Beautiful," Willow whispered, sniffling. "Of all the jobs I've ever pulled, this one is, by far, the best."

The sun set lower, coloring the grounds a golden purple, then indigo, and then greyed out darkness. The stars turned on one by one, like stolen diamonds twinkling against the backdrop of a black velvet evening gown.

The End

Acknowledgments

Our very first acknowledgement goes to you.

Yes, you, the one reading this sentence, right now. This is partly because if it wasn't for you buying this book, or checking it out of the library, or accepting it as a gift from a friend, we would never have been able to bring these villains to life. Our sincerest hope is that these stories were a balm for the more villainous corners of your gentle reader's soul.

This is also because reading these acknowledgements makes you a member of a unique coterie of like-minded readers who bother to read acknowledgements in the first place. Someone who (like the editors of this collection) wants to soak up every last word of a beloved book, like using a slice of hearty bread to sop up every last drop of a comforting stew that bubbled on the stovetop for hours. Thank you for your camaraderie, and for relishing every single page along with us.

Next, our deepest thanks to the contributing authors who gleefully lent their brilliance, bite, and moral ambiguity to these pages—you make villainy an art form. Specifically, thanks to Brianna Alers, Dave Beaudrie, M. B. Bruce, Dennis K. Crosby, Jasmine Griffin, Hannah Kate Kelley, Chance Kistler, Jonathan Maberry, Meghan Spelbrink, Robin Talamas, R. V. Thomas, Jocelyn Wallen, Morag Wherle, Alexis Wright, and Dewey L. Yeatts. Your collective imaginations have created worlds inside worlds peopled with characters who are now living out their lives inside the imaginations of our readers. What a beautiful thing you have accomplished!

Immense gratitude to our copy editor, Paxton Alyssa, whose sharp eyes kept this chaos elegant, and to our sensitivity reader, Dr. Harpreet Malla, who helped ensure that our darkness was thoughtful rather than careless.

Thank you to our cover designers, Sasha West and Paul Miehl for making sure the outside looked as dangerous as the inside, and to our PR manager, Cielo Villaseñor, for fearlessly unleashing these stories upon the world.

Finally, thank you to the villains in each of these stories, for never failing to keep heroes on their toes, and reminding us that it's always worth listening to both sides of the story.

Mental Health Resources

Because we at Divine Feminine Publishing value our readers and your mental health, we wanted to share some optional mental health resources with you:

In the US:

If you are having a mental health crisis:

Call 988 (available 24/7 free and confidential)

Text: 'HOME' to 741-741 (available 24/7 free and confidential)

If you are not in crisis, but would like to talk to someone, contact a warmline (as opposed to a hotline): warmline.org

If you are in the LGBTQIA+ community and are struggling, please feel free to text the Trevor Project at 678-678.

If you or a loved one experienced sexual assault:
Call or message RAINN: 1(800) 656-4673 (available 24/7 free and confidential)
Website: www.rainn.org

For reporting domestic violence:
Call 1(800) 799-7233
Website: www.thehotline.org

For information on how to stop child abuse:
Call 1(800) 422-4453
Website: www.childhelp.org/hotline/

To find a mental health professional in your area:
Type in your zip code on www.psychologytoday.com